PUFFIN BOOKS

TERRY ON THE FENCE

'Terry!'

'I'm clearing off! No one wants me in this house. All you do is just shout at me and treat me like a baby. So I'm leaving. For good!' yelled Terry, and he slammed the front door and set off for the common.

He knew what he was doing. He'd spend the night in his secret place, and by the morning they'd realize at home how unfairly they were treating him. He didn't even mind the rain, because he could hear his mother's voice inside his head: 'Poor little devil, drenched through, he was. It made me think.'

But things didn't work out the way Terry planned. First of all he found his hideout was in ruins, and then the deserted bandstand wasn't deserted after all. Instead, five hostile faces were staring at him, grinning dangerously.

'Where you off to, Pig-face?' said one in a croaky, cat-and-mouse voice.

'Which school d'ya go to, then?'

'Fox Hill,' said Terry.

'A Fox Hill snob,' they sneered, and their evil minds began to work. ''Ave you got a lot of stuff up Fox Hill?' they asked. 'Stuff worth nickin'? Tellies and transistors. Tape recorders. That sort of stuff...'

Terry didn't want to help them, but he was frightened. He felt guilty already, even thinking of robbing his school, but not nearly as bad as he would feel later on, when it seemed as if the gang would never leave him alone, or let him go back to being plain ordinary Terry Harmer, not very good and not very bad.

This is a very human story, about an ordinary boy caught up in a web of ugliness and dishonesty, suitable for people who enjoy a really adventurous read.

Bernard Ashley was born in Woolwich, South London, in 1935 and educated at the Roan School, Blackheath, and Sir Joseph Williamson's Mathematical School, Rochester. After National Service in the R.A.F. he trained as a teacher. He is married to a teacher and has three sons. He lives in Charlton, not far from the scene of his early childhood, and is Headmaster of Charlton Manor Junior School.

Other books by Bernard Ashley

ALL MY MEN
BREAK IN THE SUN
DODGEM
JANEY
A KIND OF WILD JUSTICE
THE TROUBLE WITH DONOVAN CROFT
HIGH PAVEMENT BLUES
I'M TRYING TO TELL YOU
DINNER LADIES DON'T COUNT
RUNNING SCARED

TERRY ON THE FENCE

*

BERNARD ASHLEY

Illustrated by Charles Keeping

PUFFIN BOOKS
in association with Oxford University Press

PUFFIN BOOKS

Published by the Penguin Group
27 Wrights Lane, London W8 5TZ, England
Viking Penguin Inc., 40 West 23rd Street, New York, New York 10010, USA
Penguin Books Australia Ltd, Ringwood, Victoria, Australia
Penguin Books Canada Ltd, 2801 John Street, Markham, Ontario, Canada L3R 1B4
Penguin Books (NZ) Ltd, 182–190 Wairau Road, Auckland 10, New Zealand

Penguin Books Ltd, Registered Offices: Harmondsworth, Middlesex, England

First published by Oxford University Press 1975
Published in Puffin Books 1978
10

Made and printed in Great Britain by
Richard Clay Ltd, Bungay, Suffolk
Set in Monotype Baskerville

Chapter One

TERRY slouched down the road with his hands in the pockets of his jeans, concentrating on the cracks in the pavement. With his duffel bag slung by the string over his shoulder he walked along the grey evening pavement, looking neither to right nor to left, determination stumping down through his thin rubber heels as he made his way along the row of privets and low walls. His Adam's apple felt swollen with the hurt of the row and there was an unpleasant prickling feeling behind his eyes. He always came off worse when there was a row with Tracey; he was always in the wrong whatever had happened. His mum thought Tracey was all grown-up and right, and he was just a little kid who didn't agree with them. Well, he wasn't. He was eleven. And it wasn't fair.

Without consciously thinking about where he was going he walked the length of his own street and turned left down towards Fox Hill Road and the common. He was confident he wouldn't bump into anyone from school down there; but to have turned right would have taken him up to the new flats, and that was a certain rendezvous. He felt both bitter and sorry for himself and he didn't want his mood broken by seeing someone he knew. He certainly didn't want to be polite and ordinary now.

Tracey had started it that morning, Terry recalled.

'Terry, take off that new shirt, that's clean for Saturday,' she'd said, bossing into his room.

She was only thirteen but she really thought she was grown-up. She tried to treat him as if she were a sort of auntie instead of a sister, and she ganged up on him with his mum whenever she got half a chance. He wouldn't mind her coming on strong about her age if she were the sort who'd stick up for him now and again.

'I wore it Sunday,' Terry had replied defensively, prepared for this attack from one of them. 'It's not clean . . .'

'And it's not dirty, either. You only wore it in the evening for Uncle Charlie. You know Mum wants it for the party on Saturday. She told you Sunday night. I heard her.' Tracey's voice had an edge of officialness about it, and a sing-song smugness which Terry hated above all else.

'Clear off!' he had said as he slammed the door. 'And mind your own!'

It was a great shirt. Even now, after all the trouble, Terry still felt a surge of excitement when he looked at it. Black, fitted at the waist and see-through, more like a performer's than a schoolboy's, it had been a lucky buy from the catalogue by Mrs Harmer. For the first birthday in his life Terry had been more delighted with something to wear than with any of his toys. It had glinted a promise at him from its cellophane wrapping at the bottom of his bed; and he hadn't been disappointed. At first curious, then excited, Terry had tried it on. It had fitted him perfectly, and somehow in that private ten minutes of strutting, posing and self-admiration in the mirror, Terry had felt himself move from one world into another, from a cheerful disregard for his appearance into a sudden awareness of himself as someone whom other people looked at.

The birthday had been ten days ago, and it had been followed by flat schooldays and unsuitable occasions when the shirt couldn't be worn – like the warm spell after the sledge has been bought, or the rain after the cricket bat. So it had been a great joy when Uncle Charlie with the shop had phoned to say he was coming over to tea on Sunday, bringing his own ham. It hadn't pleased Tracey, who would have gone out to the Club with Karen from down the road, nor Mr Harmer, who resented his wife's uncle's habit of bringing his own food, but it had delighted Terry, who was now given his first opportunity to wear his shirt for real.

'Someone's growin' up then, boy,' Uncle Charlie had said as he had relieved the Rover's suspension of his seventeen stones. 'I like yer dicky-dirt . . .' The big man, at home in his car but like a turtle on land out of it, had shuffled up the narrow front path leaning heavily on Terry's shoulder. 'Nice feel to it. Good bit of cloth, I dare say. Come into a fortune, Glad?'

From the minute he arrived to the minute he left, Uncle Charlie never stopped talking and teasing and making everyone except Mr Harmer feel like Bank Holiday, and Terry had felt secretly honoured that the shirt had been worthy of praise from the big man.

'Be a good boy, now,' he had said at the end of the evening as he sat once more at home behind the multitude of glowing dials in his car, 'and here,' he produced a fifty-pence piece as if from nowhere, no fumbling, 'get yourself a nice silk hanky to go in the pocket of that shirt. Gawd, how you kids grow up . . .'

Two metres tall and feeling like a pop star revisiting his old mum, Terry had walked back indoors, expecting to go back in the front room and have another of Uncle Charlie's Coca-Colas. But he was in for a mild surprise.

'Come on, Terry, off with that shirt and start making tracks for bed,' his mum had said. 'School tomorrow, and it's nearly ten o'clock. And hang your shirt on a hanger. It'll do for the party on Saturday . . .'

Brought down to earth again with a rush now that Uncle Charlie had gone, like a full-blown kite when its supporting wind drops, Terry had gone to his room and reluctantly taken off his shirt, tossing it with great care on to his bedside chair.

Now, as he walked along the pavement, he looked down at the cause of all the trouble. It shone back at him. It was made of some special material which gave it a sheen, and it rippled and glistened in diagonals as his body moved. He watched it and thought of the stir it had caused at school that morning. All the kids had liked it.

'Taste!'

'Old Harmer reckons himself in that!'

Terry had smiled at the remarks, even the rude ones. It felt good to be the centre of attention, like waking up on his birthday morning. Even Mr Evans, in his quietly humorous way, hadn't let him down.

'That must be some funeral you're going to, Terry,' he'd said as he gave out the English books.

Wearing the shirt to school that morning had taken some doing. First, it had led to the argument with Tracey. Then it had meant dodging his mum downstairs, and clearing off to school without his dinner money. But it had been worth it, he thought; it seemed pointless having a great piece of gear like that and not letting everyone at school see it. They all wore their new boots and leather-type jackets when they had them. And saving it up for Jason Brown's party, with his granny and all that lot there, was stupid. Anyway, once he'd worn it his mum would soon come round. She'd see it was silly not to.

The only cloud on the horizon had been a real one, heavy and black and grumbling with electricity, and Terry hadn't taken his coat. But fortunately it wasn't cold – if anything it was threateningly humid – and the rain had held off all day. Everything would have been all right, too, he reflected, if stinking Tracey hadn't put her nose in when he got back. After work in the afternoon was never his mum's best time, and the scene just now was etched on his memory.

'Mum, Terry's come home,' Tracey crowed from the top of the stairs. 'In that birthday shirt.'

That was just to remind her mother of her duty to be angry. As if he'd come home without it!

But Mrs Harmer didn't hear at first. She had more pressing problems. She was hot and tired, and in trying to do three things at once in the kitchen she had just let the milk boil over.

'Oh, sugar! That's just about all I need!'

The crockery in the kitchen sink, already piled high from breakfast and early-morning mugs of tea, shifted slightly but held firm as she delicately balanced the scalded milk saucepan on top. She pushed a nylon cloth under the almost inaccessible hot tap and began wiping up the spilt milk from the cooker. The pinging timer still repeated its unheeded warning to remove the saucepan, and three full milk bottles, waiting to be put away, trembled together on the top of the fridge as if they were chattering their disapproval of the growing chaos. Mrs Harmer swore under her breath as her arm gathered momentum. Fast, short rubs, concentrated on a small area at a time, were necessary to begin removing the hardening film of milk from the enamel, and she soon found herself short of both breath and tolerance. Her husband Jack was the fly in the ointment. He would come in late from work, see the kitchen still in a mess, and saying nothing he'd give her one of his ever-so-noble, far-be-it-from-me-to-say-anything, disappointed looks. She threw the cloth on to the work-top and went towards the hall. Surely Tracey could be more help.

She opened the door and walked slap into a moment of frozen hostility. Like alien cats the children were in aggressively poised positions on the stairs, Tracey at the top and Terry at the foot. Battle was about to be joined. But being the first to see her mother, Tracey was quicker in trying to use her presence to advantage.

'Look at him in that black shirt, Mum. The one you told him not to wear to school ...'

The words spoken from then on still circled inside Terry's head like a loop of recording tape, the argument swiftly growing into a row and the situation quickly changing from one which Terry could control to one which he couldn't, something at once foreseeable and unstoppable.

'It's all right, Mum, it's not dirty or anything ...'

Perhaps if Terry had said nothing Mrs Harmer might have taken out her frustration on the trouble-making Tracey. But as it was, Terry drew her attention to himself, placing himself in the line of fire.

'You stupid boy, what do you mean, "it's not dirty"? Perhaps not to you it isn't ...'

'It isn't. I kept it clean.'

'Do you mind letting me finish? On top perhaps it is clean. But what about under your arms? Things get dirty in more ways than getting mud on them, you know. When it's close and thundery like today you get all sweaty underneath, and that's when clothes get really smelly.'

Tracey looked at Terry and held her nose.

'You don't want to be like Uncle Reg, do you?'

Terry certainly did not. His was one knee none of the

children liked sitting on. Terry kept quiet. He'd done what he wanted, he'd worn the shirt to school, and he guessed that this was one of those times when it would pay to stand still and be told off. He bowed his head ever so slightly; that usually helped to get it over with quickly; but he didn't miss seeing Tracey slinking off to her bedroom before she came into the firing line.

'Not that it matters all that much,' his mother was going on in a tired voice. 'I've got tons of washing to do tonight, so your shirt won't make much odds. I just thought it would do nicely for Saturday as it was ...'

'Sorry, Mum.'

It was the necessary form of words because the ticking off wouldn't be over until he'd used them. But he supposed it was a bit more than that, too. He really did feel sorry for her. She worked all day at the brush-works, and she rarely sat down in the evenings. She seemed more to collapse on the settee round about ten o'clock. She led a hard life and perhaps, as she said, they didn't always do as much to help her as they could.

'All right, never mind. Just try to be a bit more help from now on, eh?'

'Yes ...' It was drawn out with a mixture of tolerance and resignation, a little bit grudging because it was so expected. But Mrs Harmer hadn't quite finished, and Terry knew what was coming next.

'Now, have you picked all the things up off your floor? If not, do it now, Terry – I want to Hoover upstairs when I've cleared up this mess in the kitchen.'

'Yes ...'

'Especially clothes and marbles ...'

'Yes.'

'All right then.'

Mrs Harmer went back to her clearing up while Terry made for the stairs, reluctantly. The trouble with being kind and helpful at home was that it was so boring. Some kids he read about could be helpful by painting fences or chopping wood, or serving in a shop. All he ever got asked to do was pick up his clothes and 'be good'. You couldn't get more boring than that, he thought gloomily.

But he was in for a quick pick-me-up. As he got to the foot of the stairs his own full-length reflection in the hall mirror suddenly caught his approving eye. Oh yes! It really was a great shirt: he looked quite old in it, someone to be looked at twice. He stopped there, and putting his head slightly to one side, winked slowly at himself, the performer and the audience in one.

'Can I just keep it on till tea-time, Mum? My shirt?'

Mrs Harmer was pouring milk into another saucepan and trying to kick the fridge door shut at the same time.

'Yes,' she called back, long suffering. 'If you like . . .'

Terry puckered his lips at himself in the mirror, his head thrown back and his arms held wide for mass appreciation. The new discovery. Chart-buster. 'The Boy in the Black Shirt.' Frenzied applause and female screams of ecstasy filled his ears, and he waved to the cameras.

'You selfish little pig!'

Tracey had appeared at her bedroom door, her face twisted with disgust over the landing rail.

'Selfish little swank, you think you can get away with everything,' she spat at him. 'Mum, don't let him. Make him take it off.'

'Shut your mouth!' But Terry had learned long ago that you didn't shut Tracey up by standing and shouting at her. You took more direct action. He charged up the stairs with his head down, his feet drumming an angry tattoo on the tolerant treads. 'You shut up, Tracey! Keep your long nose out of it!' The swank bit had angered him, but her catching him posturing in front of the mirror had been worse; that was one of the biggest embarrassments of all.

Tracey stayed where she was long enough to see the strength of his reaction before diving for the shelter of her room. She knew that with her weight to the back of the door she could still withstand Terry's attacks, big as he was. But she just had time to yell, 'Mum! Mum! Tell Terry!'

Terry wasted no more words. He lunged for the top of the stairs and swung himself round the banister post on to the small landing in a practised movement which he'd perfected some years before in the long series of battles with Tracey. But she was no novice in that same theatre of war and her actions bore the hallmark of split-second timing. The door had slammed and Tracey had thrown herself against it before he made his furious assault.

'Chicken! Open the door! Let me in!'

'Mum!' came the muffled and breathless reply. 'Can you hear him?'

Mrs Harmer, who had certainly heard the thumping, the slamming and the shouts, was already on her way. In three or four angry strides she was at the foot of the stairs adding her own loud and unhappy comments to the commotion.

'You rotten kids!' she exploded. 'Can't you see I'm worn out enough as it is? All I ask is peace and quiet and a bit of doing what you're told. And all I get is this. Quarrel, quarrel, quarrel. Terry, come away from that door!'

She was half-way up the stairs, her head on a level with Terry's plimsolls through the banisters. It was just impossible to grab his ankles through the railings: she knew, she had tried often enough before. He stood there, his back to the door, his face red and angry, his eyes filling with tears of frustration.

'Rotten Tracey!' he said. 'It's her fault. She won't bloomin' leave me alone ...'

Mrs Harmer reached the landing and knocked authoritatively on Tracey's door, while Terry, taking no chances, ducked his head in case the flailing hand was coming at him..

'Tracey, open this door. Come out here. I want a word with you.'

Mrs Harmer wiped the door with her sleeve where she had smeared it with the raspberry powder from an Instant Whip. 'Come on, hurry up.'

The door opened a cautious crack to reveal Tracey's pale but righteous face.

'Tell him, Mum . . .'

'Come out here.'

'He's nothing but a rotten selfish pig. He thinks he can get away with anything, just because he's a boy. You used to be much more strict with me . . .'

Tracey stood back in her room, holding the door open, in a compromise position of safety both from Terry's foot and her mother's hand.

'Tracey, how many times have I told you not to cause trouble? We'd live a nice peaceful life if you'd just keep your remarks to yourself. Leave him alone. You're not his mother, I am. I'll deal with him if I have to. It's none of your business.'

'That's right,' said Terry, pleased to see his sister getting ticked-off.

'And you!' Mrs Harmer suddenly turned and shouted at him, her patience completely exhausted. Her face showed all the strain of late nights, of trying to run a home and of doing a full-time job, as she returned to a familiar theme. 'All I ever ask of you children is that you behave yourselves and mind your own business, and that's all you can ever not do . . .' She was too tired and fed up with them to put it any better. 'If you can't get on with one another, keep out of each other's way for God's sake! I've got enough on my plate without stupid quarrelling kids! And the sooner you two realize it the better.'

There was a moment's pause while Mrs Harmer's shouted remarks rang round the small landing, sinking in, before she shifted her weight ready to return to the milk downstairs. She sighed. Another crisis over.

But Tracey was unable to resist the temptation to have the

last word. 'He gets away with murder,' she said in a low sulky voice as she began to shut her door.

'I do not!' Terry lunged at her but he was a slam too late and the hardboard panelling took the force of his battering hands.

'Stop it!' shrieked Mrs Harmer. She was really angry with them now, and frustrated at the situation suddenly getting out of control with so much to do and so little time before Jack came in.

'Spoilt little baby!'

'I'm not!' Terry deeply resented Tracey calling him a baby. She had always held her two years' seniority over him like some sort of debt he owed her.

'Yes you are, Mamma's little baby!'

'I'm not!'

'Where's 'our dummy, 'ickle baby?'

'Shut up!'

'Change 'is nappy, then?'

'You're asking for it!'

Mrs Harmer's shrieking voice reached a new high. '"Stop it!" I said.'

'That's what you are! A little baby!'

'No I'm bloody not!'

That was the limit for Mrs Harmer. She whacked at Terry's head and caught him a stinging slap on the left ear. She was already furious and shaking as a result of the total disregard from the pair of them, and now she was both shocked and ashamed at hearing one of her own thoughtless swear-words coming back from the boy. Somehow she always imagined that he didn't hear what he wasn't supposed to. Perhaps it was because he had never copied them in her hearing before.

'How dare you? I'm not having that, Terry Harmer, not from a little boy like you.'

Tracey opened her door again, disappointed at having missed the climax. But the sight of Terry in tears and holding the side of his head told her all she wanted to know. A faint smile and a knowing look crept onto her face, an expression on tiptoe ready to vanish the moment her mother looked round at her.

'You've gone too far. I know I'll never go to heaven for what I sometimes say, but that's no reason for you to start using bad language. Tracey's right, I give you too much of your own way. You wore that shirt when I definitely told you not to, and now you start coming the old soldier up here . . .'

Tracey's smile broadened and settled complacently on her face as she turned back into her room, her task of bringing Terry to book seemingly completed. She left the door wide open so that Terry would know that she was hearing it all while she brushed her hair at the dressing-table and hummed softly to herself.

Mrs Harmer went on, a bit more like a mother now instead of an angry woman. She was quickly calming down now that Terry had put her in control of the situation once more: and there was also the undoubted satisfaction of having clouted someone for the frustrations of the past five minutes.

'You're still my little boy, Terry Harmer, and while you're in my house you'll do as I say and you'll act decent. Now is that clear? Is it?'

She stood with her hands on her hips, leaning forward, her eyes boring into him. Terry, his head still ringing with the unlucky blow, and his eyes full with both the pain and the hurt of the injustice, felt his stomach suddenly leap over in angry rebellion. That's it! He pushed past his mother. He had had enough. To hell with the consequences. He didn't care any more. It was the sort of extreme mood he'd seen kids in at school when they'd shouted at a teacher. He thumped loudly down the stairs and snatched up his duffel bag from the bottom banister post.

'Terry!'

'I'm clearing off! No one wants me in this house. All you do is just shout at me and treat me like a baby . . .' He got to the front door, almost too choked to shout the words out. 'So I'm leaving. For good!' He threw the door shut behind him with all the force he could muster, clattering the letter-box and starting the wind-up bell ringing.

The slam shook through the house as slams always did, but tonight, being tonight, it carried through to the kitchen in just sufficient strength to stir the crockery in the sink. With a shifting, settling clatter the china pyramid collapsed, sending the milky saucepan bouncing off the rim of the sink to clang loudly across the kitchen floor, spreading a pool of dirty white water with it. For Gladys Harmer it almost drowned Terry's parting shot. But not quite. Anger and frustration had lent power to his vocal chords. He pushed open the letter-box flap and yelled at them both at the top of his voice.

'Bloody good-bye!'

Chapter Two

MRS HARMER was sitting on the kitchen stool, defeated, when Jack came in through the back door. He was a wages clerk at the local cable-works, and Thursday was a busy and a late day for him, so it was nearer six o'clock than five when he eventually nosed his car into the narrow space in the right-of-way at the back and walked, head down, up the rain-spotted concrete garden path. His customary shout of 'Aye, aye,' as he opened the back door was usually heard throughout the house, and everyone who was in at the time was expected to reply in some way: it was Jack's idea of what a happy family should be like. But his call was cut off on his lips tonight as he saw first the saucepan, then his wife, in their motionless and unusual positions in the kitchen. He threw the two comics and the plastic brief-case he was carrying on to the top of the washing-machine and stepped over the puddle to put an arm round his silent wife. She looked up at him and tried a weak smile.

'What's up, Glad?' he asked quietly. 'What's happened?'

Mrs Harmer blew her nose on a crumpled tissue. Her protective and defensive attitude towards him still tried to assert itself.

'Oh, nothing much. I'm just fed-up ,that's all.'

But he couldn't be fobbed off that easily, and she might have known it.

'What is it? Work? Someone upset you at work again?' He crouched down and looked up at her tearful face, as he would to an upset child. 'If so, you know what I think about that . . .'

Mrs Harmer sniffed loudly. 'No, it's not that, Jack. It's

the children; well, Terry really. He's just being bloody awkward, that's all.' She avoided his eyes and looked down at the floor.

'That's all?' Jack stood up again. 'Look at the state you're in, and look at the kitchen, upside down. You can't say, "that's all". Where is he?'

He made to move towards the hall door but Mrs Harmer restrained him with such a hard grip on his arm that he felt forbidden to go any farther for the moment. She stood up and pulled him back towards the stool.

'Sit down here and I'll make you a cup of tea, Jack. Hold your horses, and I'll tell you all about it.'

'Good God and little fish-hooks, something's really wrong, isn't it?' The family knew very well that the exclamation was never meant as flippantly as it sounded: it wasn't heard often at home but when it was it usually meant a hot time for someone. 'Has Terry been playing you up again? Come on, Glad, what's up? Out with it.'

Jack sat on the stool and put his hands into the pockets of his nylon mac. He watched his wife skirt the puddle and awkwardly fill the electric kettle from the cold tap. She looked awful, slightly hunched, smaller than her metre and three-quarters, and older than her thirty-five years. Her hair was scragged back and her pretty face was drawn and blotchy, the lifeless eyes accentuating the lines beneath them. A deep frown marked her brow like a sign of caste, and he noticed her hands trembling as she plugged the kettle into the socket.

'You look terrible, Glad,' he said. 'Come on, it's no good trying to defend him, let's have it.'

Mrs Harmer stood facing the stove and with the tears of frustration welling up again in her eyes she began to tell her husband what had happened since she had come in from work. She went right back to Terry's leaving for school in the black shirt that morning, and Jack didn't say a word as she reluctantly told the whole story, unravelling it slowly and cautiously like a bandage off an unhealed wound. She knew he found the children's behaviour to her hard to believe, and even tonight, sympathetic though he was, he had a slight look of being about to play it down. The children always seemed to behave one way for her and another way for him, and he rarely saw what she had to put up with. He even grinned slightly when she told him about Terry leaving home. He was an unpredictable man. He might have blown up at the news, but today he laughed: perhaps to comfort her, she thought.

'Well, he'll come back when he's hungry. Boys usually do. Anyway, I'll have a go at him when he comes in. And I'll go up and sort Tracey out now. She's old enough not to stir things up.' Then he did something strange, something he'd not done for a long time. He turned her to look at him and held her face in his hands, like a connoisseur with a rare vase. It seemed to her like an action in a romantic film. His hands still carried the tang of the coins he'd been counting all day. But it was good, like old times, and already she began to feel better.

Jack kissed her, dropped his hands, and walked towards the kitchen door. 'I'll just go and see Tracey,' he said. 'Pour out that cup of tea, eh?'

Gladys smiled at him through the tears, sniffing apologetically. 'Yes, O.K., Jack. I'm sorry I made so much fuss. But, you know ...'

'Yes, I know.' He said it finally. It was all over. As Terry had known he'd had to say he was sorry earlier, so Jack knew the right things had to be done now to weather the emotional crisis. They had been done, and from now on life could proceed smoothly.

'Got something decent for tea?'

Gladys looked round at the wreck of the kitchen and sighed. Whatever happened there was always the next thing to do. But she felt better, and she made light of her failed attempt to get them a more interesting meal.

'Would you settle for fish fingers and Instant Whip?'

'Any day,' said Jack, 'cooked by you . . .'

Gladys smiled again. This was like the old days. It was almost worth all the bother . . .

The common which divided the once fashionable upper part of the borough from the lower riverside stretch was itself divided in two, not by a boundary but by a dramatic change of terrain. The 'flat common', laid level like a smooth green bedspread, stretched from a row of tall town houses at the foot of Fox Hill across eight hundred metres of unenclosed land to a bandstand and a straggly line of ancient gorse bushes, where it suddenly disappeared from view and became 'the ravine', a steep-sided sloping valley leading, now the crumpled bedcover trailing to the floor, down towards the docks. Small boys, dogs and old-age pensioners were the flat common's most frequent users, with regular cricket matches on summer Sundays gracing the well-sprung turf with sporting purpose. Overlooked by the elegant front row of Victorian residences, it retained something of the promenade atmosphere of former years, when those who walked upon it did so both to see and to be seen. By contrast, the ravine was for those who sought more privacy: sweethearts in the shade, schoolboy Indians stalking cowboys in the gorse, and from time to time a solitary man or woman sitting still or walking slowly among the bushes.

However bright the day the lower slopes of the ravine were always dark and cheerless. The top branches of the knife-scarred trees met overhead, and under foot the dust and stones of the valley bottom lay exposed by generations of running and kicking feet. At its deepest point, just before the first streets of gloomy dockland houses marked the lower limit of the common, a metal-covered brick drainage shaft echoed up the tricklings of an underground water-course, dank and unworldly. To Terry and the boys from Fox Hill it was an eerie, menacing place. Being the lowest point of the common many of the chasing games gravitated down to end there, on the drain cover, but none of the children who lived in the streets above the ravine ever stayed there for long. It was always good to get back up to the bright openness of the flat common again. Sometimes the menace they felt was far from imagined. If you weren't known and accepted by the boys down there you could soon discover what an animal on the run feels like: and even if you were accepted – through a football team or a youth club – you didn't stay longer down there for more than a shouted 'Wotcher!' You could sometimes see the look in a friend's eye change unpleasantly when he was with his older brothers and their mates.

It wasn't Terry's intention to go right down there. He had a favourite spot higher up in the ravine, not far from the flat common, where he planned to bivouac for a while, just long enough to show his mum he was grown up and could get along on his own. A small clump of gorse bushes overhung a narrow gully high up on one side of the valley, and it was possible for a boy to be concealed under there, as alone as in a Western landscape, yet with the comforting sound of London Transport not too far away. It was far from comfortable: London feet had eroded the gully long ago, and smooth stones trickled down the slope like water every time anyone moved: but it offered privacy and, with the plastic sheet in Terry's duffel bag, it could give him reasonable cover. It was just luck that he had kept the sheet in the bag for the next game in the garden. Terry had this place in the back of his mind all the time as he walked down the flattening slope of Fox Hill Road towards the common: he could even vaguely see in his head the shape of the gorse bushes and how he might fix up his plastic roof. Yes, he told himself, he had a plan, and by the morning they'd realize back at home how upset he felt about the unfair way he was treated.

The late spring sun was hidden, and a flat thundery light was spread without shadows over the common, tinting everything with the two-dimensional colour-television look of pale green English scenery. It was coming up for six o'clock and the place was unusually empty.

Terry had that uneasy feeling that he shouldn't be there. Used to being one of a crowd, it was a strange sensation, not very pleasant. Everyone was somewhere else. It was like going down the High Street on a Sunday morning. Only the road was busy, with home-bound cars and full buses in a line nose to tail; but nothing on the road had any connection with the common; it all filed past without a look to right or left from anyone.

Terry crossed over on to the grass by a zebra crossing, and suddenly, almost as suddenly as a swift cut from one scene to another in a film, he had that feeling that he had run away. It was crossing the main road, away from his local pattern of streets which brought it into focus. Anyone looking for him would probably stop short of the road, concentrating on the building sites and the empty houses up Fox Hill. They wouldn't think to come down to the common for some time – and when they did they'd have a job to spot him under the bivouac in the dark. It would probably be nearer the dawn when they found him huddled under the bush. Then perhaps they'd realize how serious he felt about the unfairness at home. He shivered. He wished he'd thought to pick up his coat with the duffel bag and the plastic sheet.

Ahead of him lay the flat expanse of green, then, in the distance, the still dock cranes and the haze of Greater London on the other side of the river. Somewhere between, down and out of sight, lay the Thames and its attendant wharves. He would see it all more clearly from the top of the ravine, and then not at all from his camp in the gorse. The distant view was as familiar and as accepted as the wallpaper at home, yet made remote by the dividing river. 'The other side of the water' was a world away, its only significance in its creation of atmosphere – bright, sunlit and near; or hazily cold and distant. This evening the scene looked ominous. It was hung low with dark smoky-looking clouds, and Terry had the feeling that over there, too, in all those hidden streets, thousands of people were hurrying to the shelter of their homes.

It was going to storm. It had been in the air all day, but now it was as close and as certain as the dusk. Terry headed across the plateau of grass and made for the ravine. He could survive getting a bit wet, he decided. In fact it might help. His mother's voice sounded inside his head. 'Poor little devil, drenched through, he was: it made me think . . .'

Terry stumped on across the grass, quickly putting a reasonable distance between himself and the road, cutting himself off. Already the traffic noise was reduced, only the heavy sounds of the buses carrying across in any volume, and he was suddenly aware of an aeroplane, up there in the darkening clouds, banking slowly for its final approach to London Airport. The already strong feeling of being on his own was heightened by these sounds of communal travel, but with resolution stemming from a stern reminder of his grievance he ran the last few metres to the edge of the gorse and the top of the ravine.

First he glanced down to check on his prickly camp. Yes, it was there, speckled yellow with sparse flowers, but looking shorter and thinner, and more obvious as a hiding-place than he'd thought it would; and he was mildly surprised to see it farther down the steep side than he remembered. He looked out over the river again. The sky was even darker now, and in the middle distance, on the grey Thames itself, a small liner twinkled with cabin lights, nosing her way slowly downstream. Probably going to Australia, he thought, filled with people leaving their old homes behind. Just like me. A sudden shiver contracted his shoulder-blades.

He dropped crab-like down the stony slope to the gully. The gorse there was certainly thinner than he had thought, but it still reached across the gully from either side, and it would give some protection. It was impossible for anything bigger than a dog to enter it from above without getting scratched to pieces – this was one of its advantages, there was only one entrance to defend in war games – so Terry scrambled round the bush on the right to the wider and deeper access below. He slipped the duffel bag off his shoulder, then, like anyone going into hiding, he looked around him before crawling in to inspect his bivouac. The whole ravine was deserted. In the gathering dusk lights shone out from the first row of houses at the bottom, pale yellow oblongs on the pavement, and in the distance the top mast lights and the funnel of the liner seemed to glide past the roof-tops above them. A front door slammed, and someone started calling a boy called Leroy for his tea.

Feeling more lonely than he had ever felt in his life, Terry scrambled on his hands and knees up into the secluded gully. With his head close to the earth the slithering of the loose stones sounded loud as he moved. He pricked his hands on a low sprig, and he suddenly feared for the safety of his precious shirt. He pulled himself closer to the earth. It took his eyes a few seconds to adjust to the dimmer light.

But his nose reacted at once. Poo! He might have known. Blast! Any place that was secluded enough to be a good place to hide was also private enough to be used as a public convenience in an emergency, or when someone was too lazy, or too involved in a game, to go home. Filthy swine, whoever it was. He couldn't live with that! He backed out of the gully quickly and stood up. Charming! Now he'd have to find somewhere else.

Terry picked up his duffel bag and moved back up the slope, above the chosen gorse bushes once more. He looked all around him, but there was nowhere else like this. With a sigh he dropped down onto his haunches. It was this sort of thing going wrong that could send him home with his tail between his legs. Blast! Blast! Blast!

As if that wasn't enough, at that moment the weather turned on him. The day's dull threat finally became a reality and the first large spots of thundery rain began to fall, cold fingers through his shirt pushing him to find cover. There were no flashes, just a long rumbling growl, a menace in the throat rather than the sharp snap of jaws, but he knew better than to ignore it. And finding shelter from the rain wouldn't be enough, he knew that. He would need to find shelter from the lightning, too. That ruled out the trees – he'd be better off getting wet than risking standing under them. He looked around and it was instantly clear that he was left with a straight choice – back across the flat common to the road and the shop doorways, or under the green dome of the bandstand. He looked at the distant road, then at the bandstand, then at the road again. Something more than just where to keep dry hung on his decision. Going back to the road and the shops really meant going home, he told himself. But getting under the bandstand stood for a refusal to give in, time to think out his next move at least.

He decided on the bandstand. He hadn't run off for nothing. There was a second's hesitation while he wondered whether or not it was safe from the lightning under there, but he guessed it had to be: they wouldn't be allowed to put them up without lightning conductors, or in a summer storm you'd see the bandsmen diving off in all directions to get away from their metal instruments.

With a sudden flash of lightning acting as a starting pistol he put his head down and began to run, spurred on by the following clap of thunder which echoed around the sky in a a series of rippling cracks. He ran swiftly over the slippery grass towards his objective – the bare frame of ornate green ironwork which stood lifeless in the rain, waiting, like some huge shrub, to flower with colourful uniforms in the summer. He only just made it. The next flash, brighter than before, took the colour from the grass before him, and the deep boom that went with it with the awful finality of a hydrogen bomb, spurred him to leap up over the last metre of grass and land sprawling on the screeded floor of the bandstand. Panting, he scrambled to the centre of the concrete circle and crouched down beneath the tall and elegant metal canopy. He was soaking wet. His shirt clung coldly to the front of his body like a creased black skin, and his jeans clutched round his legs like wet hands. Another electric-white flash lit up the common and an instantaneous crash shook the earth. Terry screwed his eyes shut tight, terrified, as the elements demonstrated their huge power over the civilization of south London, and the urgent hissing of the downpour sounded like silence in his ears when the thunder stopped.

Terry opened his eyes in time for the next bright flash, a jagged arrow which left a purple image on his retina. And then he saw them. Five faces, staring, smiling at him from the filled-in section of the bandstand, squirting derisive laughter at him in the huge wave of thundering sound.

His first reaction was to shut his eyes again, to tell himself that they weren't there. Surely he'd been alone on the common. But a second, deeper, instinct told him to get away, quickly. You didn't stop to argue with a gang of hostile kids down here. In a fraction of a second he was on his feet and running towards the bandstand steps – but swift as he was, he hadn't the advantage of anticipation, and the others had. One of them was blocking the only way off before he'd gone two metres.

'Where you off to, Pig-face?' The voice was croaky, just broken, but with a cat-and-mouse lilt to it.

'Duff him, Les!'

'Put yer boot in!'

'Gob on 'im!'

The chorus was giggled, but sinister.

'Shut yer mouths!' High, drawn out, and firm, the leader's voice halted the suggestions.

Terry stared up into the strange and frightening face

before him. Two slitted blue eyes held him there, a pair of flaking raised eyebrows and an open 'what're-you-going-to-do-about-it' mouth, chin up in a mocking query, dared him to move. That close, and afraid to step back into the others behind him, Terry registered two other features in his frightened mind. The older boy's skin was paper-thin, drawn across his forehead like a very old man's, and the only hair he seemed to have grew in a thin dead lock high up on his head.

'Si' down. All of yer.'

'Yeah, si' down,' a West Indian voice echoed behind him.

Terry did as he was told. His heart was beating fast and his stomach churned over and landed somewhere down in his bowels. He decided to play along with them. There were times when it didn't pay to be brave. He'd been in this sort of situation once before, when a gang of boys had trapped him in the ravine and made him fight one of their younger brothers – a tough little kid much smaller than him. Terry had offered little resistance, he'd been beaten easily and he'd cried quickly, but he'd got away with little real hurt but to his pride. Again now, like any animal against a stronger creature, he knew instinctively when to assume an attitude of submission.

'You ain't from our school.'

It was a plain, aggressive statement, and Terry, intuitively playing the situation, decided not to reply. But he looked round to where the voice had come from, somewhere behind him to the left. The four boys, three white and one black, all round about his own age, were sitting leaning against the back partition, their legs outstretched and crossed at the ankles, their hands in their pockets. One of them was smoking a cigarette with the stub-end held claw-like by the tips of his fingers so as to get the last centimetre out of it. He stared at Terry and took a last deep drag, casually flicking the butt at his head. Terry ducked and it missed, to the scorn and amusement of the others.

'Which school d'ya go to, then?'

It was the older boy, the leader. Terry turned back to face him, his head on a level with two tubes of trouser worn high above heavy boots.

'Eh?' The boy spat a white gob at Terry to remind him that he'd asked a question.

Terry dodged the spit and answered up sharply. He had to play along till he could make a break for it.

'Fox Hill,' he said in a quiet, straight voice, keeping both pride and criticism out of it.

'Ugh!' scorned a voice behind him. 'A Fox Hill snob!'

'Wassup with Napier then, mate? Not good enough for yer?'

Terry's immediate reply was tactful. God, you had to be tactful. These kids could be more prickly than the gorse. It was also the truth.

'No, it's just not near where I live.'

Terry knew Napier, and the area it served. They wrote something about the problems of the place nearly every week in the local papers. It was very different from Fox Hill.

Napier Junior School was down in the middle of the run-down Queen's Dock Estate, the whole area now left high and dry, stranded with the dockers' families when the tide of commerce receded from the London docks. The papers called it a 'sink school', and said that, like the area in which it stood, it was in that first stage of decay when people were still involved in it and were expected to make the most of it. Fox Hill Primary was half a kilometre farther up the hill from Terry's house. While the one was old and exclusively dockland, dark, grim and depressing, the other was a post-war bungalow with an intake of children from round Terry's streets and from the smart detached houses nearby. Fox Hill was by no means new, but it was light and airy, and when it was mentioned in the papers it was as a show school that was often chosen for exhibitions of children's work and for music festivals.

'Where d'yer live then? Up them snobby 'ouses?'

'Palmerston Road.' Terry left them to judge for themselves. He wouldn't call his terraced house snobby.

'Got a garridge, 'as it?'

'Yes.' Terry was on the defensive now. 'An old asbestos one at the back,' he added, trying to beg pardon.

'Oh,' a mock affected comment came from behind. 'Arse-bestos, at the back!'

Even Terry joined nervously in the whooping laughter this provoked. He wasn't averse to being on the laughing, whip-holding side himself when the opportunity arose, and he envied them their amusement.

'Fox Hill poof!' The black boy put him firmly in his place. 'Stop laughing at our jokes.'

'Belt up!' Les, the older boy, whose face hadn't shown even the glimmering of a smile, brought the kangaroo court unpleasantly back to order. He took a heavy-booted step towards Terry. 'What y'doin' down our ravine then, nosing round? You nicked suthing and come back to lift it?'

Terry didn't quite understand, but he made the mistake of frowning too innocently.

'Come off it, Pig-face, you know what I mean. You've 'id suthing down the ravine an' come back to find it. Or you've just 'id suthing. Suthing like that.'

'I haven't!'

''Course you 'ave. I ain't bloody daft. You come over 'ere when it's gonna pee down with rain, in your little black slippers, without your coat, with your little bag – an' y'go scramblin' under them bushes, then y'come shootin' out again straight away. Who you kiddin'? What's down under that prickle bush? Eh?' He thrust his pale, drawn face down at Terry, his wet lips glistening round brown teeth. Terry's eyes widened nervously. This big kid was dangerous.

He was sorely tempted to tell him about the mess under the bush; but better sense checked him just in time. They'd only take him down there and rub his face in it, the mood they were in.

'Nothing. Honest. Nothing.'

'Bloody little liar!' A heavy brown boot kicked Terry hard on the fleshy part of his left leg. It numbed more than it hurt, but Terry cried out in reaction. 'What you come down 'ere for, then?'

Terry racked his brain for an answer. He knew he was going to have to box very clever. To say that he'd run away from home would probably sound snobby to them, the sort of thing posh kids did in books, but all the same he knew that he had to say something – and quickly, before they thought he was stalling and tried to kick an answer out of him. His brain worked fast to pick the right words, to tell them what he was doing without putting his foot in it.

'I was going to sleep there. I've gone off from home. I was looking for somewhere to camp.'

There was no response from the others; no sound from behind, no change in the disbelieving expression on the wrinkled face before him.

Terry decided to use the support of a likely lie to try to convince them. 'But it was goin' to rain so I come up 'ere.' Deliberately, he broadened his south London accent to a more pronounced cockney, and he consciously made a grammatical mistake. In his anxious state he was prepared to do anything to narrow any gap which these boys felt existed between them. He'd start swearing soon.

'Oh, yeah? Stinkin' little liar! You're up to suthing!' Les's mouth twisted back into an unpleasant sneer. 'You don't fool me, you little swine.'

'It's true!'

'Come off it!'

Something snapped. 'It's bloody true!' Terry shouted at

him, his indignation beginning to rival his fear. He looked round in desperate appeal to the four boys behind him: they were more his age; couldn't they understand? But there was no chance there. No one was grinning now, no flip remarks tumbled out. Their expressions had hardened into the scowling frowns and tight mouths they wore to frighten their mothers.

'Get stuffed!' the smallest of the four pushed out of the corner of his mouth. 'We don't bloody believe yer!'

'Lying little wallie!' said another, who was wearing half a plastic football on his head like a clown, his own mark of individuality. 'You ain't told us a word o' truth since you come 'ere.' He got to his feet, leaning on the boys on either side to loud groans. 'We don't like snobby little liars. That's why I'm gonna kick yer teeth in. Sorta teach yer a lesson . . .'

'Yeah . . .'

'Don't dirty yer boots, son!'

This was it! It had to be now or never, Terry knew. He'd got to get away quickly. The cats had finished playing with the mouse. Now the killing was to start, the real fun, and he wasn't going to hang around for that if he could help it. All the time he'd been there, answering their questions and taking their abuse, one part of his brain had been sizing up the possibilities of escape. There was no way out behind him: the bandstand's back was filled in with plywood, and the four toughs were there. There was unlikely to be a way past the uncouth bulk of the big kid by the front steps. So that just left the sides, bounded by fancy railings about a metre high. If he could jump up and get enough impetus before they grabbed him he could vault that easily, and chance a steady landing on the grass. It had to be that. There was no other choice. He'd worked out which way he'd go. Being right-handed his body wanted to go to the left, to use his left hand for the strong grip on the rail and his right for the more delicate job of steadying his body on landing. So he knew just what he had to do. The big problem was getting going, taking off from his seated position on the floor. Now, the boy making a move from behind had decided him. It had to be now. There was no choice any more. He daren't wait till they got too close.

He was lucky. A sudden flash of lightning and a stroke of good sense came to his aid just in time. As everyone blinked in the brightness Terry suddenly threw his duffel bag at Les's surprised head. He scrambled to his feet, pushing the concrete with palms and soles, and he ran the five or six metres to the railing.

Les caught the bag expertly above his head in both hands, rugby style, but it distracted him for three vital seconds. Three of the boys scrambled to their feet as swiftly as Terry had. The boy with the plastic bald head darted forward and threw himself at the black shirt. But by then Terry was leaping for the rail.

He had no time to think about anything, to worry about the rail being slippery with the rain; he just had to go, whatever the consequences. His grip held as his heart leapt, and in a fine gymnastic vault he flew over the railing and landed, running on three limbs – two feet and a scrambling hand – on the wet grass. He put his head down into the heavy rain and he raced for all he was worth across the flat common.

If he expected to be pursued by disappointed yells and a chaos of bodies he was mistaken. There was no confusion, no tumbling about like outwitted guards in a film. A high and mocking Indian whoop came from one of the boys, and it was quickly taken up by the others while the leader cleared his throat noisily and spat. Now there'd be some fun. The rabbit was running, and they knew without doubt that they'd get him. There were five of them, and the common was wide: they could cut him off with ease before he ran a hundred metres.

'Get 'im!' said the leader, quietly.

There was another general whoop, but softer this time,

more purposeful, followed by a slight pause while they drew fresh breath and made swift decisions about direction.

'Shall we duff 'im, Les?'

'Just get 'im!' Les croaked, a new twist appearing on his white and ugly face. 'I want that Pig-face dead or alive!'

Chapter Three

JACK HARMER sat sideways in an armchair in front of the television, one leg over the arm, trying to look relaxed – but obviously ill at ease. Despite his light-hearted front with Gladys he didn't like not knowing where one of the kids was: and he didn't like the idea of Terry raking round the streets out of sorts with the world. He couldn't name it, but he felt a vague, rolling unease in his stomach. His fingers twisted the wedding-ring round and round on his left hand and his foot bounced up and down in the air. His face was tight and a frown was folded into his forehead.

A grinning reporter on the regional news programme introduced a group of yodelling milkmen from Berkshire as Gladys came in with a mug of tea.

'Rubbish!' said Jack, trying to excuse himself for sitting watching by making some critical comment. 'The stuff they dish up! When they're not making hay out of somebody's troubles they're insulting our intelligence with something like this . . .' He glared intently at the set, willing somebody to make a mistake.

'Oh, I don't know . . .' Mrs Harmer soothed him by placing the tea in his hand. She was always quicker to recover from an upset and carry on with the routine of life. 'They do their best to cater for all tastes, I suppose. They can't please everyone.'

'They never please me.'

Gladys tactfully decided not to ask him why he was watching it, then. It didn't do to be too clever with him. Anyway, she knew why he couldn't settle to anything. It depressed him when family life wasn't as smooth and straight forward as he thought it ought to be. And she knew he wouldn't really relax until Terry was back.

The yodellers mercifully gave way to the weather forecast, delivered by an earnest young man in a modern suit. 'Local thunderstorms have broken up the long spell of dry weather,' he announced to a drenched south-east. 'Heavy rain is expected to continue well into the night, clearing before dawn in most areas, but bringing with it the danger of flooding in low-lying districts . . .'

'And reports have already been received,' the studio anchor-man took it up blandly, 'of two fatalities: a cow drowned in a ditch outside Maidstone, and a golfer struck by lightning at Hertford; so wherever you're out and about this evening –' he put on his grave face – 'the message is, take care!'

Jack Harmer scalded his hand with tea as he leapt out of the chair. 'Do you realize Terry's out in this?' he demanded, almost blaming Gladys for not being more aware of it than he was. 'I want him home. Come on, I'll get the car out . . .'

It was almost as if he had been waiting for the news of the storm, ready to jump up on cue: almost as if the storm was just the excuse for action. He strode towards the door, slopping tea as he went. Gladys Harmer's eyes followed him, her mouth tactfully silent.

'He should never've been allowed to go off in the first place with this storm brewing . . .'

Again Gladys bit her lips shut tight. Suddenly it had all swung back on her. It was her fault for allowing the quarrel; it was her fault for having to give Terry a good ticking-off for his bad language. She felt like the woman who put everyone to so much trouble by allowing herself to be murdered. But it was pointless arguing. Jack was in no mood for reason. You couldn't win with him when he was in this frame of mind.

'Where d'you reckon? Up by the Court flats?' Jack was half into his noisy nylon mac.

'Could be . . .'

'Eh?'

'Yes, all right, the flats. He knows he shouldn't go up there, but I expect that's where he is . . .'

'All right then, the flats. So long as we know what we're doing.' He covered the kitchen in four impatient strides. 'I'll bring the car round to the front. Get your coat on and be ready.'

With his head down he pulled the back door shut behind him and headed along the narrow pier of concrete to the asbestos garage, and within a minute he had launched his Escort into the storm. Gladys fumbled with two unsuitable coats on the hall-stand to find her short black mac and stood poised by the front door – remembering, just before Jack pulled up in the street, to call upstairs to Tracey.

'We're just going out to look for Terry. We won't be long.'

Without waiting for a reply she hurried out to the open door of the car, and found herself at the corner of the street before she could slam it shut. Whirring wipers threw off the heavy rain as fast as they were able, just about keeping pace, and Jack leaned forward in his seat to peer through the downpour. Seeing anything in this was going to be difficult, let alone a wet boy in a black shirt.

A sudden white flash froze them in their anxious attitudes, like some giant photograph, and the loud following crash spurred Jack on to the next deserted corner.

'He does know not to stand under trees, doesn't he?'

'Well, you've always told him, Jack, on holidays and that . . .'

'Well, I hope he remembers. I don't like electric storms – never have – and there's no sense taking chances.' There was still this rolling fear in his stomach, and he could only guess it was the lightning.

Gladys Harmer nodded silently. Jack was a careful man: a bit finicky even, over some things. He always pulled out all the electric plugs at night; he turned the water off when they went on holiday; he climbed a ladder the correct way, hand over hand gripping the rungs, not the sides in case a foot slipped; things like that; things her own more carefree family had never worried about. Uncle Charlie had always found Jack's ways amusing; but then Uncle Charlie usually found something comical in everything. All the same, she could see the sense in Jack's caution where lightning was concerned.

'There's no point taking chances. Life's chancy enough as it is without asking for trouble. Even if the odds are only a million to one, something could happen to him, we both know that. So let's find him and get him home. I hope to God he's got the sense to get inside somewhere.'

In which case we won't see him from the car, Gladys thought. But it was a thought she kept to herself, like many others. Experience had taught her that there were times when it paid to tag silently along. If Jack was worried, she'd be worried. She knew in her heart, though, that the danger from the lightning was slighter than Jack thought – and that wherever Terry was, angry still or licking his wounds – he was physically perfectly safe.

In the worst nightmare Terry had ever had, remembered when all the others had been woken away, he had been chased across a cleared site by a tall man in a raincoat who roared loudly in the sort of voice his dad put on to frighten him. There were no words, just a long shivering roar which tailed off to a whimper as the breath ran out, and then the roaring started again louder, nearer, as the man made ground on him. Terry had put every ounce of energy into his running, but he had made no headway; it had been like running on a roller; and his shrieks for help, directed at his mother's blind back on a first floor balcony, wouldn't, couldn't, come out. The roaring man had got closer, gaining ground fast, and Terry, in a state of terrified despair, had felt the man's nearness, heard the horror in the voice at half a metre's range. And then he had woken up, clammy with fear, and run into his parents' room still not knowing which world he was in – the real or the imagined.

Now he had the same terrified feeling, the panic of being pursued, the desire to stop and scream just before being caught that infants have in games of chase. The flat common stretched out before him in such a wide void, with the safety of the road so far away, that however much effort he put into running – and it was total – he seemed to be making no gains on the space before him. Running down an alley or along a pavement at least gives the impression of getting you somewhere. He didn't look round to see where the gang was: he could hear them, whooping and catcalling with the same scaring effect the Red Indians, or the Chinese tin-bashers, or the Scottish pipers, have on their enemies. Weak legs and a searing throat, staring eyes blinking in the heavy rain, an adrenalin-supercharged system urging every muscle to carry him forward fast, this was Terry as he raced for the main road. The rain ran off his flattened hair, it stuck his see-through shirt to his pumping chest, it squelched in his plimsolls on the soggy grass; but worse, it clung in the fabric of his sopping jeans, making them heavy and awkward, and his legs tired quickly as they fought to overcome the added resistance.

He knew he was losing when he heard the triumphant voice over on his right, the tallest of the four pursuers drawing level twenty metres away on a course which must cut him off from the road.

'You've 'ad it now!'

'Bring 'im down, Micky!'

'Duff 'im!'

The supporting voices came from behind, not far behind, and Terry knew they'd have him. And that wasn't defeatist. It was just plain fact. So what did he do now? Stop and put his hands up? Throw a punch at one of their stupid heads?

Kick a crutch? He knew that few pursued creatures once on the run will stop and fight unless they're cornered: while a metre separates the hunted from its prey the difference will have to be run. Suddenly, like a hare being coursed, Terry changed direction in an instinctive attempt to delay the moment of the kill. He ran sharp left and headed back for the ravine, his legs aching almost unbearably now and his breath being sucked in in hoarse animal rasps. Momentarily, the storm helped him. In the teeming rain on the clear common several strides at a time were being covered with heads down and eyes closed, and he gained a very small advantage when he switched direction.

'Cut 'im off you wallies!' yelled the longer-legged Mick, but the others had lost those few seconds and Terry's dash for the ravine opened up an extra metre between them.

The ravine was now about eighty metres away. What Terry hoped to do when he got there didn't enter into his panicked thinking. It offered no refuge and as a terrain for flight it was worse than the flat common. He could only end up down in the Queen's Dock Estate, enemy territory, and he didn't stand a ghost of a chance in climbing the steep far side to escape into neutral streets. But he ran on. It was that or give up.

For a fleeting moment he thought he might make it unimpeded, but he'd forgotten about Les, and as he mentally whipped himself across the final stretch of flat grass, flagging now like a racehorse at the end of a three kilometre chase, he suddenly saw the hunched figure coming at him from the curtain of rain which covered the bandstand. Les could have been an early cave-dweller chasing an injured deer, long arms in front, body bent over, head thrust forward. He didn't shout. He menaced with his very silence. He ran in a straight course to cut Terry off, heavy boots smacking violently into the wet grass. The kill was to be swift and sudden – the shooting-out of a snake's fangs, the darting tongue of a fly-catcher, the sharp squeeze of a trigger. In a few strides he was within reach, arms stretching out for the grab, eyes bulging, mouth open in a snarl. But the hunted had one final dodge left in him. Even if he didn't make it he could try one last change of direction, one last bodily twist. As the long fingers grabbed at his shoulders, Terry drew his body in and twisted to the left in a matador movement; the fingers which clutched at his shoulders were denied that extra grip, slipping off the wet silk surface, and the older boy was sent a metre beyond his prey. He turned for a second charge swifter than any bull, but he had lost momentum, his body balance was wrong, and by the time he was in a position of forward thrust again Terry was at the top of the ravine slope.

Terry wasn't planning any more: he was just running. He simply threw himself forward down the slope with the forlorn hope that his mum, his dad and a couple of policemen were waiting for him at the bottom – the only way this nightmare could end for him. The near miss with Les seemed to have given extra strength to his legs, the steep slope pulled at him, and he threw himself down it without hesitation. As he ran something Uncle Charlie had once told him flashed into his mind. 'The fastest way to run down a hill is like your gurkha. They're only small but they go like the clappers. They don't run down a hill like you do – sticking up straight like a lamp-post on a slope. No, your gurkha runs down at right angles to the ground, throws himself forward. That's what gives him his fantastic speed . . .' Terry had thought about it at the time: it had seemed impossible: he'd remembered his own way of running down this very ravine, slamming his feet down and holding his body back to put the brakes on to stop himself falling over. He hadn't thought any other way was possible. Perhaps now was the time to try. With the big boy pounding and snorting behind him he needed every bit of help he could muster. There was nothing to lose. The ground dropped away from him in a rough and uneven one-in-ten slope, but he thrust

his body forward like an aeroplane altering its trim, his sodden jeans and squelching plimsolls pumping beneath his single-minded gaze to carry him forward and down. It seemed to work. He was going at a terrific speed, but because of the angle of his body he was able to keep control. It was easier than he had thought, and he knew it was working because he could no longer hear Les's heavy breathing in his ear – just a distant shout of 'Come on, 'e's over 'ere!' For the first time since he had been cut off on the flat common he began to think he would get away.

At that moment another flash seared into the ravine. Too late, it lit up a large gorse bush through the rain; it was dead in Terry's path, reaching up with its prickles shining wet in the sudden light, too close to avoid. There was no stopping. At this headlong speed there was only one thing to do, and no time to think about it. With a kicking push-off Terry leapt over the bush, sheer panic giving him the height and the confidence to clear the spiky obstacle. His legs kept running as he soared through the air, his arms spread out like wings to give him balance, his stomach turning over as it did when he jumped off the top board at the baths. He seemed to hang in the air for seconds as the gorse glided harmlessly beneath him. But his body had tipped forward in the air, and Terry suddenly knew that he was going to hit the ground simultaneously with his hands and his feet. Oh God! He saw that the bush had concealed a stony gully, a treacherously uneven surface where he'd have to land. Down he went, the slippery stone and the rivulets of soil in the gully flying up at him in sharp focus. First his hands hit, sliding forward on the loose surface, next his toes caught, and then, with a breath-crushing smack, his chest skidded down the gully like the body of a crash-landing aircraft. As the air was knocked out of him he was gripped round the chest with a sharp squeezing pain. He yelled out in agony. But his forehead struck a large smooth stone jutting out from the gully's side, and after another blinding flash of light, either the lightning or from within his head – he couldn't be sure – there was only darkness.

There was no pain now. The body in shock anaesthetized itself, and Terry, coming round and drifting off in a fuzz of unreality, saw just the white light once, and heard the rushing of water, deep down and echoing underground, as he was half dragged, half carried, out of the bottom of the ravine and into the grey streets of the Queen's Dock Estate. But he distinctly heard a breaking voice before he passed out again.

'Come on!' Les said. 'Get 'im back to my place. I've gotta idea!'

The Harmers' car pulled up alongside a grey concrete development which was being grafted on a grand scale on to the side of Fox Hill. It was on a site which, since the nineteen twenties, had been in turn a flourishing lawn tennis club – with terraces of green courts and rectangular box hedges – a war-time Nissen-hutted A.T.S. camp, and, most recently, a post-war estate of thin-walled prefabricated houses. Now, groaning under tons of thick concrete and the steel framework of high-rise flats, the former tennis club was finally and permanently giving over to housing, only the very gradual change from green to grey making it possible without protests and petitions from the local residents. This was where some of the families from the Queen's Dock Estate would eventually be re-housed. Meanwhile, it was regarded by the local children as a superb adventure playground, with mounds of sand, mountains of shingle, labyrinths of sewage pipes, and flights of stairs climbing to heaven. And for a while, the one completed and inhabited twenty-three storey block of flats – Court House – had provided them with high-speed lifts for launching themselves into space. Of late, however, the security patrol had added its own cops and robbers element of adventure, and angry chases with capture involving the threat of a trip to the police-station gave an extra thrill to the less timid children.

This was where Terry sometimes came to play after school. He wasn't supposed to any more, now that his mum knew where he went, and since Mr Marshall's warning in school about playing on the site. But the lifts were too great a temptation to resist, and there were still a few lengths of sewage pipe to slide down. Mrs Harmer knew this from the grey dust on his jeans.

So here they were, she and Jack, in the air-bubble of the car peering out on to a seemingly deserted site. Jack made visibility better by wiping the film of condensation from three windows with his hands, leaning forwards and stretching backwards in his seat to cover the greatest area quickly.

'That's better!'

He brought into focus a vertical column of early lights from Court House – squares of brightness tinted in pastel shades by lamps, curtains, and the flickering blue of television – each light signalling a husband home, a family tea, or a relaxed lounge on a sofa.

'Well, if he came up here he's either under those big trees on the far side, or he's in one of the blocks of flats. There's nowhere else he could be.'

Mrs Harmer nodded. 'I expect he's waiting somewhere for it to ease off a bit to make a dash for home.'

'Yes, well it's the trees I'm most worried about. I'll check under them and you check the block with lights. Do the top floor and the bottom. He won't be anywhere else, unless he's in someone's flat.' Still the stomach churned, the vague unease tingled in his limbs. 'I'll meet you outside the lifts as soon as I can.'

'All right.'

'Then we'll check the empty blocks . . .'

'Yes.'

'Come on then, no time to waste.' Another bright flash dulled the flats' lights to insignificance; but the thunder was a little slower on its heels. 'I think it's moving off. But don't take chances. Take your ring off. Then look snappy. If he's not here we've got a lot of looking to do.'

He took off his watch and his own ring, licking his finger to slide it over the knuckle joint, and put them into the glove compartment. Then he was gone, head down, his mac flapping behind him like something out of a creepy film, across the unmade roads and high kerbs towards the far side of the site. Obediently, Mrs Harmer struggled with her scarred wedding-ring for a while, but it was never meant to come off, and dismissing Jack's instruction, she left the car and did a fast straight-legged run to the foot of the inhabited tower block, Court House.

Fifteen minutes later they were both back in the car, heads and legs soaking wet, and with the back seat still unoccupied. He wasn't there. He hadn't been under the trees, nor under any of the concrete mixers or pipes or closed workmen's huts. The unfinished flats were securely locked at the bottoms, and Court House had shown no signs of life along its sad no-man's landings.

'Where to now, then?' Jack asked. 'Where else does he go? You know his playing habits better than I do. Hasn't he got any special friends? Someone whose house he might have gone to?'

'I don't know, Jack. He's a quiet boy. He plays with a lot of different boys from the school, but no one special I can think of...' It suddenly struck her how little she knew about Terry these days, the things he did, the company he kept. 'Perhaps we ought to try the common. I think he gets down there sometimes. Otherwise, I'm not sure. Unless he's round at your mother's, or Uncle Charlie's...'

Jack frowned. He hadn't thought of that. His one concern had been to get Terry back; Terry's reason for going off had been of secondary importance; but when other people got involved in it – even family – you found yourself having to account for everybody's actions. And you always came out of it looking a bit stupid. Family quarrels were for families, immediate families. Everyone else was an outsider and had no right to be involved, not by anyone. It might be different when someone needed protecting from a bully, like a battered baby from a cruel parent; otherwise, dirty linen was best washed in your own machine, with the door closed.

'Oh God, we don't want Mum involved. Nor your Uncle Charlie. Especially Uncle Charlie. He'd make a right meal of it.'

Gladys ignored the criticism. 'I'm not saying he has gone to them, am I? There's just a chance he might have, that's all. Anyway,' she added as he turned the key and the car coughed obediently to life, wipers awake and starting work, 'let's have a look down on the common before we start worrying about that ...'

Chapter Four

THE rain, which had momentarily helped Terry twice in the past ten minutes, was no friend to him now. It forced everyone indoors. The narrow right-angled streets of the Queen's Dock Estate were deserted, left to the puddles and the overflowing drains. Only the snails were out on the few bits of green. There were no adults standing in doorways or tinkering with old cars to tell the gang to leave the struggling kid alone. Half the houses were boarded up anyway, corrugated sheets over doors and criss-crossed planks over windows, but those houses which did show signs of life – with mangy cats and streaky milk bottles huddling on doorsteps – were firmly closed against the wet world outside. So Terry's plight went unseen as the boys forced him quickly along the uneven pavements with his right arm twisted spitefully up to his shoulder-blades. Like a dog on a noose, the more he struggled the worse it hurt, and with his head aching and a retching feeling in his stomach, he soon gave up all but a token resistance and allowed himself to be marched on his heels along the shining pavement. But his senses, heightened by fear, took everything in. He heard everything that was said, and he saw everything there was to see.

'Wotcha gonna do with 'im, Les?'

'You'll see.'

'Y'can't take 'im 'ome. Your mum'll murder you.'

''E ain't goin' 'ome.'

Les hissed silence at them while they passed a seedy paper shop on a corner. 'FAGS AND MAGS. Cheap smokes.'

'Les . . .'

'Shuddup! Case my ol' man's come for 'is paper.'

There was silence while they passed the shop, taking no chances. One side window, with 'Charlton Rule' squirted across it in aerosol paint, was boarded up, too expensive to replace yet again, and it was hard to see whether anyone was in the shop or not.

Les kept Terry's arm forced hard up his back to make good speed along the street, while the others kept pace on either side with occasional unnecessary thumps and pushes. The smallest, a fat boy with dirty blond hair who had to run to keep up, made up for his lack of height by kicking at the backs of Terry's legs from time to time.

The street they were in showed fewer and fewer signs of life as they went along it. The boarded doors and windows with their official messages, 'Gas Off', 'Elec. Off', began to outnumber the thinly curtained windows, and cookers and cans had grown rust in more and more of the narrow front gardens as one by one the tenants had gone into temporary accommodation to await the flowering of the giant bean-stalks of flats. Opposite the first stretch of railway-sleeper dock fence a notice on a dead café served as its own obituary. 'Queue served in strict order. No places saved.'

'You ain't goin' in the docks? There's dogs in there . . .'

'No, I ain't.' Les gave Terry another painful jerk to get him to his destination quicker. 'But I tell you what. If you don't bloody shut up it'll be you I fill-in 'stead of 'im!'

Terry twisted and struggled again. In the march along

the street he'd been scared, but somehow the threat of serious violence he had felt in the bandstand had seemed to be receding; with his fall he somehow thought he'd earned a quick release when he got the chance to explain his truthfulness to them again. Now with Les's words the old fear returned. These kids meant business. And with the fear came a fresh hatred. Uncle Charlie was right. No-goods like this ought to be strangled at birth.

Suddenly, Les stopped. One second he was giving the impression of marching Terry on at high speed; the next, he'd stopped.

'Quick!' he said. 'In 'ere. Don't let no one see yer.'

They were outside another house, one like most of the others down the street; door corrugated over, windows boarded, damp green slime up the walls. A strong smell of wet soil and slugs crawled up from the front patch and a

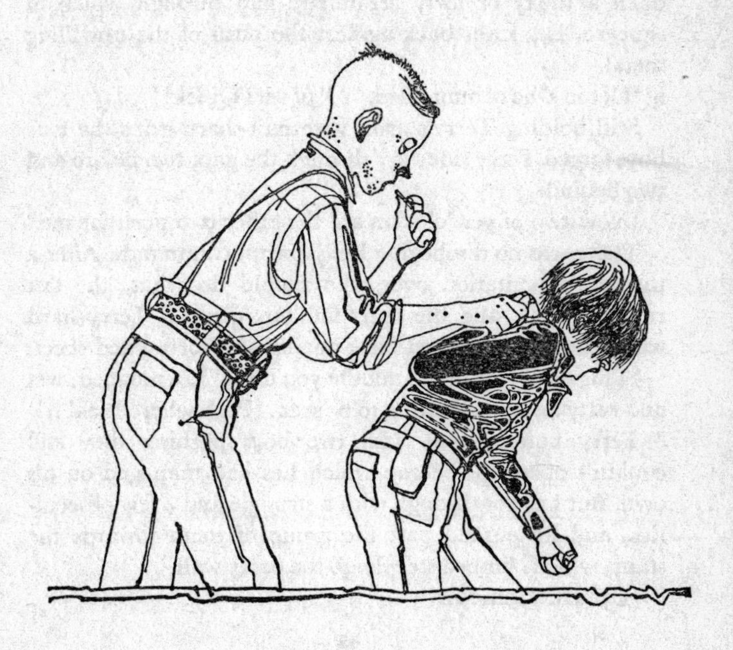

rangy privet swayed uncertainly in unclipped freedom against the decaying garden wall. A defiant daffodil grew dustily out of the rubble. Ducking to avoid the wet bush the boys pushed Terry up to the front door.

''Old 'im!' Les ordered curtly. He let go of Terry's arm and started pulling at one side of the corrugated sheet. The sudden release of his arm was no relief to Terry: it had been twisted up his back for so long it had become numb in that position, and when the other boys pinned it to his side in response to Les's order it sent an acute shooting pain from his elbow to his shoulder. He yelled out, loudly.

'Shut yer mouth!' A boot on his ankle hurt almost as much, but he winced silently. He was learning the rules fast.

Les pulled hard against the left side of the silver-grey sheet. The galvanized nails had been removed and it was possible with some effort to pull back the tall barricade and open a thirty or forty centimetre gap through which to squeeze. Les leant back against the push of the unwilling metal.

'Get in!' he commanded. 'All of yer! Quick!'

Still holding Terry's arms with nail-sharp grips the four boys forced Terry sideways through the gap, two before and two behind.

'Now two of yer 'old 'im an' the other two push for me.'

There was no disobeying Les's abrupt commands. After a moment's hesitation over who should do what, the fast runner, Mick, and the short fair boy gripped Terry hard while the others pushed back against the corrugated sheet.

'This side! Not in the middle you divs!' Les moaned, wet and ratty and not wanting to be seen. 'Push where I 'eld it!'

Terry noticed that with two boys pushing they still couldn't open up the gap which Les had managed on his own. But Les got through with a struggle and a few obscenities, and he pushed past the group of them towards the stairs, which climbed steeply up the party wall.

'Up 'ere! Come on!'

Although he had been forced there against his will, Terry still felt a strange feeling of having invaded someone's privacy by being in the empty house. It was like going into his nan's, his mother's mother's, after she'd died: the very walls seemed to question the intrusion. In fact this house was very like his nan's: a bit smaller perhaps, but built to the same pattern; and it wasn't all that run-down. It couldn't have been empty for long. There was a faint smell of damp wallpaper, of an empty house in cold and wet weather, and the floorboards were dirty in the middle where the varnish had stopped under the hall carpet, but there was no muck in the house, no piles of brick dust or charred papers, no evidence of it being used as a lavatory. It would take a little time for that.

After their exertions the steep stairs took the wind out of all of them, and the last step up, from the stairs into the back bedroom, was the last straw for them all.

'Bloody hell!'

'Thank Gawd!'

'I'm knocked up!'

It was nothing to how Terry felt.

'Didn't know about this. 'Ow long you 'ad this place then, Les?'

'Slick Brylcreem! This ain't bad!'

The back bedroom was clearly Les's private place. Spread newspaper moulded an old wicker chair to Les's shape, and the iron grate was filled with very short dog-ends. The walls displayed once-glossy footballers, a couple of girls from a calendar, and a rough dart-board shape sprayed on with aerosol paint, all targets for Les's darts. There was little need for a curtain: the grimy sash window filtered the light down to a dull grey.

Les hovered uncertainly in the middle of the room while the four others grouped themselves round Terry over by the door. No one was certain what was expected of him. Les seemed to be thinking out what to do; not generally, but next. Terry watched every muscle on the tight face, every movement of the small folded eyes. Whatever Les was deciding it was going to be about him. A prisoner, a hostage, a victim, he was going to be subject to Les's god-like decision.

'Right!' Les said after a few moments, before the others began asking him questions again. 'Turn round an' face the wall.'

Without a word the gang turned Terry in a rough blind-man's-buff spin and pushed him close up to the small pink roses on the yellowing wallpaper.

'All of yer!'

Four pairs of eyes narrowed in suspicion. Three mouths set firmly in a line; but one, Mick's, broadened into a grin. The tallest and the strongest of the four, he wasn't far off challenging Les one day.

''E's gonna shoot us!' he said in mock disbelief. Two of the others snorted laughter at the wall. The smallest spat at a rose, very unsure now.

'Shuddup!'

They did as they were told and stood silently facing the wall, only Mick getting a casual lean into his stance. For Terry there was some small comfort in the others being included in Les's command. But it had been ups and downs all evening, and he wasn't really hoping for anything any more, except, just faintly, for a sudden reprieve – Les and the gang getting fed up, maybe, or having to go home, telling him to clear off, with perhaps a kick up the backside to help him on his way. He stared intently at a join in the wall-paper which ran down through a line of roses, a couple of millimetres out – like a geological fault threatening disaster.

There was a creaking sound from behind him, which he put down to Les prising out a floorboard, followed by a scrape as Les fiddled with something, then a bang as the floorboard was replaced with the final stamp of a foot.

'Right!' said Les. 'Turn round.'

The boys obeyed the instruction; three of them eagerly, impatient to see what Les was up to, Mick turning that bit slower, not to be impressed; Terry was last, eyes half closed, very apprehensive.

A metallic click opened them wide.

''Ey, Les!'

'Slick Brylcreem!'

'Where d'y'get that, Les?'

But Les was answering no questions. Not now. He stood facing Terry in a poised attitude of attack, feet apart, one in front of the other. His right arm was thrust out with the fingers extended, palm uppermost; and lying down the length of his hand, white-bone handled and shining sharp, was a wicked looking flick-knife with a fifteen centimetre blade. It was so close to Terry's face that he drew his head back in alarm and knocked himself against the wall.

Les held his aggressive, dominant, position for long enough to impress them all – the four docks' boys with his style, and the kid in the black shirt with his serious intent.

'Right, now jus' you listen, Pig-face. I'm gonna ask you some questions. An' I want the truth, right? One little lie out've you an' I'll chiv yer, right?' Terry stared back at him, unblinking. 'Right?' Les thrust the sharp point to within a centimetre of Terry's face, between the eyes. Terry shut them and nodded. 'Right, si' down then, an' listen.'

Terry slid down the wall, shivering. He was drenched through, they all were, and his clothes stuck coldly to him. He was scared, and he was uncomfortable. He liked his comforts – an electric blanket, clothes that weren't rough, big bath towels. He always shuddered when he remembered a story of Uncle Charlie's from the Second World War, when a group of soldiers he was in, cut off from their unit in France, had come across a deserted farmhouse, all of them caked in mud and filth from running and fighting in their uniforms for a week. They'd found a tin bath and boiled some water on an old wood stove; but while it had been

Uncle Charlie's turn to soak himself a look-out had spotted the Germans coming, and Uncle Charlie had had to scramble hot and wet into his rough uniform and run for the woods. Terry always shivered at the thought; he had an idea he'd have preferred to dry himself properly and give himself up. He felt just as demoralized now. With an aching head, chest, and arm from the fall, still feeling sick, and soaking wet, his resistance was as low as any interrogator or brain-washer could wish. He sat huddled against the wall with the other boys standing belligerently on either side, and Les leaning over him in front, menacing with the flick-knife. No fear, he'd co-operate.

'You reckon you go t' Fox Hill, do yer?'

He nodded. 'Yeah, I do.' There was no 'reckon' about it.

'All right then, what's the 'eadmaster's name?'

Were they checking up, or did they want the information? Terry wondered. Either way there was only one answer.

'Mr Marshall.'

A sudden hoot of derision echoed in the small room.

'*Mister* Marshall!'

'Please, *Mister* Marshall, good morning, *Mister* Marshall . . .'

'Can I lick your boots, *Mister* Marshall?'

Mick kicked Terry on the thigh. ''Ere, wallie, are they all mister up your school?' He didn't wait for Terry to nod his head. 'We ain't got none of them at Napier. There's old Shadbolt, an' old 'Arvey, an' old Priddis – an' Bandy Bandish, the 'eadmaster; an' a lot of old women. But we ain't got no *misters*, 'ave we?' He went on sniggering, trying to give the impression that he had the whole staff eating out of his hand.

The others were still playing with 'Mister Marshall', with heavily sarcastic and obscene suggestions. It put Terry in mind of a brush he'd had with Mr Marshall himself – over some minor infringement of the school rules – when the headmaster had picked on some small unimportant point and made a meal out of it, taking a quite unexpected tack. It was disconcerting. You didn't know where you were.

'What's your teacher's name, then?'

Terry hesitated. It was Mr Evans. 'We call him "Old Evans",' he said at length. Again there was a riot of amusement.

'Good afternoon, *Mister* Old Evans.'

'Please, Old Evans, can I go lavvy?'

Terry shut his eyes and let out a long pent-up breath. There was no winning with this lot.

'All right, belt up!' Les tossed the next question in casually, like an experienced soldier with a grenade.

''Ave you got a lot of stuff up Fox Hill?'

It had a similar effect. The room was instantly filled with an explosive tension, shutting the others up suddenly as they saw what Les was leading up to.

'I dunno. What stuff?'

'Come off it, Pig-face. You know what I mean. Stuff worth nickin'. Tellies an' transistors. Tape recorders. That sort of stuff...'

Now Terry saw the drift as well. He didn't know what to say, how to answer. Yes, there was a lot of stuff like that. But it didn't seem right to tell them.

'Well, there are a few things. I think there's a telly. And a radio...'

He got no further with his evasions. Suddenly the point of the flick-knife was pressing against his cheek, and Les was breathing stale butt-end breath in his face. Terry's head and shoulders were gripped from either side and his legs were pinned down to the floor. There was no joking now. The jokes were over. They were in deadly earnest all right. He'd been daft to relax his fears even for a second. He was within that second of being slashed, he knew it.

'Don't you get clever with us, son. Either there is a telly, or there ain't. There ain't no "I think" about it. Now, you've got about ten seconds to tell us, so don't muck us around. What stuff 'ave you got up your school, an' where is it?'

Terry swallowed; but he didn't need as long as a second to think. Under these circumstances even Mr Marshall would have told them. It began to pour out.

'There's a big telly on a stand; and there's six transistor radios – one between two classes; and there's a couple of cassette recorders. Hang on ...' He paused for a moment while he searched the time-table in his mind. He was sure there was more. '... And there's a record player; and a set of chime bars.'

'Stuff chime bars!'

'Ding-dong,' said Mick.

'And a film projector,' Terry added, getting up to Friday afternoon in his mind. 'And a slide projector. A film strip thing ...' There was a longer pause while Terry racked his brain for anything else. But that was all. He couldn't think of any more.

'Is that all?'

'Yes.' Terry felt guilty already.

'Nothin' else?'

'Only more chime bars,' said Mick. 'Ding-dong.'

Les squinted hard at Terry. 'You sure?'

'Blimey,' said Mick, 'that's enough, ain't it? We ain't got none of that down Napier ...'

'Only 'cos you've nicked it,' put in Plastic-head. 'There's nothin' worth nickin' down Napier no more ...'

'There ain't a stick o' chalk they don't chain up ...'

'All right!' said Les. 'Stop makin' us cry. Now, where's all this stuff kept?'

With a sinking feeling Terry realized that this might be his chance to put himself right. To refuse to help them further, or to give them false information, might make up a bit for telling them what they'd wanted so far. But the moment soon passed.

'The radios are in Marshall's office, in a cupboard. I

dunno about the recorders and the slide thing. The telly and the record player are in the library – locked up.'

There was a long silence while Les thought something out with a frown. He looked round the room, at his chair, at the bare floor, at the grimy window. Then he looked hard at Terry. The others waited to see what he was going to do, Terry apprehensively, the others with a fidgety excitement. Terry was presumably about to hear whether he was going to be released or not. Now that he'd helped them he deserved it, he thought. His main worry was whether he'd get away without them all having their parting shots at him, their last kicks and punches.

'What's your name, Pig-face?'

Les had suddenly sprung to life again with a jerky gesture and an angling of his head like a snappy television crook.

'Terry Harmer.'

'Right, 'Armer. I'll tell you what the score is. An' you lot listen an' all 'cos I ain't a bloody record player . . .'

Les had everyone's undivided attention.

'We're gonna do Fox Hill School. Tonight, in the rain, while everyone's keepin' dry.' Four faces lit up. 'Pig-face 'ere takes us up there an' shows us the layout. Then we do it. If we're quick we can be in an' out an' back 'ere before anyone's old lady starts sussin' nuthin' out. We lay the stuff up somewhere till tomorrer; then while you're all in school I 'ave a word with a bloke I know an' I fix up to unload it. Right?'

'Yeah . . .'

'We can make a good few quid out of them trannies – easy to shift, them. Dunno about nothin' else. But it'll keep you lot in faggies for a couple a' weeks, an' I can use a few quid meself . . .'

'Yeah. Good idea, Les.'

'Yeah . . .'

There was another short silence which Terry daren't break, however shocked and outraged he was at his inclusion in their plans. He suddenly sensed that he was the subject of their thoughts.

'An' if you're wonderin' about 'im, 'e comes with us – all the way. Right in. Part of it, all essept the split.' He turned to stare into Terry's wide, frightened eyes. 'Then you can't do nothin' about it, right, 'cos no one'll believe you wasn't in on it. Your word against five. An' against this an' all!' The flick-knife darted forward again, snake-like. 'We know where you live, an' we'll chiv yer – real bad – if you open your gob.' Terry looked scared, but Les obviously thought he needed one final act of persuasion. He suddenly threw his head back and pulled his grimy collar down his throat. 'We'll chiv yer like this!' Round his throat, like a wide white ribbon with a livid ridge along the centre, ran a long scar, a surgeon's scar with stitches, the start of the new skin which formed part of his neck. 'Worse than this! Right down your mush!'

Terry couldn't speak. There were no words he could bring out of his numbed mind; no voice available to carry them, anyway. Just a loud, fast-beating heart. The silence went on, almost unbearable, until it was broken impetuously by Mick.

''Is mum done that,' he said suddenly. 'Didn't she, Les?'

Les turned slowly to grip the ambitious Mick with a look of angry hatred. He was two years older than Mick and he didn't have to take that.

'Not for the purpose!' he said, holding him with his snake eyes, his voice low and toneless to convey the message that he was still the one who called the tune.

'Oh no, not for the purpose,' Mick agreed wisely. 'Just to let Pig-face know you ain't soft . . .'

Les went on staring at him, his eyes telling him that he hadn't been far off a chiv himself.

'No,' he said at length. 'Soft I ain't.'

'Right,' said Mick, eager to get over the hurdle he had

foolishly erected for himself. 'So that's it. Up to Fox Hill for them trannies . . .'

'Yeah.'

'An' some o' them chime bars,' added the black boy. But nobody found it funny any more.

Chapter Five

FROM the Court flats the Harmers' route to the common took them back down Fox Hill, past Terry's school, and round a recently introduced one-way system of small streets to the road which divided the flat common from the lines of Victorian villas.

It was a route which also took them past Uncle Charlie's corner grocery shop, and while Jack was not perverse enough to make a long diversion, he was grateful for the screen of rain which would enable them to pass it unobserved. Uncle Charlie's large Rover was parked outside, moored to the kerb-side like a liner among a fleet of tugs, but there was no sign of the old man through the 'special offer' windows.

The main-road traffic was much thinner now, and it took the Harmers very little time to cruise the length of the flat common and round to the ravine boundary. Gladys kept her window wiped with a tissue and peered intently out. But the common was bare, the trees sheltered nothing but sodden litter, and the bandstand stood like a lifeless skeleton.

'He's not here, Jack, I know he isn't.' Jack grunted. 'Of course he could be back home by now . . .' Jack grunted again, his eyes aching from having to squint through the rain, keeping one eye on the road and the other on the doorways on his right.

The rain was as persistent as it had been for the past three-quarters of an hour; but the thunder and lightning seemed to be playing catch across the sky rather than bouncing down to earth, and Gladys was tempted to suggest they might go home and wait for Terry to return from whatever hole he'd crawled into. The whole business suddenly began to look a bit silly, unnecessary, and she started to feel rather like she did when she had run hard for a bus at the terminus and then it hadn't gone for another ten minutes. People looked at you and smiled sympathetically but you knew they thought you'd made a bit of a fool of yourself. The storm was easing off and they might just as well go home and wait for him to come in, she thought. But even as she half opened her mouth to make some sound of contact before speaking this thought, the common suddenly flickered with blinding bright light and an immediate crack rocked the car with the force-wave of its electrical discharge. It must have been very close. It reminded Gladys of the war, when everyone had thought the planes had gone and then a late bomb had exploded.

'Ooer, I thought it was passing over . . .'

Jack just grunted again. There were times when thoughts raced too quickly to slow them down with spoken words. He stopped the car and frowned out through the slap of the wipers. He didn't like this one bit. There was danger of some sort in the air, and his old fear had come to life: his fear that the family would be separated at some crucial moment, and that he wouldn't be there to protect and to comfort. It was a frustrating feeling, and it turned his inside over with a strange, longing, sensation. Now, in the centre of the storm, seeing the potential danger as being in the thousands of volts of electricity flashing about them, he wanted to envelop his family with his arms and hold them tight against the danger.

'Come on,' said Gladys, 'let's check up at your mum's and Uncle Charlie's. But a hundred to one he's safe and sound somewhere.'

The last huge flash over the flat common convinced Les that he was right. As he pulled Terry roughly by the arms against the flow of the gutters he knew that few people would be mooching about Fox Hill looking for villains this evening. Anyone with any sense had his head in the dry, kipping down in front of the telly, or lifting his arm in a pub.

Now the raid was on there was silence among the boys. If someone had shouted at them before they had made their plan they could have let the kid in the black shirt go, and run off somewhere with kicks and shouts of abuse and raised fingers. But with the kid involved in their plan now, and with a lot of loot to lose if they failed, they wanted to attract no attention to themselves at all. Only Les had known what was in his mind before. Now they all knew, and it was up to all of them to make it work. They might get bored with it if things didn't go right, but up to now they were all with Les. The exception was Terry. With Les's scaly hand gripping his arm, forcing a good pace through the oily rain, and hemmed in on all sides by the silent gang, he was filled with that same sense of shame and foreboding he felt when he had laughed about his mum or his dad with other kids. Breaking into his own school, treading all over Mr Marshall's room with their wet feet, stealing the transistors and the cassettes, it was fantastic, like the sort of nightmare you didn't believe in even when you were having it. His row with Tracey and his set-to with his mother paled into insignificance against this.

There was usually some way out of a tricky situation; you could say you were sorry, save up for a new whatever-you'd-broken, or stick it together, clear off for an hour. But this situation wasn't going to go away, and whatever happened afterwards, whatever he told his dad, he was still going to catch it either from Mr Marshall and the law or Les with the knife. His dad might believe him, but there was no reason why anyone else should. He got on all right with Mr Evans, for instance, but he wasn't all that well-in; he wasn't one of those boys all the teachers wanted to make a monitor. And Mr Marshall hardly knew him. He was sure he'd go on the bare facts rather than give him the benefit of some huge doubt.

Terry weighed it all up in his mind as he was pushed along the mirrored pavements, and he came to the conclusion that he had no choice really: his only salvation lay in a successful raid and a safe get-away. At least these kids seemed to know what they were up to. They might be scum but they weren't thick when it came to doing a bit of thieving. Yes, it might all work, he told himself, and then he could forget it, put it out of his mind, return to normal, be himself again. He began to feel convinced. Looked at like that, it was really the only thing that he could do.

Putting any sense of shame aside, as he felt he was entitled to, he began to think positively about the mission. He thought about the geography of the school, the location of the caretaker's house, the most sheltered route into the grounds, and the best way into the building. He pictured the most direct route to the headmaster's room once inside, with the least number of intermediate doors to force, and the white cupboard where he knew the radios were kept. He found himself beginning to think about the whole thing as an accomplice would, and he very nearly spoke about it as he was hurried along. Only the gang rule of silence on the move shut him up. So, in the grey streets of the Queen's Dock Estate, in the pouring rain, at his lowest ebb, he found himself taking that important step over the boundary between the 'us' of his previous law-abiding existence and the 'them' of what Uncle Charlie called the criminal class. His head still ached and his arm still hurt, and he told himself he wasn't going to make things any better by dwelling on what he was about to do. He shut his eyes and he sighed. There was a first time for everything, he supposed.

Jack and Gladys had known better times, too. Getting an idea across to Jack's mother wasn't as easy any more as it might once have been. She spent a lot of time on her own, and it took her a while to adjust her thoughts to cope with other people's problems. She could be a funny old stick, and

Gladys had never quite lost the feeling that old Mrs Harmer wondered whether she was as good a housewife as she ought to be. Jack hadn't long left his mother's after his customary pay-day visit on the way home from work, and at first she was surprised to see him again so soon.

'What's up, Jack? Have you left something behind?' she asked as she opened the door to him. Then she saw Gladys. 'Oh, hello, Gladys. You haven't come for the ride on a night like this?'

Gladys, over-sensitive, wondered if the old girl thought she was out gallivanting and neglecting the children. 'No, Mum. We're just having a little look round for Terry.'

'Why, isn't he at home?'

'No, Mum,' Jack replied, squeezing past her portly figure as she held open the door. 'We wouldn't be looking for him if he was . . .'

'No. Where is he then?'

Jack ignored the pointless question and tried to put the situation over to her slowly and without complication. 'He went out to play before it started to storm and we wondered if he might be taking shelter here.'

'But it's pouring down with rain.'

They were in the back room now, packed in with the furniture, the nick-nacks and the photographs, and Jack's mother had shut the door and sat down. Already they felt claustrophobic. Terry clearly wasn't here and they wanted to be away: but having stirred up the calm of the pond they had to stay and wait for the mud to settle before they departed.

'We didn't want him to get wet running home,' Gladys explained. 'If he was sheltering with you we wanted to give him a lift.'

'If he's out in this he's going to get soaked to the skin,' Jack's mother observed in a wise voice. 'He's not out to play in the storm, is he?'

'No, I shouldn't think so.' Jack struggled to keep the

exasperation out of his voice. It was terrible, what age could do. 'I expect he's taken shelter somewhere.'

'Yes.'

There was a short silence while the room filled with thoughts of departure.

'Yes,' the old lady repeated. 'I expect he's taken shelter somewhere. Mind, I don't see much of him these days – but whatever else he may be he's not silly enough to stand about in the wet . . .' She looked at Gladys with a look which suggested to her daughter-in-law that his lack of silliness could only have come from Jack's side of the family. Gladys smiled.

'Cup of tea, Jack?'

'No thanks, Mum.' He took a step back towards the door and bumped into his wife.

'Gladys? Cup of tea?'

'No, Mum, thanks. I think we'll just drive around the block and see if we can see him . . .'

'He'll catch his death of cold if he's out in this.'

Gladys took a deep breath. 'Well, I expect he's found shelter somewhere . . .' The words weren't worth the effort of repeating them. But she went on saying the same thing yet again.

'Yes. He'll turn up for tea if it's something nice . . .'

Again Gladys sensed a faint air of criticism. 'I expect so. Anyway, we'll just have another little look . . .'

'Yes.'

With each comment Jack and Gladys backed away up the hall until at last they were at the door.

Old Mrs Harmer peered out past them. 'It looks set in for the night. He'll have to make a dash for it sooner or later.'

'Yes, Mum.'

They were just about to get away when the old lady's final comment revealed a perceptive eye out of keeping with her woolly remarks.

'You haven't lost your wedding ring, have you, Jack?'

Jack stopped short and looked at his bare left hand. Gladys shot him a meaningful glance. She could imagine what the old girl would read into that. Thank God she'd kept her own on.

'No, of course not. It's in the car.'

'Oh, I see.'

But she didn't. Neither did she see, because her eyes weren't that good any more, as the car drew away and she took her customary look up and down the street before going in again, a small gang of wet boys hurrying round the corner and pushing one of their number up the street in the direction of Fox Hill Road.

Passing his gran's was the nearest Terry got to making a break for it. He had known all along that her house was on the direct route between the ravine and Fox Hill School, but he hadn't seriously considered an escape attempt. Les still had the flick-knife handy – he continually reminded Terry of his intention to use it if necessary – and Terry certainly didn't fancy hammering on his gran's door with his face ripped open. He'd have escaped for nothing then. But something emboldened him to chance his arm with a bit of bluff. Perhaps it was the way his mind had begun to accept the fact of what he was going to do, this insidiously growing feeling of being a member of the gang, however much against his will – and his conscience was reacting against it. Perhaps it was just the sense of outrage which hit him again as he found himself being force-marched towards a crime past his own gran's house, in his own familiar pattern of streets where these yobs had no right to be. Whatever it was, he suddenly thought he'd try to upset their plan somehow; and as he passed number forty-two with the familiar chipped oval enamel number on the brown door, he abruptly stopped.

'My gran lives here,' he announced in a falsely bold voice, 'and I'm going in. See you . . .' There was just a chance they'd come to their senses when they realized they might be seen through the net curtain – or that his familiar voice might be heard by an Amazon of a super-gran who stood behind her innocent looking front door just waiting for people to be rotten to her grandson. There was just a chance they might scatter in all directions and leave him to walk up the short concrete path and ring the bell.

But Terry was to learn that one of the unpleasantest elements of tangling with crooks, even young novices like these, is the element of surprise they bring to a situation. If you square up to a thug with your fists he'll have kicked you in the crutch before you give that vital area the first thought of defence; or if you're ready with hand and feet he'll butt you on the bridge of your nose with his hard forehead; or if he does none of that he'll spit at you, or stamp on your toe or let two sharp fingers fly at your eyes. He's always ready with the next unexpected and unacceptable move. So Terry, expecting a few moments' parley and a rash of preliminary threats at the least, suddenly found himself cracking the back of his head on the pavement, with Les's ridged boot pressed hard across his throat and the flick-knife pricking at his cheek.

'If y'want it now, Pig-face, y'can 'ave it – 'cept you'll be drippin' blood all over the 'eadmaster's carpet. There ain't no out f'you so stop poncin' about. Get it?' Les thrust his boot further into Terry's throat and momentarily cut off the supply of air. 'Do yer?'

Terry tried to nod, but he could only blink his eyes in submission and assent. The four other boys stood above him, casual and seemingly unconcerned in the pouring rain. Les was dealing with Pig-face and no one else felt the need to interfere. A transistor apiece at least was going to be good pickings from tonight's bother, and an almost professional calm had settled over all of them for the time being.

'Right, then git up an' git goin', and don't try nothin' else, right?'

Terry got up and croaked something softly. They moved off again in the pouring, rumbling and flashing storm. No one said anything. Terry, soaked to the skin like the others, had come to ignore the wet as a fish does the water – he'd been in it so long it had become his element – and even his push to the pavement had added little really to his wetness. Only the pain in his throat increased his discomfort. Les's boot was partly responsible. But apart from that his Adam's apple had swollen with self-pity and with the strange pain of suddenly realizing what the protection of his parents meant to him.

Terry's was not the only pain up Fox Hill way. Only a street or so away the pain which Uncle Charlie felt at that moment was a long, dull ache, and he was rarely without it when he was alone. He knew what it was. It was the pain of growing older into another era, the ache of nostalgia for earlier days. Like a man suddenly made redundant, a docker employed as a milkman, or a lighterman shut in a foundry, he found himself virtually in a different job, even though the sign over the door hadn't changed for twenty years.

He hated supermarkets. However, in line with most other small grocers up and down the country he had had to go over to the new way of doing things. He had had the old oak counter ripped out and a line of flimsy metal racks put down the middle of the narrow shop to satisfy the modern demands. He had cut out the fresh meats and installed an extra deep-freeze. If people expected self-service and pre-packed goods, he told himself, that's what you had to give them or you went out of business. Unfortunately, the re-arrangement of the shop had left him without a satisfying job to do all day. No longer could he stand behind his counter, his hands spread flat on the polished surface and inquire into the needs of his customers personally, packing their baskets and listening to their troubles. Nor could he impress the children any longer with his skill at knocking and catching the cornflakes off the top shelf, or expertly pull the wire back and down through the tight cheese, accurate to the half-ounce. No longer did his fingers lovingly stroke the eggs as he boxed them, or his hands show off the quality in a slice of bacon as he held it out, proudly and silently, to speak for itself like a diamond necklace. All that was gone. Now he had the choice of hovering about like a store detective, occasionally filling the shelves, or sitting on a stool like a computer operator pushing buttons at the check-out.

He didn't like the choice, so he did neither. He resented the enforced change so much that he filled the shelves overnight and he employed a school leaver to sit at the check-out; and he spent his days in the small back room playing at the paper-work and backing a few hunches on the horses, selecting his runners in the mornings and sometimes watching them romp home in the afternoons. He was no longer a poor man, and he found himself taking more and more time away from the shop on one pretext or another, chasing up a delivery or following a favourite at one of the racecourses within driving distance. But what made him really happy was when a customer couldn't make her mind up in the shop and he felt invited to go to her assistance. Or when he was making someone laugh at a family tea-table. At those times he was in his element; being a real grocer, or being an uncle. He asked for little more.

When Gladys and Jack arrived he was sitting on a large wooden chair, lifting jars of marmalade out of a large cardboard box and putting them on to the wire shelves. His mind was years away and his belly was aching with nostalgia; but company was always welcome, and when the private knock came and he had satisfied himself that he wasn't about to admit a burglar, his natural cheerfulness welled up inside to drown the melancholy thoughts.

'Hello, Glad, hello, Jack. Come to borrow a cup of sugar? Here, you don't want a thousand packets of curry powder, do you? I've only over-ordered b'ten. Put an extra nought on the end!'

Gladys did try to smile. 'Oh Lord, have you? No thanks, Uncle Charlie . . .'

'Well come in for Gawd's sake.' His sharp businessman's eyes looked into their serious faces. 'Hello, you look in a bit of a two-and-eight, the pair of you. What's up? You look as if you've lost a quid and found a Green Shield stamp!'

They filed into the shop while Uncle Charlie carefully re-bolted the door. A quick anxious glance told them that Terry wasn't there. In as few words as possible Jack told him the same version of the story that Gran Harmer had heard, while Uncle Charlie rested his unsteady seventeen stone against the check-out and scratched his smooth bald head with the cap of a ball-point. When Jack had finished, the big man, who clearly didn't take the situation too seriously, hitched his slipping braces up on to his shoulders and tried to pass some of his immense reserve of assurance on to the worried pair.

'Well, if he ducks in here out of the wet stuff I'll give you a tinkle and you can come and fetch him. Don't worry. He'll be all right. He's got his head screwed on the right way. No flies on him. You can bet he won't be standing about in this lot waiting to be struck by lightning. Give him credit for a bit of sense . . .'

'Yes, of course,' said Gladys, brightening. However old you were it was always good to get reassurance from someone like Uncle Charlie.

'He's a good boy, Terry. I've got a lot of time for him. Streets different to some of the little tykes I get in here. Sticky-fingered, the lot of 'em, and cheeky with it. I'd like to get a good old-fashioned stick across some of their backsides!' He pushed himself up off the check-out with a groaning effort and hobbled over to the box of marmalade. Gladys thought fleetingly of Terry's cheeky departure from the house earlier, and reflected how little other people knew of the inner workings of even a normal family. And a good job too, she thought, or all the kids in the world would be written off as monsters by people without children.

'Anyway, no panic, Glad.' Uncle Charlie raised his voice above the click-click of the little pricing stamp which had made the stub of pencil behind his ear redundant. 'You go home and make yourself a nice cup of rosie. He'll turn up sooner or later. When he's hungry.' He caught the darting look of anxiety on Jack's face. 'And don't do nothing stupid, for Gawd's sake. If he hasn't turned up by eight give us a shout and I'll have a cruise round the streets in the motor. The police won't be too pleased if they get called out in the wet while young Terry's watching the telly in one of his mates' houses, will they?'

Jack reacted sharply. 'Of course not,' he said. It was disconcerting to have his thoughts read by the worldly-wise old boy. 'We just thought we'd call at one or two likely places...'

A few minutes later they were gone, sitting silent in the car as it cut a swishing path through the oily streets back to the house. Each of them hoped to walk in and see Terry sitting curled up in an armchair in front of the television as if nothing had happened; but each had a nasty feeling that that wasn't how it would be.

Meanwhile Uncle Charlie started on a crate of tinned potatoes, his lonely thoughts reflecting once more on the world he used to know, when people talked to one another, when cat's whiskers hadn't been superceded by transistors, and where values weren't recorded in computer language. For a few minutes, old as he was, he thought about his mother, God bless her. And every now and then, when the storm lit up the shop, he thought of Terry.

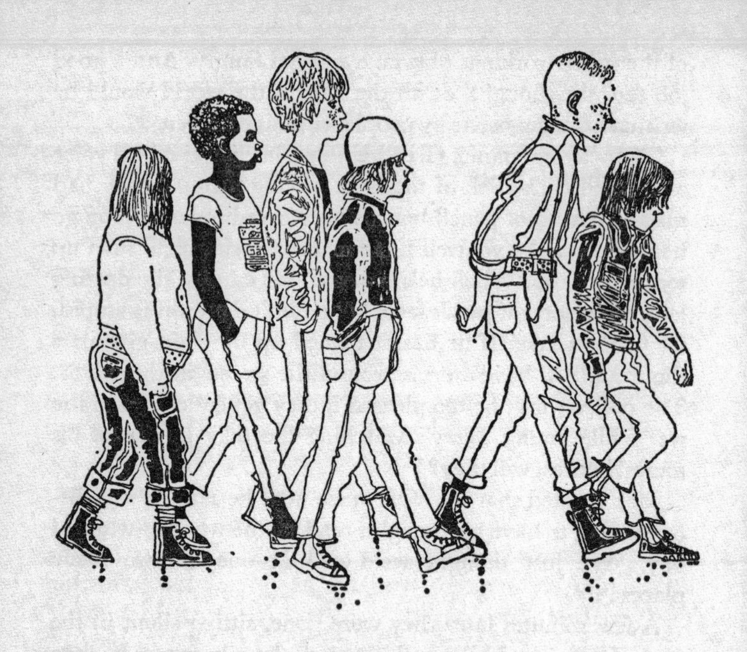

Chapter Six

THE rain began to ease a little as the gang approached the final corner before the school. Terry still led the way, so closely followed by Les that the slightest hint of him making a break for it in any direction would have led to swift, and, Terry had no doubt, vicious action. Les was like a stage gunman, when a hat or a raincoat or a jacket pocket does nothing to conceal the fact that he's holding a weapon at somebody's back. Wet as he was, it couldn't be for comfort, or to keep one hand dry; the only point in him keeping one hand in his jeans pocket was the long, wicked flick-knife lying dangerously ready to spring.

Very little had been spoken since Terry had been got down on the pavement outside Gran Harmer's. Mick and the others formed a silent escort at the side and the rear of Terry. None of them thought it was worth planning much until they could see their objective before them. This scheme of Les's was already a rare exception to their usual spur-of-the-moment activity.

Although he was out of his own territory Les knew enough of the lie of the land to recognize the corner before the school. He suddenly stopped and with exaggerated interest pretended to read the collection times off a handy pillar-box. His eyes were directed at the enamel rectangle, but his voice was directed menacingly at Terry.

'Right, Pig-face, before we go round this corner, I want the best way into this stinkin' school, right?' He punched three sharp knuckles into the region of Terry's kidneys. 'An' I don' wanna be led up to the bloody caretaker's door, neither. Get me?' The three knuckles went in again, and a sickly numbness spread itself down through Terry's body, weakening him at the knees. But he kept his mouth shut and he stayed on his feet. 'So let's 'ave it – straight!'

Terry knew that the next thing he said would finally cast him with the gang or against it. Up to now he'd been forced along at knife-point, without having to say anything. Admittedly he'd thought round all the possibilities and he'd joined them mentally by working out a plan for getting into Marshall's room with the best chance of success; but he'd not actually said yes, and he'd not said no, and because of his escape attempt outside his gran's they still weren't to know he wouldn't finally refuse to help them, and risk the consequences. Now he'd been asked a question. Very forcibly. And now they were waiting for his answer.

For a second or so he looked into Les's accident of a face, at the hooded eyes, and the sneering mouth which plastic surgery couldn't help because the wound went too deep. All around him Terry could sense the tension in the others. Mick pretended to be biting his nails, but there was nothing left to bite; Plastic-head pushed the hemisphere of ball back off his forehead a fraction, like a cowboy waiting for trouble; little Blondie squared himself up to look tough; while the fourth lad, the wiry black boy, wiped the back of his hand meaningfully across his moist nose. They were about to embark on something now, they seemed to say – either a job, or a beating-up. And it was all down to Terry which it was to be.

Like every creature born, Terry had the basic instinct to preserve himself against injury or death; and he regarded Les's knife as a bigger threat to this basic desire not to get hurt than the more remote possibility of his parents or the police sometime finding out about the raid. If it was a choice between definitely getting hurt now, or perhaps getting hurt later, the decision was easy.

'There's two ways in,' he began in a toneless voice, running his finger round the wet plate on the pillar-box to show the rectangular shape of the school premises. 'The front way's in Paget Street, round the corner half-way down on the left between the houses.' The others had grouped round, fixing the layout in their minds from the wet map Terry was drawing. 'The caretaker's house is just inside, behind the other houses. The back way in's the best. There's no open space to cross, like in front. It's in the next road up, Hazledene, on the right . . .'

There was a short silence while the new knowledge sank in; and as it did it had the effect of slightly changing their attitude to the kid who'd given it: not much, but a bit.

'All right then, kid,' said Les. 'Round the back it is. But I warn yer, one little trick an' you're gettin' it, right?'

'Yeah!' said Mick.

'Yeah!' echoed the others in various notes of menace. But the short blond boy, who'd drawn his boot back for another kick at Terry's calf, stamped it down instead. It was a little bit different now.

'All right,' said Les. 'Now tell us the layout.' Terry opened his mouth. 'As we go! We can't stay 'ere no longer or someone'll think we're puttin' dogs' muck in the letter-box or suthing.'

Dennis, the black boy, laughed. 'Lord, man, that's better'n some o' the letters my 'ole man gets!'

'Yeah, I know,' said Mick in a throw-away voice, not to be outdone with the quick remarks. 'My old man sends 'em!'

That creased everyone with laughter but Les and Terry, who both had too much responsibility creasing their foreheads to pay any attention to the banter.

'Belt up!' said Les. 'And come on!' He pushed Terry forward and the group crossed over the side road and walked quickly on to the next corner. As if by some agreed plan they all suddenly began walking on tiptoe. They were within hearing, if not within sight, of their objective, and like cats on the prowl they muffled their pads and sharpened their outlines in preparation for the pounce.

Fox Hill Primary School was completely hidden from view, almost as if the planners had decided it was best kept from the public gaze, a modesty which was not intended. The original school, opened in 1902, had been sited within an enclosing square of well-built Victorian houses, with a broad opening in the middle of Paget Street giving an impressive view of the tall, ornate building. But in 1940, when the children were safely evacuated to the country and auxiliary firemen slept in the class-rooms, a stick of German bombs fell short of the target docks and, as well as leaving empty sockets in the rows of houses, hollowed out the school like a drill in a wisdom tooth. Twelve firemen died and three never walked again. But within two years of the end of the war the school was back on its feet, a new one-storey building for infants and juniors, and new houses – at first temporary pre-fabricated bungalows, and later small town houses – filled in most of the original gap in Paget Street so that only the locals, or people passing at playtime, were aware of the school's existence.

The bombs brought about a social change as well. On the other side of Fox Hill Road, where the bombs had also fallen, the destruction had been repaired by a speculative builder with grand ideas, and amongst the remaining villas he placed a small estate of large square neo-Georgian houses with elegant doors and small-paned windows. Within fifteen years the whole area around the school had become a smart place to live, a posh address, what Mr Marshall called a cricket table on the football pitch. The nearest corner shop became a delicatessen, the second-hand junk and light removals man became an antique dealer, and the new state school became *the* place to send their children for all the occupiers who had spent every penny on the house. Mr Marshall now had the strongest Parent-Teacher Association in London, plenty of money for transistors, televisions and tape recorders, and a high rate of admission to the local grammar school.

He also had a lot of children, like Terry, who weren't quite sure where they fitted into the scheme of things.

It was a good building, almost revolutionary in its time in breaking away from the London County Council pattern of three-storey-schools with central halls and classrooms leading off them. Fox Hill had a large hall standing on its own, and twelve classrooms built in a square, facing into a central quadrangle, and linked by a corridor which had once been an open reinforced glass veranda. The head's room, the staff-room and the office were at the front of the square, facing the Paget Street entrance across a small car-park. The hall was tacked on at the rear, hard by the backing row of houses in Hazledene Road. Two playgrounds flanked the school, the infants' on the left and the juniors' on the right, the whole establishment inset into the surrounding square of houses like a block in a geometric puzzle.

Terry intended to break in through the hall at the back. The side wall of the hall was fairly secluded, and the windows there were pivoted at the sides and opened upwards and outwards, while the handles inside were simple affairs, set centrally in the bottom of the metal frames and easily opened by a knife up the crack. In fact, as many boys knew, it was often done on a Saturday morning when Mr Evans wanted to drop the sports bag into the locked school – and it was only now that Terry felt surprised that no one had used this knowledge for some criminal or mischievous reason before. It had never crossed his mind. As for the knife needed for the crack, they certainly had that with them. Terry was hardly likely to forget the knife.

'Where we goin'? Round the stinkin' block?' Mick asked suddenly, tension coming out in impatience.

'Shuddup! The kid's gonna tell us, ain't 'e? Cloth ears!'

Terry had learned the lesson not to wait for a painful prod before doing what he was told. In a fast but low voice, a conspirator now, he told them the first part of the plan that had formed in his mind.

'The next road up is Hazledene. There's a back way in up an alley between the houses. You can . . . we can . . . easy climb the gate, it ain't high, and we can get into the hall through a window. It's easy. You can do the catch with that knife. Then we'll have to see what doors are locked inside. I dunno about them . . .'

'Don't worry,' said Mick. 'Dennis'll put 'is 'ead through them . . .'

'Watch out it ain't yours I put through,' growled Dennis, not amused.

'Belt up!' Les could see the danger of even the slightest disunity in their ranks. 'We're on to a soft touch 'ere if we play our cards right.' He turned to Terry again, flicking the rain out of his eyes with his fingers. 'What about the caretaker? Where's 'e likely to be? An' the cleaners? What about them?'

Terry hadn't thought about the cleaners. He mentally reckoned the time since he'd left school earlier in the afternoon. That had been a very long time ago; time enough for his whole life to have changed direction. 'No, they won't be there now. It's only the caretaker. But 'e's got eyes in his bum . . .'

'Naughty, naughty,' sneered Mick.

'. . . But he'll be in his house now. I expect . . .'

'You hope, you mean,' Les reminded him nastily. 'But 'e don't know us, remember. You're the only one 'e'll know if 'e sees us!'

'Yeah, there ain't no way 'e'll be able to pick us out,' said the small blond boy to convince himself.

''Cept for Dennis,' added Mick. 'An' y' can't tell 'im from all the others, can yer, Den?'

'Pick your nose an' eat it!' Dennis retorted in a low growl, no more appropriate insult springing to mind.

Mick let it go at that. He wasn't ready for a fight with anyone just yet.

'Come on!' Les croaked at them. 'Let's get inta the 'all out of this bloody rain. I'm just about up to 'ere with it. Let's get this job done an' 'ome!'

Without saying any more the small group turned the corner into Hazledene Road and hurried along it to the alley between the houses.

Mr Jarvis, in the well-furnished comfort of the caretaker's house, took his large bunch of keys from their hook by the front door and called to his wife in the kitchen.

'Inge, I'm just going over the school for ten minutes. That flat roof on the hall doesn't like too much rain . . .' It was no criticism of his school: it was just a fact, like a pet cat not liking fish. 'I won't be long if it's all right. Or I might have to put a bucket down on your floor . . .'

Inge, who cleaned and polished the hall, said something in reply. It might have been in English, if she was pleased, or in German if she wasn't. Mr Jarvis didn't catch it – he had his bad ear to the kitchen; but he could guess well enough. A tall, serious man, wearing a blue bib and brace beneath his shiny-worn jacket, with a wide brown belt round his trim non-drinker's stomach, he stood under the porch of the school house and looked out at the sheet of tarmac which separated him from the school. The sky was slightly lighter now, but still the rain fell, and the sound of swallowing drains filled the air. The flat, black, and shining surface of the staff car-park was raised in a goose-flesh of rain, and the modestly porticoed front entrance of the school still seemed a soaking away. Suddenly Inge was behind him at the door.

'Do you have to go this minute? The rain won't fall for ever, and your supper is right ready.'

Ernest Jarvis looked at the sky, he looked at the swimming tarmac, and he looked at his school. Duty called; unfortunately, so did his wife – his war bride with the Teutonic temper. He didn't apologize. He turned up the collar of his jacket and jumped the puddle outside the porch.

'I won't be long,' he called. 'Keep it hot.'

Even through the rain and the cotton-wool of his poor hearing he heard a torrent of angry German pouring out after him, finally dammed by the slamming of the front door.

'The hall!' he called out into the wetness. 'I must just check the hall.' Then, head down, selecting the right key from his bunch, he ran across the car-park to the school.

Terry, and Les's gang, were at the hall already. The tubular frame of the back gate had provided a good handhold, and the padlocked handle a convenient step. Les had sent Mick over first, in case Terry had tried to make a last run for it, then he had sent Terry, and then the rest. But Terry had so conditioned himself for what was to come that he had gone over the gate almost willingly.

It wasn't until they were at the first hall window, hidden by the angle of the P.E. equipment store, that a renewed and heightened sense of what he was doing hit Terry like the

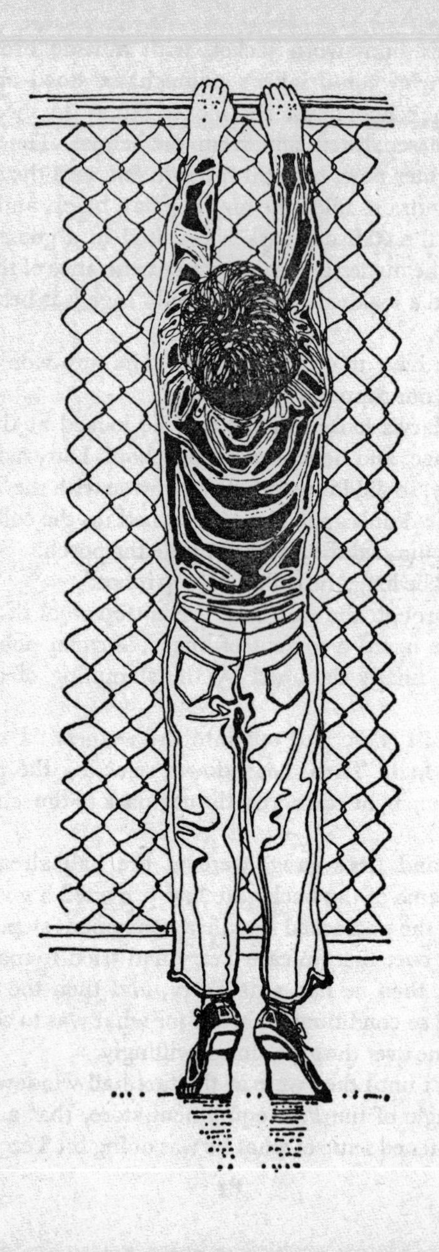

sudden stomach-turning pang of having forgotten Mothers' Day. If Mr Jarvis came right this minute he might just get away with a ticking-off, for playing on the school premises after hours; but from now on, from the first fiddling with the hall window-catch, he was going to be in much deeper, hotter water.

Les cupped his hands round his eyes and looked in through the running glass. The others, all but Terry, did the same. There's no evidence like that of your own eyes, they knew, and no one should be trusted too far, especially the dodgy leader of a dodgy gang.

The hall was bare, and dry. The dinner chairs were stacked in mathematically equal piles along the top end, and the P.E. mats, benches and horses were along the bottom, on their right.

'Smart!'

'This ain't a school, is it?'

'Yeah, it's just the hall,' Terry said from behind them. Then to soften the sharp edge of difference between his school and theirs, he added, 'We have to have our dinners there as well.'

'Cooked 'ere?'

'No, they bring it in containers . . .'

'Like ours . . .'

'Prob'ly all cooked the same place . . .'

'Yeah . . .'

'Bet they taste better up 'ere.'

'Yeah.'

Les stopped the drooling. 'Shut up about bloody food an' let's get them radios. That's what we're 'ere for. All of yer shut yer noise 'less I ask y'suthing. We don't want no one nosin' round 'fore we even get started . . .'

Shaming them by his own activity, as their mothers would by working round their idle feet, he slipped the slim blade of his flick-knife up into the crack in the bottom section of the window-frame, just beneath the handle. It was too easy. The handle obediently lifted, and, with finger-nails in the crack, the window was pulled upwards and outwards to make an aperture about fifteen centimetres wide.

'Slick Brylcreem, 'e's right!' said Mick. 'It's like openin' my sister's money-box . . .'

'Yeah . . .'

Plastic-head beat an excited tattoo on his bald pate, and Dennis and Blondie punched each other and laughed. Mick was right. It was laughably easy.

'Right, Pig-face, you're first. Get in an' pull one of them chairs over 'ere to the winder. Make it easier for the rest of us.'

Terry hesitated; this next step was the biggest step of all.

'Go on, y' can't pull no tricks now.' Les gripped Terry's arm above the shoulder to push him forward towards the window; but he changed his mind suddenly and swung Terry back to face him. He fixed Terry with an intent stare, eyeball to eyeball. Terry saw the caked sleep in his hooded, lashless eyes, the blackheads round his greasy nose. It was a moment of complete contact, of one-hundred-per-cent communication between two people. Les spoke with a new seriousness, an earnestness which marked the change from what had been an opportunist plan – which could be abandoned at any time – to a criminal activity which involved breaking and entering with intent to steal. With a suddenly deepened understanding of his grim position Terry listened.

'Don't go thinking there's any way out now, Pig-face. You're in this right up to your neck with the rest of us. You're the kid who comes 'ere, you're the one who showed us 'ow to open the winder. You're in it worser than anyone, so it's all down to you to get us in an' out safe with them trannies. An' remember – if it all goes off O.K. you're laughin'. If it don't . . .'

'Come on, 'urry up!' complained Mick. 'Let's get in the dry for Gawd's sake!'

'Yeah, come on, Leslie,' said Dennis. 'Once we're in this

place we can't be seen from none of that row of houses. I feel like I've got my trousers down out here.'

In a swift movement Les rounded on them, gripping Terry's arm painfully tight.

'Shut yer traps! I'm just makin' sure Pig-face knows where 'e stands. 'S'important. I know what I'm doing.' He yanked Terry round to face him again. 'Right, get in, right? An' remember what I told yer . . .'

With a push he released Terry in the direction of the window. Terry wasted no time, he risked no impatience. He ducked under the window-frame and stood up with his head inside the glass. Immediately, the familiar hall smell of coconut mats hit him with a strange sort of friendliness, and he couldn't stop his stomach churning over with a shaming feeling of betrayal. The only thing to do, he told himself, was to stop thinking about it. He gripped the hard, thin edge of the window-sill and with a jump took his weight on his hands, in the position of a gymnast on the parallel bars. The window-pane sloped in behind his head and cramped his movements, but by shifting his weight from hand to hand as the metal cut into his palms he got up enough sideways momentum to swing his left foot up on to the sill, and with an awkward wriggle which threatened to hurt his crutch on the handle catch, he straddled the metal bar and dropped clumsily to the wood block floor.

As he felt the hard smooth blocks beneath his hands, coldly familiar, he realized with a shooting pain in his stomach that his chance had come. The change from being in the wet to being in the dry, or the sudden muffling of the rain, or just the P.E. lesson feel of the floor, made him realize at that instant that momentarily he was alone. He was in, and they were out. Now, if he were quick, he had his chance. He could shut the window on them and run into the school and put all the lights on, attract the caretaker, and take a chance on who the police would believe. Or he could hold these windows shut from the inside until they gave up and went away. It stood a good chance of working, unless they came up with something unexpected.

Terry got on to his hands and knees. This was not a choice he would have to agonize over. He had to get up and slam that window shut now, or not at all. The chance wouldn't be there for longer than three or four seconds.

He looked at the grain in the block floor, groping in his mind for an answer to what he ought to do. He ought to shut the window. And he ought to do it right now, quickly. He *ought* to . . .

Slowly, Terry got up, his back to the window. Les was in behind him in an accomplished flash, without waiting for the chair he'd asked for. He wasn't taking any chances on what Pig-face might do. He couldn't know, but there was very little danger of Terry doing anything to upset their plans any more. He had already been so hurt by his fall, frightened by the knife, and demoralized by their treatment, and he was now so involved – past the point of no return in his mind – that he'd given up all hope of doing anything like the right thing by any standards he knew. He was seeing things very simply now. It was easy. He was in the school to help this gang to steal the stuff he'd told them about. His mind had become conditioned to it. He didn't believe in miracles, and he couldn't think his own way through any course of action which would get him out of this mess on the right side. Whatever he did, he knew he wouldn't be seeing far enough ahead. They were bound to win. And no magic wand would spirit him back to an understanding mother and a dry towel inside his own front door. He had been made to believe that his only hope was for the raid to be successful, with a clean get-away, and he had stopped complicating things by trying to go against that way of thinking, by giving any serious consideration to the possibility of getting away any more. He stood and waited meekly while the others followed Les through the window.

Plastic-head, the last of the sodden group, swung over the

sill hurriedly and his supporting hand slipped. He let out a pained and obscene cry as he fell on to the catch, clutching at his crutch and dancing to derisive laughter on the hall floor.

'C'mon, stop muckin' about,' Les complained unsympathetically. 'We don't want no one to see us from them 'ouses. An' you don't know where the caretaker is for certain, so shut up!'

Plastic-head suffered in silence and the rest confined their mirth to wide and knowing smiles. Les was right. No more mucking about. The raid was on in earnest now. For real. For them all.

And that included Terry.

Chapter Seven

MR JARVIS turned a heavy key in the rim lock at the front door and let himself into the school. Unaware of what was happening a few doors away he stood on the large mat in its metal-framed well and turned down his collar with his finger-tips, shaking his lapels and kicking the water off his trousers as if he were taking out his discomfort on a disobedient dog. 'Bloody rain,' he muttered. But he was really as cross with himself as with the weather that moment, for he had only come without his mac on account of its being in the kitchen on the far side of his wife. He straightened up and looked round the quiet entrance lobby. Despite the rain it had that tranquil after-school atmosphere he loved; a peaceful calm punctuated only by the electronic click of the clock which governed the playtime bells, and the quiet bubbling of the air in a tank of tropical fish. He exhaled loudly, contentedly, and looked around. He supposed if he were quick he could check the hall and return to his meal before a real Teutonic mood set in. Say, two minutes, and he could be clear of the building, even allowing for all the doors.

It was a small pool of water on the lino tiles beside the tropical tank which saved Terry and the gang from discovery that soon. 'Hello, what's that?' Wiping his feet thoroughly on the mat as if a class of children were watching, the caretaker walked over to investigate. He hoped to goodness it wasn't a leak in the tank: that was a job and a half to repair. Still breathing noisily he ran his stubby finger round the seam of the tank. He couldn't be sure, but he was inclined to pronounce it dry. Still, best be certain. His hands were still damp from the rain so he found a dry spot on his bib to rub one finger thoroughly before starting again.

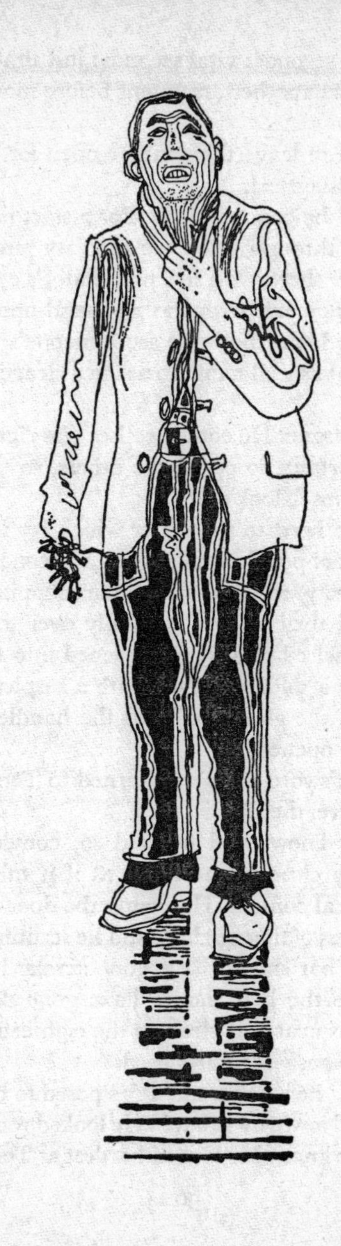

That all took seconds: vital seconds: just time enough for the gang to settle another argument before moving in from the hall.

Mick wanted to leave the window open for a quick getaway; but Les disagreed.

'No, shut it!' he commanded. 'For a start it ain't quick, gettin' six of us through – and we can easy push them bars on the door over there.' His sharp predator's eyes had spotted the emergency exit with the push-and-open bars. 'Besides, if anyone looks they can see someone's got in if we leave it. Y'might as well hang up a sign as leave that winder open.'

Mick didn't argue. He could see Les was right; but what was more important, so could the others, so there was no sense making himself look daft.

They paid no heed to the water which lay in blisters on the polished floor: people would know someone had been in the school anyway, so why waste time mopping up? With Les in the lead they walked stealthily over to the double swing doors of wired glass which opened into the corridor. Cautiously, like a soldier dealing with a suspicious car, Les looked through the glass and tried the handle, just out of habit. The door opened.

Surprised, he swore softly and turned to Terry. ''S open. Is someone in 'ere, then?'

Terry didn't know, and he said so, convincingly. Les pulled his body close to the door, as if it might yield its secret by physical contact. He swung the door slightly with his hand, careless of fingerprints, and he scrutinized the gap where the lock bar should have gone across. He looked at the floor where the bolt should have gone down into its socket. It was as neat and clean as the eighteenth hole on a golf course, obviously regularly used.

'I don' get it,' he whispered. 'It's s'posed to be locked, i'n it? But it ain't. Now why's that?' He looked round at everyone, but no one knew. He looked hardest at Terry, who was beginning to feel that Les might think he was leading them into a trap. 'Eh? Why ain't it locked if it's s'posed to be? The caretaker at Napier'd get 'is cards if 'e di'n't lock what he was s'posed to lock.'

'Yeah!' said Mick in a loud voice. 'They've 'ad so many break-ins that school's locked up like a prison now.'

In their tense state nobody reacted to his observation except to hiss silence at him.

'If someone does 'appen to be 'ere we wanna know about 'im before he knows about us, right?'

Les turned his attention back to the doors and the seemingly empty corridor. The corridor ran on either side of the hall door for about twenty metres, where, on each side, it turned at right angles away from the hall, down past the classrooms. Directly facing the hall door was a wall which separated the corridor from the quadrangle, as it did all the way round the square of the building. The corridor had clearly been no more than a covered way once, a long veranda along which children had walked, run and queued in all weathers. Now bricked in, with wide windows letting in light from the central quadrangle, it was still only a one-sided thoroughfare, opening on to classrooms on the outside and a forbidden formal garden on the inside.

It took Les a moment or so to realize that the pattern of the building allowed anyone on one side of the school, or in one corner, to see into the corridor all round, and that from window height – from the waist up – he stood exposed to anyone who entered the square of corridor.

'Geddown!'

The gang obeyed as one man: there was no clever remark, no mucking about now. Terry, in a seizure of panic, got down the lowest, behind the others. Jarvis! It must be! He crouched there with his heart pounding like a shivering rabbit. There was no escape now.

''S all right. It ain't nothin'. Not anyone. But there's winders all round so we'll 'ave to keep down . . .'

Terry started breathing again. He should have warned them about the windows.

'Right, what's-yer-name, which way do we go for the 'eadmaster's room?'

'Eh?' Terry couldn't grasp anything for a few seconds: he still had visions of old Jarvis or Mr Marshall suddenly appearing round the corner.

'You, Pig-face, Tony . . .'

'Terry . . .'

'Terry.' Les said it sarcastically, applying mock patience like a film of oil. 'If it ain't too long since I told you what you was to do, which way is it to the transistors and that? Left or right?'

Terry thought for a moment of the position of the headmaster's room at the front of the building. It was almost opposite their position now, just to the left of the entrance lobby as they faced it. It could be reached from either direction. They had to go through the swing doors into the entrance lobby before turning sharp left, and there wasn't a centimetre's difference in the route to the left or to the right of the symmetrical building.

'Either way,' Terry said. 'The room's over there.' He pointed to its position. 'But we've got to go through that door first . . . '

Les took it in. He nodded. 'All right. Foller me. Keep close together. An' keep down, below these winders . . .' He set off to the left, bent double, moving fast, a comical sight but deadly serious.

Terry was pushed to follow him by Mick, who still found time to turn in his doubled-over position and give a warning to Dennis.

'No biting my bum! Cannibal! I don' want the plague!'

'You mean the Black Death!' snorted Plastic-head, joining in the undisciplined banter. There was a general laugh which Les, in his urgency, didn't bother to check. They were almost there, and he'd rather risk the noise than stop them all for another rollicking. It was like kids in school who made more noise shushing than the original talkers. Besides, he had a lot on his mind. He didn't like that door being open; that didn't seem right.

If he could have seen round three corners, into the entrance lobby, he might have held them crouching there, or sent them scuttling back to the hall and the emergency exit. As it was he crept on along the left-hand route, leading his gang towards their objective. His choice of direction was going to prove crucial. But he couldn't know that just then.

It came from the roof-light, Mr Jarvis decided. The water. It didn't come from the fish-tank at all, it was just coincidence. Across the top of the entrance lobby a roof-light, shaped like a little glass bungalow, gave both light and height to the small area. Slatted windows ran along both sides of it, and one of these sections had been left partially open, letting in an occasional drip of rain to form the small pool by the tank. Pleased with his discovery, but at the same time cross with Mrs Brown for leaving it open, he turned the window handle on the wall with a speedy expertise, looking the other way, and the low-geared slats slowly closed. He studied the pool on the floor and decided to leave it for Mrs Brown to buff over with her machine in the morning. He'd have to tell her, of course, and she wouldn't be pleased, but that was too bad.

Satisfied, he headed for his main objective, the hall. If all was well there he could still hurry back for supper before he was really missed. He unlocked the swing doors into the veranda corridor and pushed his way through.

In that same corridor, to his right and not thirty metres away, the six intruders were hurrying to where he was standing, all of them bent double and moving like a string of guerrilla fighters. He had only to turn right and they would more or less walk into his arms.

He turned left. As usual. He was a methodical man, and

the classrooms were numbered from one to six down that side of the building, then from seven back to twelve along the right-hand corridor; his route, therefore, was determined by years of checking things off in order, as the Army had taught him. He walked along quickly, not patrolling tonight, with his set purpose in mind. He passed the six classroom doors without really seeing them: they were all shut with an empty waste-paper basket set neatly outside each door, and there was no irregularity to draw his attention to any of them. Only one room drew his attention, in a minor way. That was Mrs Snellgrove's, the deputy head's. Next to her wooden name-plate she had hung a small cardboard notice. 'NEW BOX OF STRAWS PLEASE.' Mr Jarvis made a mental note to put one out before school in the morning: she could have one without any bother; she was deputy head, and she didn't use them for Art and Craft. Then he turned the corner which led to the hall.

By now the gang was almost at the point he'd just left, the swing door to the entrance lobby. Mick was remarking on the name-plates.

'Gawd, they 'ave their names painted on the doors 'ere, like down the doctor's . . .'

'They couldn't do it down Napier,' said Plastic-head. 'No one hardly stays long enough. There'd never be time for the paint to dry.'

'Come on! And shut up!' Les was at the door to the entrance lobby, his voice tight and thin as the tension within himself grew to meet the climax he was seeking. Tentatively, he tried the door, suddenly recoiling from it as if it were a trapdoor on to a long drop. It gave.

''Alf time! Look at this! 'Nother door not locked!'

He screwed his eyes up and looked at it with a deep distrust. The others followed his eyes, but only with mild interest, as if they were glancing at the hundredth case in a boring museum. It'd be all right. He shouldn't panic. After a careful inspection of the door, round it, through it, and a checking look along each of the wings of the corridor, he decided to relax. It all seemed to be all right, didn't it?

'They ain't very partic'lar in your dump, are they, son? All these doors left open.' He made a disparaging chucking noise with his mouth. 'Come on. Ain't my fault if they're bloody stupid.'

Terry didn't know whether to be pleased or sorry at the caretaker's negligence. There were fewer hold-ups this way, less damage having to be done; but every hurdle crossed took him that much nearer to the ultimate goal, that much closer to finding himself running off in the rain with a school transistor under his arm.

Still crouching down on his haunches Les pushed the door further open and waddled through – for all his criminal intent and sinister threats putting Terry in mind of a little girl playing the part of the baby in a game of mothers and fathers. A similar thought must have occurred to Mick.

'Come on, "Dozey".' He pushed Terry in the back. 'After "Big Ears"!'

Terry waddled awkwardly through the door himself, and the rest followed behind while Mick whistled 'Heigh-ho, heigh-ho' through his teeth. But it wasn't funny. Terry's clinging trousers brought a new discomfort in this position as they stuck coldly to fresh parts of his legs, and he could feel his black silk shirt beginning to steam across the shoulders. His legs ached and his eyes felt raw and stinging. But the physical discomfort was nothing to the fresh bout of mental torture he was about to have to go through. For suddenly something Terry saw sent a cold shiver surging down inside him. It was a picture on the wall of the entrance lobby, a painting neatly mounted on black sugar-paper which he'd done for the class project on American Indians. Pinned there, looking so normal with its neatly printed label, 'Buffalo on the Range by Terry Harmer 4E', it had the unwelcome effect of triggering in his mind a fresh, cold assessment of what he was doing.

This was insane; it was unbelievable, diabolical. He knew what he should have done now. He should have stood up to them, taken their kicks. He should have called Les's bluff with the knife. He should have shut them out of the hall when he had the chance. If anyone could see him now – his dad, his mum, Tracey – they'd have fifty fits. He shuddered with disbelief. He closed his eyes and forced a pressure of sound inside his ears to shut out the sight and the sounds of the moment, as he always did when a diabolical thought needed wiping out.

But nothing went. When he stopped nothing had changed. Here he was, in the school, taking part in a raid, and for the moment there was no way out of it. He couldn't think of even the beginnings of a plan. So what could he do? Nothing. He cursed himself for his lack of ideas, for his blank mind which wouldn't, or couldn't, think positively about his problem. He would just have to be carried along with events, a match-stick in the gully, and hope for a miracle to rescue him before he went down the drain with Les and his gang. But it was a forlorn hope, he knew.

Les looked round the small entrance lobby. There was a door immediately to his left, and another, to the paper stock room, to his right. 'Which door?' he demanded. 'C'mon, we're like the fish in that tank in 'ere.'

'That one, on the left,' Terry replied, snapping back to the needs of the moment. '"Inquiries." It leads to the office, then Mr Marshall's room's through that . . .' Still crouching, he indicated the door which stood by the side of the fish-tank.

Les looked at the featureless wooden door and frowned. 'Bet this one's locked,' he muttered.

'Well, there's one way to find out i'n't there?' said Mick, sliding down the opposite wall to sit on the floor. ''Urry up, 'fore my bum gets cold!'

Les took no notice, but he crouched at the door and tried the handle. He was right. It was locked. 'Cobblers!' he said, and he sat back on his haunches and looked at the door as if it might open on its own if he thought enough evil thoughts about it.

'Well, wotcha expect?' asked Mick, more than a little pleased now that something was going wrong with cocky Les's perfect plan. 'It's not like nickin' suthink off a barrer in the square. When y'plan to break in somewhere you've gotta be up to acherly breakin-in! Thought you knew that!'

'Get stuffed!' said Les. 'Shut up, I'm just thinkin'.'

'Well think quick. We can't sit 'ere for ever . . .'

It was the farthest he'd dared go against Les; but he left it there for the moment. The time would come, not today or tomorrow, but it would come, and he'd show this lot how to do a job. Les said nothing, he didn't even look round again, but his right hand went to the scar beneath the neck of his shirt, and as he looked at the problem door he began scratching at the scar nervously.

The others spread themselves with long legs and possessive ease around the lobby – and Terry began to see a ray of hope, the early working of the miracle he'd thought could never happen. If Les couldn't open the door, perhaps the whole thing would be called off, and he could crawl home, untouched by the leprosy of real crime.

It was an anxious time, filled with everybody's private thoughts, secretly pulling in their different directions; and for a while nobody spoke.

'Stupid woman!' Mr Jarvis had put the key in the hall lock and found it wouldn't turn. He'd tried three other keys in the same series, without success, and he'd been just about to try the first key again, after checking the serial number, when he'd unintentionally put his weight against the door, and it had given. 'Stupid!' He felt foolish now, trying all those keys in an unlocked door. And angry. 'If she makes a fuss about supper I'll let her know all about this!' Mrs Jarvis was occasionally responsible for these little lapses, and he sometimes had to cover up for her where one of the other cleaners would be told her fortune in front of the rest. But there'd still be a flare-up at home, if he felt up to it. It wasn't an easy situation, having his wife work under him, and now tonight, what with the rain, and the supper, and this door, he felt really disgruntled as he went into the gloomy hall.

At first everything seemed to be all right. In wide sweeping arcs, like giant duster strokes, his eyes covered the squared plaster-board ceiling from the far end to above his head. There was no sign of damp, he was fairly sure of that. He heaved a sigh of relief. The last application of tar and small stones on the roof must have done the trick. But best make sure. With a deft flat-palmed movement down the panel of switches he put the lights on, and he walked down the length of the hall peering up at the corners of the plaster-board squares and round the lights, the trouble spots where the first signs of invading rain would appear. No, it was as dry as a bone.

'Well, barring accidents, she's all right,' he thought to himself, with the caring attitude of a ship's master after a refit. 'Good,' he thought. Still looking above him, double checking the ceiling, he walked swiftly back down the hall to lock up. 'Good!' he said aloud. Perhaps he wouldn't mention the unlocked door to his wife after all. We all make mistakes, don't we? With that tolerant thought in his mind, a tolerance born out of his own well-being, he walked head-up into the puddle left by Les. His right foot suddenly shot forward at the speed of adrenalin. 'Oh! Oh! Oh! Oh! Oh!' It wrenched him painfully into the splits position, his left knee twisted round and cracked down awkwardly on the hard block floor, and as he put out a steadying hand to keep his trunk upright, that, too, found a boy's puddle and shot away from him. 'Oh! Oh! Oh!' With a severe crack his head hit the pine floor and he found himself, a prone column of pain, looking up again at the bone-dry ceiling.

A numbing shock-wave enveloped him. As a young soldier, like children and athletes, he was as used to being on the ground as on his feet. But the man who had a struggle with his socks every morning was mentally unprepared for suddenly being flat on his back, and the shock of it was more serious than the physical pain or injury. Mr Jarvis lay there, too stunned to curse. Strangely, the first thought to flash through his mind, even before he could make the effort of wondering how hurt he was, was that he might be left there in the hall for some time. His wife wouldn't come looking for him, not tonight. Not just yet, anyhow. His second thought, laying the blame, was that the stupid woman must have overdone it with the oiled sweeping compound, leaving the floor too slippery. Silly bitch, hadn't he told her often enough? Then a string of other thoughts, all unpleasant, followed in quick succession as he gingerly tried moving his knees, lifting his head, twisting his neck, generally assessing the situation with a tender thoroughness of which only the sufferer is capable, until he decided that basically he was all right. A few sharp intakes of breath punctuated the moans as he finally sat up, his legs straight out and apart, like a toddler on the carpet, and for a few seconds he stayed like that, blinking. Then, delaying the moment no longer, and groaning loudly to help the effort, he turned over on to his hands in a press-up position and painfully struggled to his feet, while his leather belt did the creaking for his aching body.

It was not until then, his eyes staring wide with the effort at the floor beneath him, that he saw the water which had caused his downfall.

'Water?' he questioned through a slowly clearing haze. 'Where the hell's that come from?' A slow stiff-necked movement turned his head through three hundred and sixty degrees to survey the hall. The emergency door was shut, the windows were closed, and he knew the ceiling was dry. 'Water?' he repeated. 'That's funny...' But he wasn't laughing. He was all too serious, too intent now upon finding the answer to the enigma to bother too much about his aching head and limbs. Slowly, painfully, carefully – but with great determination – he walked towards the hall door. Something was up, by George, and it was his duty to find out what.

Chapter Eight

'WHY doncha admit you ain't got the first stinkin' idea 'ow to open that door?'

Les said nothing, preferring to concentrate for the moment on wiggling the thin point of his knife in the lock. He could thump Mick later.

'Eh? It ain't movin' is it?'

Les sniffed loudly and continued to concentrate on the lock. His nose always ran when he concentrated. Terry crouched still, not yet daring to hope that the whole thing would be called off, but just beginning to nurse the faintest glimmer. Dennis sat where he was, beneath the displayed project work, pulling out drawing-pins and trying to flick them into the fish-tank. Plastic-head made black marks on the lino tiles with the sides of his soles, and Blondie appeared to do nothing, but every now and then he had to make a conscious effort not to suck his thumb.

Mick spoke again. 'Y'need a bit o' wire for that. That's fav'rit . . .'

The flick-knife came out of the lock and Les rounded on him. ''Av you got a bit o' wire?'

'Nope!'

'Well then . . .' Les looked at the door again. He folded the blade back into its handle. 'Then it's shoulders against the door, i'n it?'

'You're jokin', o' course!'

'No I ain't. This don't look all that strong.'

'Don' it? Go on then, Batman. Let's see ya!'

Les said no more. He shot Mick one look, disdainful and laden with warning. Then he stood up and took a few paces back, eyeing the door, with his head held slightly down, like a bull at a red cape. Dennis held the pin he was about to flick still in his hand; Plastic-head stopped scuffling; and both Terry and Blondie stopped thinking their private thoughts and watched with deep interest. Then, suddenly, as if he were starting a paced run for the high jump, Les charged at the door, swift, jerky, and aggressive. His eyes blazed with determination and he grunted with effort at each step as his boots bit into the floor. For a moment it seemed he was going straight through it, head first. But at the last instant he turned his right shoulder to meet the woodwork; he hit it with a dull, wet thud just to the right of the handle, and with a tearing rasp the door yielded.

No one was more surprised when it gave than Les. He had really intended them all to put a shoulder to it, together; but Mick's jibes had forced him into a first solo attempt to rattle the door sufficiently to convince them all that it could be done. But it gave, almost willingly, and when he stood back off it they could see the socket hanging cleanly on the protruding bolt, with its two screws still in their metal holes.

He didn't stoop to a shout of triumph; but he permitted himself a tight, twisted grin, and he sniffed at Mick. And as Terry's faint glimmer of hope died he ordered his gang to move.

'Get in! All of yer. Quick! Outa this gol'fish bowl.'

They needed no spurring on. Seven seconds saw them all inside the secretary's room, with Les propping the door shut with a chair, carefully setting the ripped-out screws back into place; and with four pairs of experienced eyes looking round for something to pinch. The secretary was a conscientious and a methodical woman, however, and she left nothing about for a cleaner to meddle with. Her glass tray of pens and pencils was locked away, with her three-dice desk calendar and her lunch-time ash-tray. All the surfaces were clear, just a dictionary on the window-sill, and the walls were bare but for a pin-board with a time-table and an educational supplier's calendar on it.

As one, the interested eyes now focused on the inner door, which stood in the far wall in line with the one they had just come through. 'Mr W. M. Marshall, A.C.P.', announced another rectangle of painted wood.

'Terry!'

It was Les. Terry's head shot up from its sunken chin-on-chest position. Terry! What was all this? His attention hadn't been demanded like that by this lot before.

Perhaps Les, flushed with his unexpected success, was prepared to be reasonable for five minutes. 'They're definitely through 'ere, ain't they? 'Cos if they're not, we're all caught in a trap in 'ere for nothin'.'

'Yes.' Terry jumped in quickly, before Les had to be nasty again. He met Les half-way with his accent, too. 'We

’ave to come ’ere for ’em before the radio lessons. ’E gives ’em to us, or Mrs Baker does . . .’

‘Right! So come on, let’s get in an’ get ’em.’ Eager now to repeat his successful performance, Les took as many paces back as the room would allow and faced the inner door seriously, as if it were a deadly enemy he was going to kill.

‘Smash it in, Les!’

‘Paralyse it, man!’

Mick folded his arms and watched in silence.

‘Don’t do that.’

It was Terry. His words fell into the silent room like a tarantula plopping on to the floor; for a second no one knew what to do, but their guards went up like scorpions’.

‘Eh? Whaddya mean?’

‘It’s a sort of swing door. It ain’t a proper door . . .’ He could easily have let Les go charging through, perhaps hitting his head on something inside. It might have been to his advantage, he didn’t know. And he didn’t know why he should have warned him. Maybe it was because he’d suddenly been called ‘Terry’. Or maybe he feared the reprisal from an angered, wounded yobbo like Les. Anyway, like before, it was best not to think about it. Whatever the reason, he’d done it.

‘Eh? Oh, cheers.’ Les made no more of it than that. He walked over to the door and booted it firmly with his studded sole on the ‘M’ of ‘Marshall’. With only the faint resistance of the ball-catch the door swung inwards, and Les was through it before it could swing back.

‘’S only a partition,’ he announced. ‘This was all one room once.’ He suddenly put his head back round the door and smiled unexpectedly. ‘Still, I ain’t complainin’. Makes it easier for me, don’ it?’

Mr Jarvis was complaining. Bitterly. The shock of his fall, and the anticipation of some sort of bother with intruders, prevented him from thinking clearly, and he was finding himself at the mercy of his huge and unco-operative bunch of keys. The keys, which normally sprang accurately and obediently to his fingers like the beads on a rosary, kept slipping round the ring, and the right key for each classroom door was always the last one he came to, it seemed. It could have been the keys, or it could have been him. Something was up. But he didn't know what. Now every classroom would have to be checked, and the keys were hindering instead of helping.

Checking was important. There was water on the hall floor, from he didn't know where, and there was a strange, abused feel about the school, the way the car felt when he'd crashed the gears or hit a tyre against the kerb. All was not well, and he felt vaguely responsible.

He had only recently left the entrance lobby, and there had been nothing amiss there but the open roof light. The hall, too, apart from the mysterious pools of water on the floor, had seemed to be all right. That only left the classrooms to check. He had already passed six of them, on the left-hand route from the lobby to the hall, but he'd have to go into each one of them now. Meanwhile, he was going into each room on the opposite stretch of corridor, along the route the gang had taken.

There was a master key to all the doors, but Mr Marshall had borrowed that to get another cut to replace his own – which he'd chewed up in one of the doors at half-term – so Mr Jarvis was all fingers and thumbs and army curses as he fumbled impatiently with his metal puzzle.

Each room, as he checked it, appeared to be in order – in order from a security point of view, that was. There was plenty else that would call for comment. In one, a probationer teacher's, the crate of watery-white milk empties had been left in the corner instead of being taken to the front porch. In another the floor had been swept but the chairs had been left up on the desks. Even his shocked system wouldn't prevent him having a few words in the offenders' ears for these transgressions against routine – unless he had something bigger, more serious, to occupy him. Slowly, fumble by fumble, curse by curse, door by door, he worked his way back towards the entrance lobby, his brain becoming clearer, and his step surer, as he went.

Terry's own system was undergoing a fresh shock, probably the biggest so far: the shock of standing uninvited in Mr Marshall's room. He never quite took it all in when he was there on official business. The presence of Mr Marshall dominated all the conscious senses, and only by chance afterwards did something unnoticed at the time come to his mind – an after-image recorded like a camera by the retina of the eye. Like when his dad won a barometer in a works' draw, and Terry remembered that its twin was on Mr Marshall's wall. Or when he saw Mr Marshall's curtains in a material shop. Now he stood in the holy of holies and looked round with fresh, and frightened, eyes.

Terry's dad would have said Mr Marshall didn't seem to have enough to do. His desk was too clear, too neat. It looked too consciously arranged and prepared. There was no impression that he was daily dragged protesting from a stack of unfinished paper work. The desk set made of green slate (from a holiday in Wales), the rocking blotter with unmarked pink paper, the glass paper-weight which held nothing down, the telephone at forty-five degrees to the resting hand, these were the symbols of his activity. Perhaps Terry couldn't read these signs: but he could vouch for the amount of time Mr Marshall was prepared to spend on investigating crimes, both major and minor. It was important, the head always said, if the school's reputation was to be maintained. This was his job: to think, to plan in outline, to ponder, and to diligently and painstakingly dispense justice.

Already Terry was overcome by the heavy and awesome atmosphere of the small room, every second like a minute, and he felt that same walking-in-dead-man's-shoes feeling he'd had in the empty house down at Queen's Dock: only this time it was much, much worse. This was wrong, and it was real. And however innocent he was in the whole business – and there could be no doubt about that, he felt – the running-away which had led to it and the impossible position he would be left in afterwards made him feel as guilty as if he'd master-minded the whole thing. He felt himself to be well over the fence that divided right from wrong now, and once over, the fence had grown too tall for him to climb back.

The paper-weight went into Mick's jeans, looking like a boil on the thigh, and the slate pen-stand, via Plastic-head's right hand, went towards the glass face of the electric wall clock. Plastic-head swore when it just missed, leaving a scar in the wallpaper and dropping harmlessly to the carpet. But it had hit the wall with a loud crack, the noise exploding in the small room with the sudden force of the quarryman's blast in the valley which had first brought it to the surface. Everyone jumped with surprise, and a surprised Les was an angry Les. In one movement, a continuation of his nervous reaction, he punched Plastic-head on the shoulder.

'You fool!' he snarled. 'We ain't 'ere for that!'

'You'll get nickin' a bad name,' grinned Mick, 'bein' destructive . . .'

''E'll bring 'alf the neighbourhood, that's what e'll do, bein' stupid. We're 'ere for them trannies, then away. Y'can bust winders an' things any time . . .'

'No need to 'it me,' moaned Plastic-head, clutching his shoulder.

'No . . .' Mick consoled him.

'Oh, shut up you two!' Exasperated, Les turned to the boy with the local knowledge. ''Ere, Terry, which cupboard then?'

Terry. Again. And when he was angry, too. Perhaps getting stroppy with the others made him a bit more friendly with someone who was co-operating. That's nice! he thought ironically. But he didn't know. You couldn't be sure with someone like Les.

'The one over there. Under the window. The door on the left.' What was the point in resisting? He'd only get hurt, and Les would smash them all in, anyway, till he found what he wanted.

Under the metal-framed window with its filtering slats of Venetian blind there ran a low white cupboard – a piece of oak furniture which had been painted over to look modern. This was sure to be locked, Terry knew. Mr Marshall had always had to unlock it when Terry had gone to collect a radio. But to Les, with renewed confidence, that was nothing now. With a long, meaningful look at Mick he went down on his haunches and started to use his flick-knife on the lock like a surgeon with a delicate operation on an ear to perform. The cupboard was made of old, solid, wood, Les could tell; and he wouldn't kick this in very easily; he'd end up looking a right twit, hopping round the room with a bad toe. Besides, he knew he could do this one, no bother.

Within thirty seconds the cupboard door was open, the knife was back in Les's jeans, and he was at the contents. At last! He was eager, excited, and his movements were both deft and brutal, like a slaughter-man. Throwing himself forward, he delved inside. This was what he'd come for – what he'd threatened and bullied and led the way to get at: with the money he got from this he could do a thing or two – and he thrust his hands inside like some starving man grabbing at a larder of food. His eyes blazed, his nose ran, and he made a strange gurgling sound in his throat.

'Easy!' he said. He laughed, a high-pitched nasal whine. 'Bloody easy!'

Mr Jarvis had his good ear towards the left-hand wall of the corridor, which was also the side of the headmaster's room, as he made his way along the near side of the building to get to the first of the six classrooms to be re-checked. He heard the loud cracking thud as something hit the wall, and he heard the angry voices which followed it. It came as no fresh shock: he'd been keyed up for something like this each time he'd opened a classroom door. So that was where they were! And kids, by the sound of them. Right! He didn't hurry, he didn't rush blindly in; he'd been in the war; he was too old a hand to do that; instead, he quietly opened the lobby doors, slipped through them, and, fingers and thumbs no longer, he deftly locked them behind him. The old over-the-top-of-the-trenches surge of painful excitement tingled within him, and his body seemed to shed ten years as he prepared for his assault. He looked carefully at the seemingly closed 'Inquiries' door, before tiptoeing to the main entrance and securing it; then, with the precision of an infantryman fixing his bayonet, he undid the buckle of his wide leather belt. Jerk, two, three; fiddle, two, three; pull, two, three; ready! He wrapped the thin end round his right hand and in his own time he cautiously approached the secretary's door, head up, one eye squinting with suspicion, the other wide open for danger. Red alert. Battle stations.

One room away, Les was surveying the haul, dribbling with pleasure. He hadn't quite known what to expect, perhaps something that would fetch three pounds, five pounds, maybe six; but the quality of these radios was a real surprise, and his head began to fill with grander thoughts. His own school, so far as he remembered from his infrequent attendances, was wired for sound in all the classrooms. But that cost a lot, he knew, so the local primary schools had to make do with portable transistors. They were about thirty centimetres by ten, and twenty centimetres high, with long, sleekly operating pull-up aerials; there were four wavebands, and sockets for making tape recordings and for listening-in on headphones; they were excellent instruments, with polished wooden ends, carrying handles, and shining bands of thin stainless steel about their girths.

'Smart! These'll fetch a few quid!'

'Great gear, these . . .'

'Hey, clever ol' Les . . .'

''E ain't just a ugly face . . .'

There were six transistors, each labelled with a number stamped on Dymo-tape so that Mr Marshall could rotate them in use and wear the batteries evenly. Almost reluctantly, counting them out, Les gave one to each of the gang and he put one on the end of the desk for himself. The last radio, number six, he thrust into Terry's hands.

'This one's yours, f'r insurance, till tomorrer. So you're right in it with us, see? You're one o' the gang, right the way 'ome. An' you bring it down the drain cover, bottom of the ravine, tomorrer night at 'alf past four. Without fail, right? An' don' bring no one with yer! If you tell anyone, yer dad or the p'lice, you're on'y droppin' y'self in it, 'cos they won't find us, or no trannies, an' they'll think you're tellin' 'em a right little cock-and-bull story: they'll only think y'got scared of bein' found out an' made it all up. I know 'ow their minds think. Right?'

Les sniffed and stood looking at Terry, waiting for some sort of acknowledgement. Terry clutched the radio as if it were some sort of unwanted baby. He felt dizzy and sick in the cloud of bitter frustration which enveloped him like a poison gas, and he couldn't speak.

Les sniffed again and wiped his nose on his wet cuff. 'Eh?'

Terry nodded his head. It was all he could do. He'd got no choice, had he? But he wasn't sealing a bargain with any words.

The nod seemed to be enough, for Les turned away. But as it happened his silence served a more useful purpose to Les than words would have done. In the little pocket of quiet which was left to be filled with Terry's voice the unmistakable sound of someone coming in through the outer door could be heard.

''Old it!' he hissed. 'Quick! Someone's comin'! Out! We've gotta get out!'

Panic struck the small room. The intruders flew about in all directions with the same noisy effectiveness as flies in a jam-jar, getting in each other's way, cracking themselves on the furniture, knocking the radios and tripping over the carpet. Terry alone stood still, struck motionless with fear. They all shouted at once, with conflicting advice, obscenities, and volleys of insults aimed at Les. Only Dennis kept his head. With a sudden strength he pushed the desk against the door in one huge movement and braced himself to hold it firm, a prompt action which had the effect of restoring some sense of purpose to the frantic activity, until at last, amongst the shouting, Les's voice could be heard giving positive instructions.

'The winders! Quick! The winders! Move them bloody blinds an' get a winder open!'

But they found that Venetian blinds have a clattering will of their own, and their strings seem to perform every function but the one required. The slats opened and closed, one end went up without the other, and they finally jammed in a diagonal of distorted plastic. It wasn't until Mick got under the blind and held the slats off with his back that the metal handle of the window was successfully reached.

'Quick! Come on! Get out, under 'ere!'

The boys quickly formed a jostling, panicking group round Mick; only Dennis remained on the other side of the room to hold the table against the pressure of the now assaulted door.

'Let me in, you little hooligans! It'll be the worse for you if you don't open this door!' But for the excitement of the moment, which had spread to the previously cool and collected caretaker, the door might have been pulled instead of pushed, and one, or all of them, caught there and then. But Dennis's action, and the caretaker's haste, gave them vital seconds.

The bulky transistors were forgotten in the scramble through the awkward escape hatch; forgotten by everyone but Les. Terry dropped his, and the rest were left on the table, the chair, and on the carpet. It was only Les who scrambled up on to the white cupboard and through the window with anything, clutching two radios by the handles in one hand, awkwardly, like an old woman getting on a bus with too much shopping.

The hero, the rough-diamond, the stuff some V.C.s are made of, Dennis, held the door till the last moment, when, seeing the way clear, he could make his own dive for freedom. He was fast and slick, and without any encumbrances he got through the aperture with practised ease. But he wasn't followed, not into the headmaster's room. Mr Jarvis wasn't so deaf as all that, and he well understood from the shouted remarks and the clatter of blinds, that the kids were getting out through the window. Even before Dennis's push eased off from the table he left the door and ran back through to the front entrance to cut the blighters off.

If only he hadn't locked it! That cost him precious seconds. But he made good time for all that, and as he ran down the steps into the still pouring rain, he was in time to see four or five figures ahead of him in the gloom, scurrying from the building like wood-lice from a burning log.

'The gate, over 'ere, down that crack in the 'ouses!'

'Come on, 'urry up! The bloke's comin'!'

'Stop! Stop there, I said!' Mr Jarvis threw his belt down,

which was tangling his legs, and put himself into what he could remember of a sprint. The kids were fast. One, coming up from behind, overtook two of the others and was at the gate and over it a few seconds after the leaders. But another, carrying something in his hands, was slower, and the caretaker thought he stood a faint chance of catching him – and a better chance of grabbing the kid who was flagging behind him.

It was Terry who was last. He'd done enough running that day to last him a lifetime, and his legs just weren't doing what they should. He knew old Jarvis was behind him, and not very far at that, and he knew that once he was caught the old boy wouldn't go after anyone else. He wanted to run faster. He wanted to shout to someone to help him over the gate. He wanted his mum. As he ran, inhaling a mixture of rain and air, he lived again that horrible nightmare, that chase by the roaring man who gained on him and grabbed at him with long fingers, that terrifying experience of the dark hours when he ran and got nowhere, when his mother stood ahead, unseeing, unable to hear his voiceless shouts for help.

Les was at the gate before him, and there was room beneath its tubular frame for him to slide the transistors to the other side before he bunked over; but that took seconds, and his bunk was awkward, a tantalizingly slow movement which blocked the way, and spoiled Terry's run at the gate. He was going to be caught. Behind him he could hear the splashing footsteps and the heavy breathing of old Jarvis, and he tried to shout at Les; but he couldn't; he hadn't the breath for that. Quick! Quick! The fingers were gripping at him. Then suddenly Les was clear of the top bar and stooping to scoop up his haul, and Terry was crashing hopelessly into the gate. He reached for the top bar himself, wet, slippery, no grip; and he half-turned in surrender before he was grabbed from behind.

'Quick! Grab 'old, Tel! 'E's on yer! Give us your 'and!'

In a panic Terry turned back to the gate. He raised both his hands in silent obedience, and he gave what little he had left in a final effort at a jump. He'd had it. Jarvis must grab him now. But somehow his wrists were grasped by Les, and in a last-second, painful, sliding wrench he was over the gate and flat on his face on the other side.

Suddenly, one final flash of lightning lit the scene like day as he struggled to his feet: and in the roar of thunder which followed he heard the caretaker crash into the gate with a loud oath.

Thank God for that! That was it. The old man was done for. He couldn't follow through the gate in time to do any good now. With suddenly renewed energy the last two escapers made off down the road, each with a radio. One was clutched enthusiastically and in triumph in Les's rough hands. The other was held reluctantly by the carrying handle in the weak and trembling hand of the slight boy in a wet black shirt. One last comment cemented them together as they ran their separate ways.

'Don' forget. Tomorrer. 'Alf past four. On yer own. I'll be waitin' for yer, somewhere near . . .'

'Yea. O.K.' Terry's sigh was broken by a sob, which could have been through running. But it wasn't. The nightmare isn't over yet, it said.

Chapter Nine

TERRY'S part of the world was dark. Somewhere the sun was still shining, somewhere it was light, but in Terry's part of London the storm had darkened the streets early, and with the timing devices on the unlit lamps unable to cope with the change in circumstances, it was even darker than normal, concealing him in the easing drizzle as he hugged the walls and ran home.

He went over his opening sentence a hundred times. 'Sorry, Dad, I was out playing when the storm started, and I sheltered on the common for as long as I could, but when it didn't stop I just had to make a dash for it, in case you got worried.' Even to Terry it sounded too prepared, and experience told him he wouldn't get it all out uninterrupted as if it were a speech in a play. But anyway, that was the gist of it, it was his story, and he'd have to improvise around it.

The radio banged against his wet knees as he ran along, rehearsing. 'Sorry, Dad, I was out playing when the storm started . . .' His mind had rejected telling the truth some time back. It no longer entered his thinking. Les had impressed upon him too forcibly what the outcome would be if he spilled the beans. If he'd been caught or recognized it would have been a different matter. But he hadn't been, and the line of least resistance, the easiest, safest thing to do was to go along with Les and give the radio to him tomorrow. Then it'd all be over. He'd have to sit through a bit of an awkward time at school – and his dad wouldn't be too easy tonight – but that seemed better than being suspected of being a willing member of Les's gang. No one was above suspicion, not even boys from ordinary homes; there was too much evidence of so-called respectable citizens going to jail for that. Even policemen went to prison for something called corruption. So what chance would he stand? No, all he had to do was get home without being seen, hide the radio from his parents – and snooping Tracey – and just face the music for staying out and getting wet. That was it. That was the only way. Most people try to make the best of whatever situation they find themselves in, he knew: optimism dies hard: and he was no exception to one of the laws of nature.

This heavy thing banging against his knees was the only problem. He'd got to get rid of that before he went indoors: he'd never get it undiscovered up to his bedroom, not tonight.

The answer seemed to come to him in a flash of inspiration. The dustbin. He could go in the back way, along the back alley to the garage, and put it in the dustbin before he went indoors. The bin had an inner lining of black plastic, a bag the dustmen left behind each week to make removal easier, and all he had to do was lift that out, put the radio in the bottom, underneath, and replace the bag. No one would lift that out till the dustmen came on Monday, and by then he'd have retrieved it on his way to the ravine, or taken it to his bedroom in a quiet moment. He had a secret place in his bedroom that no one knew about: a boarded-over fire-place with a cover that came off if he pressed it at the bottom and eased the top out with his finger-nails. He'd hidden Tracey's shoes in there in a recent row, and she'd gone berserk trying to find them, so he knew it was a good, secure hiding-place for the radio.

All too soon he was home. He passed his turning and went along to the back alley, and within a few moments he was approaching the back of his house. He was pleased to have got there without detection, but he would have liked to put this moment off. His excuses had sounded better half-a-kilometre away. Now came the crunch. A nervous cramp iced his stomach as he ran over the lines once more. 'Sorry,

Dad. I was out to play on the common when the storm started . . .'

The dustbin was just inside the back gate, next to the garage. It was in view of the house, but it was dark enough now for him to hide the radio unobserved, and the bin was conveniently made of plastic, so his actions went unheard as well.

The plastic bag was more fiddly than he expected. His mum opened it out and turned the edge over the outside of the bin, which was easy to do when it was empty, and it settled and held its position firmly as the week wore on. But it also became distended with the weight of family refuse, and while taking it off was easy enough, getting it back was a real problem. Terry fiddled with it for four or five minutes. If he got the near-side on, the other side didn't want to stretch far enough; and if he started on the far side the whole thing slipped off when he worked round to the front. In the end he left it, his forehead sweating through the skin of rain, with the radio face down on the floor of the bin and the plastic bag half on and half off, but well covering his secret.

Now for the back door. He'd probably get murdered over his shirt, but he'd have to take that; and by now his dad was bound to know what he'd said before he cleared off. On the other hand, they might be so relieved to see him they wouldn't tick him off at all. Anyway, one way or the other this would all be over by the morning; and by tomorrow night, after a dodgy day at school when he'd have to act his heart out and not go red, he'd have got the radio back to Les and life could go back to normal.

There was just this hurdle now . . .

Inadvertently, nervousness made him push the back door as if he intended going through the hurdle rather than over it, making noise enough to wake the dead, and if he expected to get a chance to dry his hair and do something about his shirt before he saw his parents, he was sadly mistaken.

'Good God and little fish-hooks, where the hell have you been?'

Terry blinked in the white neon light. He hadn't pictured them being in the kitchen. That threw him for a start. His mum and dad were both there, standing awkwardly by the sink and the cooker in their coats. They both swung their heads round suddenly as if they had been caught printing false bank-notes. Either they'd been rowing or someone had died in the family, for his mum's face was red and blotchy, and his dad was plugging in the kettle, sure signs of family trouble. It didn't strike him that it could have been him.

For all his dad's earlier anxiety it was his mum who got to him first, throwing her arms round him and kissing his damp forehead. 'My God, look at the state of you! And your lovely new shirt! Where've you been, you naughty little boy?' She emphasized the 'little', as she did when she wanted to put him in his place; but her actions told the true story and Terry knew she was trying to be an angry mother rather than an angry woman. 'We've been really worried about you, out in all that lightning. We've been out to find you, but we couldn't . . .'

All the time she was hugging him in her enveloping arms, squeezing the wet out of him, and pushing the sodden hair out of his eyes. Suddenly, like being sick, Terry couldn't hold out any more. Reacting to an open show of love at last, after all the hatred and the threats, with a deep jerking sob which seemed to start in his plimsolls, he began to cry. It was a painful, hiccuping cry, a sudden deluge of misery made all the worse by the amount of it he was still damming back. And even that dyke was nearly breached. He came to within a sentence of spilling everything, so total was his feeling of relief at being back on his home territory again, amongst the only people he could possibly tell. But that next sentence was his father's, and it was said very straight.

'Well, we'll talk about it later. But first it's a bath, before you catch pneumonia.' His own relief at the end of an

evening of vague foreboding made him distrust his ability to speak softly. He left the kitchen to run it, and Terry, even in his misery, sensed that all too quickly the moment had passed.

The bath, Terry discovered, was a good place for reflection. It had always been a good place to play, somewhere private from everyone where even Tracey wouldn't burst in and interrupt, and he normally took in a selection of plastic soldiers who would dive in off the side, or get floated on a foam-square raft towards the horrors of the cold-tap waterfall. But that evening he just lay there and soaked, and relaxed his shaking limbs in the comfort of the warm water. Everything seemed less serious there, somehow. As the acoustics made a confident singer of the tone-deaf, so the enveloping steam and water brought reassurance and a sense of security to his troubled mind.

He was only interrupted once, when his mother came in to see that he was all right. She noticed the cut on his head, rain-bleached of blood, and the graze on his arm, but he told her he had bumped into a tree running home in the dusk, and she discreetly left him in peace with the promise of Vaseline. Otherwise, it was a quiet, peaceful time.

His mind went over the events of the past few hours: his row with Tracey that had begun it all, his trouble with his mum, and his resentment at not being treated properly, as someone who was growing up; his nightmare on the common; the chase; the old house down by the docks; the unforgettable horror of the raid on the school, breaking into Mr Marshall's room; and, finally, the escape, with old Jarvis bombing across the staff car-park after him. In the warmth of his own bath it all seemed so unreal, almost unbelievable, and he might have doubted his sanity but for the awakening cuts and grazes and the memory of one ugly, twisted face. Les.

He spent a long time thinking about Les. The water went cold and he began to shiver, but still he lay and listened to the thin, cruel voice, and saw the bitter mouth and flickering eyes of the youth with the flick-knife. 'Pig-face', it had been at first when Les'd been trying to frighten him; then 'Terry', when he was up against it with Mick, and Terry had been helping; and then 'Tel', the friendliest of all abbreviations, when they'd both been pursued by the caretaker. His thoughts stopped there. Why? Why 'Tel'? His mind dwelt on that. Why should Les have turned friendly towards him? Why had he bothered to rescue him when he could have got away himself more safely? Had it been for insurance, to save his own skin in the long run? It needn't have been; he could still have got away with the radios, and it would only have been Terry's word against his.

Terry hooked the plug chain with his toe. There were no answers to all that. All he knew, as he prepared to get out of the bath, was that he felt a bit better about things, more confident now that it would be all right. And that his feet seemed to stretch a bit further down the bath than they used to.

There was a strange atmosphere in the house that evening. Jack Harmer seemed crosser with everyone else than he was with Terry. Terry managed to get out his cover-up story uninterrupted, to his great surprise, and apart from an admonishing, 'You've upset your mother, Terry, and worried both of us; don't ever do it again', no more was said to him about the incident. But Jack went all moody and quiet with Gladys, as he always did when he thought he'd made a fool of himself with other people, and he got quite annoyed when the phone kept ringing and Gladys had to put the family's mind at rest.

First it was Gran Harmer.

'Hello? Hello? Gladys? Is that you, Gladys?' The old woman treated her phone like a bomb in the living-room, still afraid of its evil powers. 'I'm just phoning to see how Terry is. I went to phone earlier, but I lost the run of my telephone book. Did he get back all right?'

Gladys was glad that he had, or she'd have been phoning every five minutes.

'Yes, thank you, Mum. Nice of you to worry.'

'What time?'

'Eh?'

'What time did he come home?'

'Oh, a little while ago. He's all right . . .'

'Oh.'

'Thanks for phoning.'

'What say?'

'I said, he's all right, thanks Mum, and thanks for phoning . . .'

'Only I was worried . . .'

'Yes . . .'

'It was ever so wet out . . .'

'Yes . . .'

'He got back all right, then?'

'Yes thanks, Mum.'

'Where?'

'What?'

'Where'd he been, all that time?'

'Oh, just out playing . . .'

'Playing?'

'Yes, Mum, he was out playing, and he got caught in it.'

'Oh. Did Jack find his wedding-ring?'

'Oh yes, he hadn't lost it. He told you. Well, I must go now. Jack sends his love. And Terry.'

'All right, Gladys. Bye-bye.'

'Bye-bye, Mum. Bye-bye.'

Jack said no more than 'Oh' to her report that it had been his mother, inquiring after Terry. But the expression on his face, unmistakably read by Gladys, showed how displeased he was at their involving anyone else in their concern for the missing boy. His eyes didn't leave the television screen, but his drumming fingers on the arm of his chair told how little he was taking in from the box.

A quarter of an hour later the phone rang again. Once more Gladys went out into the hall to answer it, her usual job, and this time it was Uncle Charlie.

'Hello, Glad, just thought I'd ring to set my mind at rest. Has that lad of yours turned up yet?'

Gladys sat on the bottom stair. 'Yes thanks, Uncle Charlie. About an hour ago. He's all right. He'd been out playing and got caught in the rain so he took shelter somewhere. Anyway, he came in drenched, but he's none the worse for wear after a nice hot bath, so all's well that ends well.'

'Good. I guessed he'd be all right. Still, you like to be sure, don't you?'

'Oh, yes. And how are you? All right? Finished your little job?'

'Oh, yes thanks, Glad. I'm just goin' to pick a few winners for Ripon tomorrow, then I'm having an early night. Nothin' on the telly . . .'

'Don't blame you. We're only watching a load of old rubbish: as usual on a Thursday . . .'

'You're telling me. I could do a better turn myself. All right then, Glad, I'm glad everything's all right . . .'

'Thanks. Cheerio, Uncle Charlie.'

'Cheerio, Glad. Bye-bye.'

The television continued to provide a good target for Jack's eyes when Gladys told him who had rung. His grunt, however, conveyed the same message as when his mother had called, but with the added indication that he wished her uncle had minded his own business. But if the television was only an excuse for Jack, and if what was on the screen was a load of old rubbish to Gladys and Uncle Charlie, it was most certainly neither to Terry. The programme was a Scotland Yard serial about a jewel theft, and every word of it seemed to be aimed directly at him. In between the action, the police and the jeweller passed comments on the morals of the crooks who'd done the job, and when they went on about the prison sentences they deserved, Terry wanted to do nothing so much as run off to his bedroom. But he couldn't find a plausible excuse, and he was forced to sit imprisoned on the settee while his face glowed red with embarrassment and guilt.

'I think you had your bath too hot,' his mother commented, 'or you've fallen for the 'flu.'

But Terry knew he'd done neither, and his stomach churned with the thought of how he was bound to give himself away at school the next day, going red. He half thought of jumping on the 'flu bandwagon, but he knew that wouldn't do. He'd look all the more guilty not being there, and besides, if he didn't go to school he wouldn't get out of the house in the evening to return the radio. So when Tracey came in, strangely subdued and friendly from the youth club, he went to bed to spend a restless, worrying night, ridden with guilt and frustration, his relaxing bath forgotten, and a long way from feeling as innocent as he thought he was entitled to feel.

Chapter Ten

EVERYTHING seemed far too normal for Terry's liking when he arrived at school the next day. He wouldn't have minded a sign at the gate saying, 'School closed due to break-in'; or, failing that, a distraught Mr Marshall in the playground asking everyone what knowledge they had of the disgraceful affair. Anything to get it over with, to establish his alibi, to be absolved, and to carry on normally. The staff cars hooted their way through throngs of children and parked neatly in their allotted spaces, noses to the wall (because the head didn't like exhaust marks on the brickwork); and Mr Marshall's own car stood obediently in line with the rest. The school dusters fluttered normally on 'Frau' Jarvis's line, and the children gathered normally in the playground without the slightest hint of gossip about a break-in. Terry would have been happier had a police car been there, or had word got out some other way, because then he could have tested his reaction to the news, and the strength of his cover story, in the playground before the ordeal that was bound to come in the classroom. Even the dried-out storm rated little comment, so he had no opportunity even to drop in a word about not having seen much of it, being indoors all the evening. And he couldn't really bring it up himself if he was supposed not to have taken much notice of it. So he let the conversations take what course they would, joining half-heartedly into an argument about Charlton Athletic's goalkeeper, and generally trying to act normally – while keeping an eye out for Jarvis or Marshall in case he could read an expression on one of their faces.

He had made sure to dress very differently from the day

before. The black shirt was ruined, but he wouldn't have worn that in any case. He was pretty sure old Jarvis couldn't have seen much of him from the back, but there would have been no sense in tempting providence. He wore a red nylon polo-neck sweater, with grey trousers instead of the wet jeans, and a pair of brown plimsolls to replace the sodden ones. In this disguise, he looked round every few minutes for the arrival of a police car, giving absent-minded replies to a score of casual remarks from casual acquaintances.

Terry's friends at school tended to vary with his mood. He was really a bit of a loner, but he'd fall easily enough into any of the groups when he wanted to. He wasn't an 'inseparable', with a bosom pal. But he regularly swapped comics with Georgie Lee, he enjoyed rude jokes with 'Bucket' Wells, he talked records with Mark Turner and his little gang, and he played football with the lot of them. He also had a private fancy for Sharon Drew, but he had few chances for indulging that: just the odd push in the back to start a game of outraged chase. There was also Jason Brown, whose party he was going to; but Jason just happened to live nearby and their mothers worked at the same factory, and he just came in handy for wet boring days in the holidays, as a last resort. So in the playground that morning, not being in the mood for anyone in particular, Terry drifted from group to group and hovered on the fringes of each, with one eye on the road and an ear cocked for gossip.

When Mrs Snellgrove came out to ring the hand-bell he manoeuvred himself as close to her as he decently could. He thought he detected a hint of tension on her face, a slightly deeper frown than usual, but it was hard to tell; and as the juniors filed in through the double doors at the end of the right-hand line of classrooms, he walked in on his own surrounded by the vacuum of his private worries, and lined up quietly in the jostling line outside Mr Evans' classroom door.

It was a sporty day with games in the afternoon, and Mr Evans emerged from the staff-room already dressed in his navy-blue track-suit and training shoes. Terry searched his face, too, for some sign of concern, some hang-over of the staff-room gossip, but Mr Evans was as impassive as ever, merely opening his door and beckoning the front of the line in with a quiet, 'Lead in, Wendy.'

There was a board of Maths work waiting for them, put there as usual the afternoon before, and everyone got on with it in their general work books while the school quietened and the registers were called. Terry tried to concentrate, but it was difficult with one eye jumping to the door all the time, and the rapidly approaching assembly drove any accuracy with long division out of his mind.

Friday was a full assembly day, when the infants were led hand-in-hand into the hall to join the juniors, the important assembly of the week when Mr Marshall presided, leading the school in a hymn, telling a short moral story, and giving out his announcements and the sports results; it was a time when the juniors clapped and the infants swivelled their heads and fidgeted. But it was the big occasion of the week, the morning when 'the whole school family', as Mr Marshall called it, came together for the required act of worship, and it was an occasion which the short, conservatively well-dressed headmaster never missed.

Terry was dreading it. Terry could only remember one occasion when influenza had caused it to be led by anybody else. Mondays to Thursdays, yes; all the teachers took a turn in the week, some with stories, some with class plays, some with guitars and recorder groups; but never on Fridays. That was Mr Marshall's day. But Terry could see that today, when Mr Evans' class filed in through the double doors to stand in line across the back, was the second exception. For standing on the drama blocks at the front, leaning over the portable lectern, keeping a stern eye on the assembled school, was Mrs Snellgrove.

Terry felt the worms of fear wriggling in the pit of his stomach again, and he couldn't trust himself to reply to Mark Turner's whispered, 'It's Snellgrove! Old Marshall's not here . . .' Terry knew that he was, he'd seen the car – and he could so easily guess what was keeping the headmaster away from the ritual family gathering.

Mrs Snellgrove's obvious unpreparedness led to a merciful brevity. A teacher of older juniors all her life, she had little understanding of the infant world – all children under seven looked alike to her – so she made her concession to a mutual lack of understanding by being brief. The whole school sang 'Glad that I live am I' at Mr Palmer's rattling pace in twenty-three seconds by Mr Evans' stop watch; she read Psalm 23 from the back of the hymn book; and she attempted to lead the school in The Lord's Prayer, but she went wrong not looking and threw the school into a confused finish. That was it. Duty was done. There were no announcements, and before the teachers had got nicely comfortable on their Friday chairs, they were all back in their classrooms and the day proper had begun.

Playtime seemed a month away for everyone, especially Terry. He had mentally divided the day into four, punctuated by the breaks, with each session a hurdle to get over before the final sprint away at the finishing bell. He knew that with the week-end coming the pursuit would slow in pace, the worst of the sweat would be over, and the following week, with the radio safely handed over to Les, everything should be more or less back to normal. At least, that's what he hoped. One thing he was sure of: he wouldn't feel as jumpy and nervous as he did today.

But he jumped so much every time the classroom door opened that by ten o'clock he was wishing that Mr Marshall would come in and show his hand: it needn't be anything too much; perhaps a disappointed announcement with a moral about honesty; or a request for information like Police Five. Then at least everyone could talk about it, and Terry could establish himself on the side of the innocents, be indignant about the school being treated that way. It was the not knowing, the fear that he was being crept up on in the dark, that was affecting him worst of all. He could well understand why murderers were said to be drawn back to the scenes of their crimes; he could feel their need to know how careful they had been, the degree of their safety.

In the end, for Terry, it was the loneliness of his fear which became almost too much to bear. A score of times he thought of going to Mr Marshall and telling him all about it. The idea recurred in his thinking like a theme in a symphony: introduced by the unreal, ethereal flutes, a whisper of a possibility; taken up by the confident strings, growing in allure; then reinforced by the positive, dominating brass, an overwhelming need. In this scared, tense state he was several times within an arm's raising of asking to be excused, of hurrying down the corridor to tell Mr Marshall the whole, truthful story.

Surely he'd understand. Of course he would. He'd been stupid to think that he wouldn't; especially if he was told about the row at home that had started it all, the running away, and the threats with the knife. Surely he'd know the turmoil he'd been in, his reasons for not telling the truth before. But something held him back. There was still a bit of sorting out to do in his mind.

While he pretended to look up a reference book about the Sioux Indians he went over all the implications in his head. He'd be asked lots of questions, especially about the others, and he'd have to lie about the location of his capture and the origins of the gang, or he might find himself down at Napier School within the hour, going round the classes to identify the rest of them. Or he'd find himself at Deansgrove Comprehensive in a search for Les. No, that definitely wasn't on. He'd hardly be greeted by an understanding Les, with a welcoming murmur of, 'Yea, I know 'ow it is, Tel.'

'*Tel.*' That still bugged him, too, that remark over the

gate as Les rescued him; it seemed almost as pointed, as inhibiting, as the flick-knife, somehow. It was as if he'd been put through some sort of examination by Les, and he'd passed.

How to do it, then? Perhaps if he could work out a fictitious group of characters, and set the scene at the Court flats instead of the ravine, then he could truthfully tell his own part in the break-in and return the radio in the dustbin to the school. That seemed reasonable. Les would surely leave him alone if he was kept out of it.

It suddenly seemed a good idea. The best way out by far. There was no choice really, any more. The thought of getting through the day at school and taking the radio down to Les faded into a total unreality as the tension of watching the classroom door grew to an almost unbearable pitch. Yes, he'd change the names, and go and tell all he knew.

Copying a chunk out of the book about white settlers, changing the odd word but not really involving his brain, he worked on a substitute for Les. Perhaps there could be two brothers, both at work, big, and with a knife each? Or a revolver? No, not a revolver, he decided. They wouldn't believe that – not for stealing a couple of radios. But both with big knives. Yes. They could be labourers off the building site, like his dad said, here today and gone tomorrow: working where the money was. Yes, that was definitely it. After all, it was basically true, in a way; it honestly told his part in it, and yet it didn't involve Les. He spoke confidently to himself, as he sometimes did when he'd had a good idea. 'Badly good! Yes. That's it.' He would just finish copying the end of this chunk out of the book, then he'd go to Marshall and get it off his chest. If he told it now, before it was all common knowledge, and if he told Mr Marshall how scared he was of the two men with the revolver – no, the knives – then surely he must be believed. Mr Marshall, and his mum and dad, must understand. Of course they must. 'Yes, that's it.' Feeling happier than he had for a long time, he started the final sentence of the copied passage. He knew that if he gave this piece of work in he stood a much better chance of being allowed out to the toilet, and then he wouldn't have to go into it all with Mr Evans, in front of the class. His hand hurried over the page: the handwriting grew in size, twisting into a slanting scrawl. Nearly there. He was just stuck for a word to substitute for 'treachery'. Get that done and he'd go. Where's the dictionary? About three more minutes. 'Good. Yes.'

The theme had built to a crescendo. The drums came in, beating support; the war drums; in two minutes they'd stop, and he'd lead the charge into his own personal battle.

Mr Marshall was not at all satisfied with the policeman's attitude. P.C. Peters was the local policeman, the 'home-beat' man, the pupils' friend; and up to now Mr Marshall had always found him to be very good at his work. Talking about road safety, organizing a team for the Schools' Quiz, warning about the dangers of going off with strangers, he'd been very efficient and persuasive in the past. And he was usually most co-operative: once, he'd even brought a member of the mounted branch with his police horse into the playground to show the infants; and he'd often helped the juniors with their project work on the police. But this morning Mr Marshall detected a slightly cynical note in the policeman's voice, a certain blasé attitude about a real crime which was never present when he was doing his public relations work. It was almost as if an invisible barrier stood between them; or as if they were transmitting and receiving on different wavelengths. The policeman didn't look him full in the eye, and he even began to wonder at one stage if P.C. Peters secretly thought he'd made off with the transistors himself. He wasn't satisfied that the constable was treating the break-in seriously enough. The man just 'Hmmmmmm'd', and nodded, and made remarks like, 'Yes, they would . . .', and generally gave the impression that the head of the Flying Squad had been called to sort out a parking offence.

Mr Marshall, however, was used to being king in his own castle. He usually got his own way. He thought he had better begin now by putting the policeman on the right track.

'Mr Peters, I know it's nothing very new to you,' he said in his clipped tones, which had almost lost all trace of his own London upbringing, 'children breaking into a school and making off with a couple of small radios, but to me it happens to be very serious, you know. It might be common in other schools – in fact, talking to my colleagues I think we have an exceptional record here – but this is a "good" area, and thieving from the school isn't something I'm prepared to tolerate. It's got to be nipped in the bud, before it gets a hold.' He hoped he made himself clear. 'Now to my mind this has all the hallmarks of what you'd call "an inside job".' He raised his eyebrows, seeking the policeman's agreement. P.C. Peters reluctantly put his helmet on the desk and took out his notebook. 'They knew just which room to enter, and which cupboard to break into. There's no sign of them searching around to find items to steal. They seem to have come straight to it. Wouldn't you say?' He'd shame action out of this policeman somehow.

The policeman nodded thoughtfully and he wrote something in the notebook, meticulously filling his lines with indentations of blue back-sloping ball-point. 'Yes,' he said as he wrote. 'I think you've got a point there, sir. It might be worth getting the C.I.D. boys up to tape a few fingerprints. But we can only finger-print a suspect, and then only with the parents' permission. Finger-printing the whole school just wouldn't be on.' He sat silent while he finished his note, more to please the headmaster and the boys at the local paper than because it might have to be read out in court. There was too much of this going on to keep tabs on everything. 'Anyway, we'll take the serial numbers of the stolen goods, and a description of them, and we'll get them circulated in case they turn up in any of the likely places. We won't sit idle, sir. But I'm afraid there's a good network in stolen goods round here. It spread from the docks originally: you'd be surprised how much stuff falls off the backs of ships, and people in factories and offices – and schools – buy it without thinking they're doing anything wrong. So your radios won't hang around for long. No chance.' He clicked his ball-pen and prepared to write again. 'Now, how do you think they got in, sir, without forcing any outside doors or windows?' Defend, attack, play cat and mouse, he thought; it was happening all the time; it never stopped.

Mr Marshall sensed the faintest hint of blame being laid at his own door. There was no doubt that holes had been found in the school's security.

'Well, the caretaker was on the premises at the time; he'd come over to check the flat roof in the rain; so of course all sorts of doors were open that wouldn't normally be, including the front door. But Jarvis thinks they came in through a hall window, somehow; he slipped on a pool of water in the hall, you know, and there was no leak in the roof.' He stopped for a second. 'It's all a bit of a mystery. We'll have to look into the security of the hall windows . . .' But he wasn't thinking about the hall at all any more. As clearly as if he'd spoken them he could sense the policeman's reasonable suspicions about the caretaker. That was the rotten thing about something like this. Nobody was above suspicion until the true culprits had been found. 'I'm afraid that's all I can tell you at present . . .' He sat back in his chair, frowning, cross at feeling on the defensive when he wanted to attack the policeman for not having been prepared to do much. Still, he consoled himself, this might lead somewhere . . .

'Well, I'll have a word with the caretaker, sir, and I'll be requiring statements from both of you. Meanwhile, I'll mention it to C.I.D. and see how busy they are today . . .'

Mr Marshall's frown deepened as the physical flow of real anger flooded through his body. There was bound to be something more important.

'Anyway,' the policeman concluded casually, 'I suppose the stuff's insured by the education authorities?'

At that the headmaster finally blew his top. So that was it. After all the indignity of the questions, too. Hang the drudgery of finding miscreants: why bother? Let the insurance companies pay up! If they thought like that the police were no different from the criminals themselves. That was usually their conscience-saver, too.

Mr Marshall summoned all the cold authority of his profession. 'Yes, it is insured. But that's not the point, constable.' He stood up to put his head above that of the seated policeman, leaning his weight on his knuckles on the desk to deliver his lecture. 'P.C. Peters, someone in this school was involved in this burglary, a fact plain enough for anyone to see, and whether it appeals to you or not, he must be brought to book.' His voice was higher than it normally was, thinned by extreme annoyance. 'Unless the police are prepared to do a bit more to show the flag in the matter, then this criminal in the making will have got off scot-free, and he'll be laughing all the way to the bank.' He had to swallow before he could continue. 'Now you mark my words, it won't be so very long after that before you're up here again, for something else, and before we know it Fox Hill School will have become another Napier, with smashed windows and break-ins every other night.' He took a deep breath, really worked up now. 'You may not be aware of it, but this Court flats development up the road is going to be filled with re-housed Queen's Dock children in the near future. They'll get their own school eventually, but meanwhile I'll have to take them in here . . .' He pulled a face as if he'd bitten open a cod-liver oil capsule. 'And things will be bad enough without it starting before they come. Before very long my "good" families will all be going over to private schools if I'm not careful. So I want some action over this, if you don't mind, before things get out of hand . . .'

The policeman said nothing, a supreme achievement of diplomacy from an old Napier School boy.

'. . . The very least you could do is show your face in the classrooms, and say something to put the wind up the little blighters. That's not too much to ask, is it?'

P.C. Peters could already see the vitriolic letter of complaint on the station officer's desk. The policeman was always the man in the middle, attacked from both sides, whatever happened.

'Yes, I'll do that, sir, if you think it will help.'

'Thank you, Mr Peters.' The headmaster stood back, off his desk. 'Then we may as well begin with the fourth years, when you've had a word with the caretaker. He's waiting outside. I believe he's got a description of one of the boys to give you; it's not much, but it might set somebody's mind ticking . . .'

P.C. Peters was a big man when he stood up, and the sight of him walking unannounced into the classroom, followed by the small but authoritarian figure of Mr Marshall, brought an instant silence, like switching off a radio. Heads swivelled, eyes widened, mouths dropped open. Terry nearly made a frightened jumping noise, but he just restrained himself, although he couldn't stop his shaking hands from sending the book on the Sioux tumbling to the floor.

Then the whispers began.

'Look at this . . .'

'P.C. Peters!'

'It's the Bill!'

The whole point of the policeman's previous public relations work had been to create the image of the friendly law man, the man you could tell your troubles to; but today Mr

Marshall was using him as a frightener, and his success in that role was overwhelming. There were few whose hearts didn't start to beat faster, for one reason or another, when he walked in. Terry's mouth set in a firm line, he inched himself into a position where he could see without being too well seen, and he gripped the desk like a ship's rail, ready to ride out the breaking storm. What rotten timing. A few more seconds and he'd have avoided all this.

Mr Marshall observed the normal courtesies. 'May I, Mr Evans?'

'Yes, of course, Mr Marshall.'

The headmaster clasped his hands in front of him and with a wide, piercing look, which made contact with every eye in the room, he made his announcement.

'Today is a sad day for Fox Hill School,' he said in an emotional voice, 'for this morning I have to tell you, although some of you may know it already, that last night a group of boys entered the school – yes, broke into *our* school – and made their way to my room where they opened the radio cupboard and made off with two of our instruments.' He stopped there momentarily to let it sink in, while everyone looked at everyone else. Loud murmurs of outraged disbelief issued from some of the girls, and from Terry. Mr Marshall held the pause for a few seconds, an actor 'riding' a reaction, timing his lines perfectly. 'Had it not been for the vigilance of Mr Jarvis they would have made off with all six of them!' Again, a wave of exaggerated horror swept across the room like a breeze across a cornfield, those who hadn't joined in before pleased to get another chance to do so. Again Mr Marshall waited for it to pass. 'Now, we want your help, because this incident has damaged the good name of Fox Hill School in a way that I will not tolerate.' He bounced his voice on the words with the rhythmic beat of a stick on a drum. 'A rotten apple will taint the whole barrel . . . it has to be plucked out before its moulder

spreads. Doesn't it, Mr Evans?' Mr Evans, who knew about the break-in and whose eyes had been on the children's faces, suddenly realized he was being addressed and started nodding vigorously. 'Now, I want you all to pay careful attention to what Mr Peters, our home-beat policeman, wants to say to you. And I want you to give him the friendly cooperation he has a right to expect.' The headmaster turned to face the policeman and spoke to him in a loud public voice. 'Thank you, Mr Peters.'

P.C. Peters had a room of undivided attention. As he cleared his throat to speak not an eye blinked, not a muscle moved.

'Thank you, Mr Marshall. Well, as your headmaster says, two transistor radios have been stolen from the school, and we have evidence to show that some person or persons unknown from within the school may know something about it. We also have a description of one lad who may be able to help us in our inquiries. So I want you to listen to it very carefully; it may be someone you know. If it is, don't shout it out now, but have a quiet word with me afterwards.' His public voice was rather lifeless, self-conscious, like many of his colleagues' when talking to children in front of teachers, hollow sounding and over-articulated like a trade union spokesman. But he opened his notebook in a practised, courtroom manner, and he read from it. 'There were four or five boys, aged about eleven, who were seen running from the scene by the caretaker, Mr Walter Jarvis.' There was a snigger at 'Walter', but it was quickly silenced by a glance from Mr Marshall. 'One of the boys may be slightly older. One lad who was seen running off was wearing blue jeans and a black, or grey, shirt.' His voice had become slow and emphatic, then it suddenly speeded up to rattle off the last bit which didn't concern them. 'Some mention was made of a TV between the lads, but the items stolen were restricted to two Super-Seventy transistor radios . . .'

He closed his notebook to a buzz of busy opinion, while Terry's face roasted in the heat of thirty pairs of scorching eyes. Of course, they'd all seen his proud new shirt the day before – even Mr Evans had commented upon it – and Terry knew that only an initial wave of disbelief and the policeman's instructions, prevented somebody from shouting it out. But they were all thinking what he was thinking, he knew, and in a state of breathless paralysis he sat and stared hotly at the policeman. He daren't look at Mr Evans, nor at the headmaster, and he daren't return the sidelong stares of the other kids. It was a lifetime of a pause. He'd have to blink or swallow soon. But he held on, and on, until his head began to quiver with trying to keep it still, and his ears set themselves back with the tautening of his muscles; each a sign of guilt for the class to see and to recognize.

Mr Marshall himself finally provided a temporary respite in his high-pitched clipped voice. 'Yes, there's plenty to talk about, plenty to think upon. Well, now here's something else.' He leaned forward on the front desk. 'I am convinced that somebody in this school knows something about this business, and I promise you I'm going to find out who it is. Meanwhile, unless those radios are returned within the next day or so, safe and sound, I shall have to seriously consider cancelling the third and fourth year summer-term visit to Boulogne by hovercraft. Your money will be returned and I will write to your parents to tell them why. They'll see that I mean to stamp this out. If the school can be treated in this way I don't see why the school should put itself out to arrange pleasant days out and involve itself in all that extra work. So, if you know something about it, or if you think you do, or you suspect someone, then I want to know. And remember,' he added, to ease their consciences, 'it isn't telling tales to give information which leads to the return of your own, your school's, property.'

That was it. He'd hit them where it hurt, and the shocked silence which followed his announcement could only be the prelude to a storm of accusations. The Boulogne trip, an expensive one, had been on the cards since the beginning of the spring term, and money had been collected on a weekly basis for some time. It was an out-of-the-ordinary trip to commemorate their second year of French at the school, a big carrot made juicier by repeated dangling, and its threatened withdrawal did all that Mr Marshall intended it to in putting their loyalty to the school above their personal friendships. If it was Boulogne or Harmer, then Boulogne would be sure to win. Terry knew that. He waited for the first voice to speak. He began to wonder who it would be. Just a few seconds more and he would be given up for the French trip – too late, now that he had lost the initiative. His story would take more believing now, he'd have lost credibility – all through finishing his work!

But just before the Judas revealed himself, a disembodied voice crackled into the room. It was the personal radio clipped to P.C. Peters' tunic, calling him to more urgent things, and he had to ask to be excused while he stepped outside to answer it.

Mr Marshall escorted him out with a final, 'Let me down, 4E, and you're letting yourselves down, remember . . .' and then the door was closed; but not before Mr Evans had purposefully walked across the room with a quiet, 'I'd like a word with you, Mr Marshall, if I may,' and Terry knew that his goose, if not cooked, was about to be put in the oven.

'Own up, Harmer!'

'Yea, go on, Terry Harmer. We know it's you!'

'Look at 'is face! Red as a bee'root!'

Any goodwill the class might once have had for one of its own had evaporated; the disbelief had gone. Now they were like a pack of hounds, snapping at a cornered fox: baying for their treat. Terry protested. What else could he do? What fox doesn't fight till beaten?

'Where's your black shirt today, then, Harmer? You was swanky enough in it yesterday.'

'Me Mum wouldn't let me wear it.'

'Oh yea? Where was you last night, then?'

'Indoors.'

'Doing what?'

'Watching telly . . .'

'Oh yea? Whatya watch?'

'"Scotland Yard"...'

'That was late. What before?'

'"Top of the Pops"...'

'Oh yea? Who was on it, then?'

'Er...'

'He don't know! You didn't see it, did you? It was him. Go on, Harmer, own up!'

'Yea, own up, Harmer! An' bring them radios back, or you're in for a right duffin'!'

'Why should we suffer 'cos you're bent?'

'Yea...'

'Evans knows. He's gone to tell Marshall!'

'Good job.'

'But you bring 'em back, Harmer. Or else!'

The sight of a fist being shaken at him was one thing, that was just the driver-to-driver language of annoyance which Terry had seen even his father use. But the bony fist thrust under his nose, hard white knuckles meaning business, was another. And Terry needed no more hateful reminders to tell him that he was well and truly between two stools: between this lot, and Les and his gang: and while he was suddenly relieved by the temporary rescue of Mr Evans returning to the classroom, he knew that his problems were far from over. He couldn't just tell his made-up story any more; he had to get the radios; there was no compromise way out. A terrible 'wait-until-playtime' atmosphere hung in the room, and he knew that the time had come, Les or no Les, knife or no knife, 'Tel' or no 'Tel', for him to open up his heart to someone. And he was really more relieved than afraid when the summons came, and he was called by the secretary to go and see Mr Marshall in his room, to return to the scene of the crime.

Chapter Eleven

THE deliberate delay in sending for Terry enabled Mr Marshall to do two things: it enabled him to take Terry's record wallet out of the filing cabinet and skim through it, and it gave him the opportunity to set the scene in his room so as to make the maximum impact on the boy. He began his preparations as soon as he had finished talking with a rather puzzled Mr Evans.

The class teacher's information that Terry's appearance the day before fitted the caretaker's description had led both the masters to speculate on the chances of the boy being involved in the break-in. Speaking quietly, rising and falling on the soles of his training shoes as he had expressed his concern, Mr Evans had been quick to make it clear that he didn't necessarily suspect the boy of being involved; he merely fitted the description: but neither had been able to deny the other children's reactions during the policeman's short talk, and, being experienced in the ways of children, they had both known that the eyes of the innocent often give away more than the mouths of the guilty. They had also realized, a trifle guiltily themselves, that when it came down to it neither of them knew too much about the boy in question. He was one of those quietish, middling-ability children who teachers find it difficult to write reports about, or to discuss enthusiastically with parents. To both of them he was one of those quiet grey ones in the middle.

The two men had stood in the corridor, against the window, looking out on to the quadrangle as if they were discussing the shrubs.

'He's a bit of a lone wolf; he does what's asked of him without putting himself out too much; he's not often in trouble. But I don't really know him. He sometimes plays football in my first team, but he hasn't got a regular place...' He'd paused while a girl passed behind him with a register. 'I met his parents at Christmas: quiet, interested people. Very pleasant to talk to . . .'

Mr Marshall had frowned and scratched the top of his head with the frame of his glasses. 'Yes, I've met them, too. But I can't quite put a face to them. I seem to remember an older sister . . .'

'Tracey. In my class first year here. Pleasant enough, but not outstanding in any way . . .'

A silence had fallen between them; everything, it seemed, had been said.

'Well, all right, Mr Evans. I'll have a look at his records, then I'll send for him. Meanwhile, don't say a word yourself . . .'

'No. O.K.'

The two men had parted company without saying more, like spies after a clandestine meeting; Mr Evans to quell a riot, Mr Marshall to prepare his room, and his mind.

Terry's records weren't much more help than Mr Evans had been. They noted his father's job, and his address, but running all through them, right from the infant reception class, was a heavy vein of 'average' remarks – 'fairly quiet', 'quite well-behaved', 'reasonable standard of work', 'average ability'. Not much to go on there: no history of petty pilfering, no prison records in the family. He could see from the address that Terry wasn't from the smart, post-war development to the west of the school; and he knew that his parents weren't forever up at the school with one complaint after another. But all that still left Terry something of an enigma; a quiet, average boy, who nobody seemed to know particularly well; the sort whose name he'd be likely to mix up with two or three others, even after six years.

'Give me five minutes and you can go and get him,' he had told Mrs Baker, and he had set about arranging his room.

He put the slate pen-holder in the middle of his empty desk, he opened wide the violated cupboard, and he arranged the four remaining radios in an impressive window-display on the white top. Then he uncapped his fountain pen, turned his notepad over to a fresh sheet, straightened his shirt cuffs, and sat waiting on his plumped-up cushion for the boy to arrive. He even thought about putting on his academic gown, to give a judge-like look, but it was at home, being ironed. So he sat and waited patiently for Terry to arrive, deciding on the best way through to this quiet enigma of a boy.

Mrs Baker was very good at escorting children in to see the headmaster. She never involved herself. She never knew what he could want them for; it might have been for a golden star or for the stick; she was always polite but decidedly non-chatty. Not that Terry was in any doubt about the reason for his summons; nor, in truth, was he fearful about it any more – it was more likely Les, or the kids in his class, who meant him harm. And he had no doubt at all that Mr Marshall would believe him. He had to. It was the truth. His only crime had been in not speaking up sooner: and anyone could be excused for that, under the circumstances.

Mrs Baker knocked on the headmaster's door. 'Here's Terry Harmer, Mr Marshall,' she announced, and after a moment's pause for a curt 'Come in', she gently propelled Terry by the middle of his back into the room to stand before the straight-spined figure of the headmaster.

The interview began by Mr Marshall playing an old, useful trick that he used nine times out of ten on such occasions. He began by saying nothing at first, he held his eyes down, while his nose wrinkled beneath his slipping glasses as if what he was reading off the record card before him was something unfit for decent people to see. It gave the child time to realize where he was, to be overcome by the awe of being there, and today, for Terry to take in the carefully arranged evidence which sat like stage-props in the room.

The headmaster usually held that position for a few seconds, judging the moment to begin speaking.

After nearly twenty seconds he looked up from the record wallet and removed his reading glasses; he stared piercingly at Terry; and he played his second trick. 'I believe you have something to tell me,' he said. It rarely failed. Only the hardest cases, or the most innocent, could resist the implication that he knew everything, and he was just giving them a chance to confess. And Terry was no exception. He was the ripest fruit for plucking in the orchard.

'Please, sir, about the radios?'

Mr Marshall nodded. 'About the radios.' It had worked again.

'Yes, sir. Please, sir, I do know about it.' There was a pause, while the courage to plumb the deepest part of the murky pool was summoned. 'I've got one at home, but it wasn't my fault. They made me do it.'

Terry stopped. He needed some reaction, some feed-back, before he went on. But the headmaster's face gave nothing away. 'Yes? Go on, boy.' He placed one hand on top of the other on the desk and prepared to listen.

'Well, please sir, last night I had a row with my mother, and I ran off, up the Court flats ...' He kept his voice steady only with the greatest effort; the wave of self-pity which had been building up for the past seventeen hours was suddenly threatening to engulf him, and was only being held at bay by his need to lie about certain aspects of the matter; but his eyes narrowed with the pressure of moisture, and the numbness around his mouth slurred his speech slightly. 'And I got caught by these ...' He stopped suddenly. He couldn't make it two labourers any more, not with old Jarvis's evidence. He put in a little sobbing sniff to cover his pause. '... By these kids, one big one and four others, not from round here, all with flick-knives, and when they found out what school I came to, they asked me questions about it.' The story was gushing out now, and it felt so good. 'They

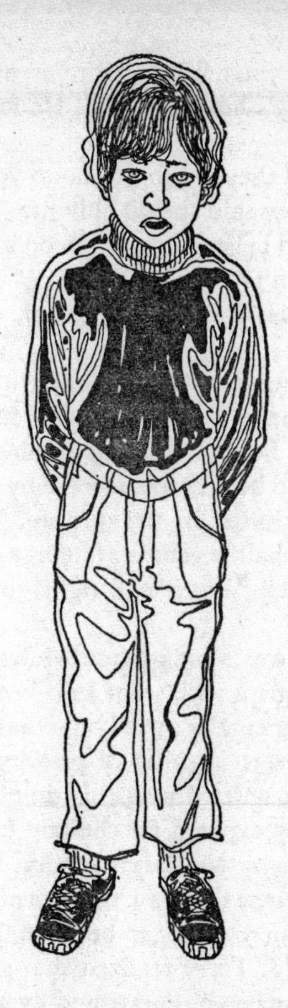

made me say what stuff we'd got – things they could sell – and they forced me to help them get in and get them. And they made me take one radio . . .'

'To keep for yourself?'

'No, sir . . .'

'To sell?'

'No, sir, to make me still a part of it, so I wouldn't tell on them . . .'

'I see. And did you tell? Do your parents know?'

'No, sir.' Terry's head dropped. He felt bad about that, now.

'And what did they say they'd do to you if you did tell?'

'Please, sir, they said they'd chiv me – cut me up – and they said no one'd believe I wasn't in on it from the start.'

'And you weren't?'

'No, sir!' It was a vehement denial, with hair swaying and eyes filling.

'And tell me, what have you done with the school radio you were ... made to keep?' Mr Marshall's tone was friendly-neutral; he was still questioning, keeping all the options open; he'd been made a fool of by kids before.

'Please, sir, I hid it in the dustbin. Under the plastic bag ...' Mr Marshall's eyebrows fought a duel with his hair-line, then retreated. 'But it's all right, sir. It didn't get too wet.'

'I see.' There was a long pause while Mr Marshall first tried to come to grips with what he'd heard, to understand it, then while he mentally sorted out what he still wanted to know into some sort of order of priority. When he spoke again it was in a quiet drawl, this time the trick question being deliberately exposed for the boy to see. 'And if you hadn't been seen by Mr Jarvis in that flash of lightning, would you have come to see me this morning?'

Silence spread across the gap between them like a sheet of ice, hard and cold. Terry realized that going across it was going to be a slippery business: and even telling the truth wouldn't necessarily improve his footing. He hadn't been going to tell, then he had; but it had been a late decision; he'd had plenty of time to tell him before all the threats came out in the classroom. He didn't know how to answer.

Mr Marshall then made things worse by trying to help him. 'This morning, when you got up, were you coming to school to tell me all about it, or not?'

Terry swallowed his indecision. But while it made answering easier it did nothing to help the answer itself. Mistrusting his voice, which would carry unintentional overtones of bravado, or shame, or not caring less, he just shook his head.

'No?'

'No, sir.' It was a quiet, cautious, whisper.

'I see.' Then, picking up the quiet tone, leaning forward, almost lying across the desk, the headmaster asked, confidentially, 'So what were you going to do with the radio? Keep it?'

'No, sir!' The ice was broken with a crack. 'I had to take it down – up – to this big boy tonight. He wanted it.'

'And if you don't?' Mr Marshall gently reminded him that he wasn't on safe ground yet.

'He's going to get me with the knife, sir.'

'Oh, is he?'

The headmaster sat up straight again, still refraining from comment, and moved on to his next area of questioning.

'Where do these boys come from, do you think? Did they give you any idea of their names? Or their school? And what did they look like? What were they wearing? The police are going to need to know all this . . .'

But Terry was shaking his head from the first question on. This was information that no one could expect him to give, not in his dangerous position. Marshall must know that.

'You don't know? Or you're not prepared to say?'

The silence again, the ice; too thin now even to put the slightest pressure on. The interrogator sensed it, and wisely kept off, for the present.

'One more thing. The caretaker tells me that you were helped over the gate by one of these boys, to enable you to get away. If that is true – and I've no reason to doubt Mr Jarvis's word – can you tell me why he should do such a thing for someone he'd been bullying, especially since, presumably, he'd got what he wanted?' The fingertips were together, the hands resting on the desk, almost in an attitude of prayer; but the eyes were wide open and alert.

Even as Terry answered, as honestly as he could, he knew that perhaps there was a part of the truth that was eluding even him. But the straight answer, the acceptable, understandable answer, was simple. 'Please sir, he was scared that if I got caught he'd get found out himself.'

'Yes, I see. Of course.' Still no comment, but another change of tack. 'And what was this about televisions? The caretaker said someone shouted something about televisions. This gang didn't think they'd carry away one of those, did they?'

Terry shook his head, frowning. This had puzzled him when the policeman had said it. 'No, sir. Please, sir, I don't remember anything about televisions. They just shouted to get out through the windows and run for the gate, and L . . . – one of them – shouted at me to help me over, like I said...'

Mr Marshall looked at his hands. 'What did you say his name was?' he asked, casually.

Terry shut his mouth, stood still, his head down. He wouldn't be tricked like that. He'd gone as far as he could. No one, nothing, would budge him further. There was a long silence, like waiting for a television to warm up, but nothing was going to force Terry into saying more. He waited, submissive, for Mr Marshall's next question; or maybe the verdict. Perhaps even the sentence.

When the headmaster himself broke the silence it was, indeed, in the judicial manner. His voice was even, well-measured, kindly but firm; and the words it carried made a brief, lucid, summing-up to the situation. It was, even if Mr Marshall thought so himself, rather neatly put.

'Well, Harmer,' he said, looking the boy squarely in the eyes, 'I may regret saying this later, but I think I'm inclined to believe you. Inclined, mind you, not entirely convinced yet. However, I think you found yourself, if your account is to be believed, in a very difficult position. These boys were bullies, and you were afraid of them, and who's to say how anyone would react in such a situation? Probably only the inner voice of your conscience can say how well you really conducted yourself.'

Terry's inner voice at that moment, however, was rather busy interpreting the headmaster's words. What was he saying? Was he for him, or quietly having a go at him? You couldn't tell till the last minute. He cocked his head slightly and paid careful attention to every word.

'So, you went through with what these people demanded?' He stopped for a moment while Terry nodded agreement. 'Well, I can understand your fear, and possibly your reluctance to tell anyone about it . . . but I must confess that even so I can't bring myself to condone all your behaviour. I find it hard to believe, for instance, that there was absolutely nothing you could do to prevent what happened from happening . . .'

So that's it. He's against me, Terry thought. Good God, he should've been there . . .

'. . . that you couldn't have shouted to Mr Jarvis for help, or broken away from them . . .'

Are you kidding? Terry wanted to blurt out; there was only that chance in the hall, for a second, and . . .

'. . . or, having been involved, that you couldn't tell your parents; and I'm hurt that you should feel that you couldn't tell me . . .'

But I was going to, I was just coming . . .

'I think you acted rather like the flash of lightning that revealed you. You know what a flash of lightning is, don't you? It is a charge of electricity taking the line of least resistance to the ground . . .'

Eh?

'. . . and that's exactly what you did. *You* took the line of least resistance. You took the easy way out, the way that involved you in the least danger, the least trouble, the least moral effort . . .'

He's barmy. I've been worrying myself sick deciding what to do . . .

'However, perhaps you think it's easy for me to say all that when it wasn't me who was up against it . . .'

You're dead right . . .

'And who knows what any of us would do when faced with a difficult situation like that?'

You can say that again . . .

'So, for the time being, we'll suspend judgement, perhaps just giving you the benefit of the doubt. But you must realize that your parents must know, and the police will have to be involved – indeed, they are already. And I must say I don't feel very much inclined to sit back and quietly kiss good-bye to one of the school radios.' He drew in a deep breath and fixed Terry with his most serious look. His voice now was quiet and grave. 'You must think about what you've done, Harmer: you must go over it in your mind, ponder upon it, and you must ask yourself, "Did I do right?" "Have I done my best, at every stage, for my school – and most important – for myself?" For these are questions that only you can answer . . .' For a few seconds he held Terry there with his eyes while his message sank in. 'Meanwhile, home you go, Harmer, and retrieve that school radio from your . . .' (he could hardly utter the word) '. . . dustbin . . . and hurry back by playtime. Do you understand?'

'Yes, sir.'

'As for the other radio, we'll have to see what course events take, but we won't press the point for the present.'

'Yes, sir.'

'Now, do I need to send anyone with you? You're not going to do anything foolish again, are you?'

Foolish? 'No, sir.'

'Very well then. I'll see you on your return.'

'Yes, sir.'

'All right then. Dismiss.'

Terry almost ran out of the room. In spite of the headmaster's criticisms of the way he'd behaved, the sense of relief he suddenly felt at having at least told someone about it, having shared part of his problem, was like nothing he'd ever experienced before. You must have to be very deeply in trouble, he realized, to understand how nice it is to be back to normal, or nearly so. It was a great feeling. As for the part of the problem that remained, well, Les knew he'd nearly been caught. He might guess he'd been recognized, or that something had given him away. Les would just have to be content with the one radio: he surely wouldn't push his luck for the other. Anyway, it'd be too late by then. The radio would've been returned. And the chances were he'd never see Les again, anyhow. And if he did – well, he'd protected him, hadn't he? Marshall might try to push it a bit in a little while, put on a bit of pressure for the other radio, but he'd said his piece, he knew the score, and he wasn't likely to do much more about it without making sure Terry was safe, was he? Neither were his parents – or the police for that matter. No, it was over, almost. Surely.

He suddenly felt like a man who'd won the pools. He ran out of the forbidden front entrance of the school and across the car-park without feeling the ground beneath his feet. He'd get the radio, bring it back, and then perhaps he'd even ask Marshall to say something to the other kids in his class. Put things right with them. Yes, he would. And then everything would be all right again. A new surge of the heady delirium of relief spurred him on. It was like waking up from that chasing nightmare, when his mother really was there after all; he'd shouted for help and been heard. It was marvellous! With a leap and a cry of 'Come on you reds!' – the first triumphant shout that came to mind – he ran out of the gate and down Fox Hill Road.

Mr Marshall watched him disappear through his Venetian blinds. He was frowning, but he was fairly satisfied, and he might almost have left the matter there; the appearance of a group of children to read to him, or a crisis over stock, or a class to teach, might have left him to just tie up the loose ends later; but, unfortunately for Terry, he had left himself with nothing to do before playtime but sort this matter out, and seeing that there were still twenty-five minutes to kill, he decided they'd be wisely spent seeking relief from one nagging doubt. He wasn't entirely satisfied that he'd gone as far as he could into this television business, there still seemed to be a slight element of mystery there, and the more he thought about it the more he came to the opinion that the boy's reason for being helped over the gate was perhaps a trifle glib. He went over the sequence of events, as he understood them, and he concentrated his mind on the boy's story, from the very plausible row with his mother to the strange affair of the escape at the end. There was certainly something that didn't quite ring true about it. Something to do with this television business. As he was thinking, and without really seeing it, he stared absently at the boy's record card on his desk. 'Terence John Harmer.' His eyes kept reading the name as his thoughts took him over the school, up at the flats, out at the gate. It was all very puzzling. The record card showed a reasonable home background, a quiet, well-behaved boy, with no reason for anyone to disbelieve him. Then, why? Suddenly, in a flash, in that 'eureka!' moment, without his realizing how, the answer appeared before him. It had been there all the time. Literally. On the record card. Good God! Of course! Why hadn't he seen it before?

With scrambling fingers he picked up his telephone and buzzed through to Mrs Baker.

'Yes, Mr Marshall?'

'Would you be kind enough to ring the caretaker's house and see if Mr Jarvis has finished his breakfast, Mrs Baker? If so, I'd like to see him again, please, before Terry Harmer gets back.'

'Yes, Mr Marshall.'

'And tell him it's urgent, will you? There's one last thing I want to ask him, which will affect the way I handle this situation from now on.'

'Yes, certainly, Mr Marshall.'

The headmaster returned the phone to its cradle, dropping it gently from his fingers the last few centimetres. Then he sat and thought, undisturbed, about the puzzle of this Harmer boy's behaviour, until a muffled tap at the door heralded the arrival of a puzzled Mr Jarvis.

'Ah, come in, Mr Jarvis. Just a little point I want to clear up.' Mr Marshall stood up and indicated the upright chair he was to sit on with a stubby gesture of his hand. Experienced in the ways of the headmaster, the caretaker thought he read the sign: a broader sweep, or even a hand on the back of the offered chair, and he'd have been about to be asked a favour; but this morning's gesture could well mean that Marshall was about to lead up to a complaint. Mr Jarvis still felt far from happy himself about the hall door being left unlocked by his wife, as his empty stomach testified – and he secretly wondered that the third world war hadn't been heard across the car-park. Perhaps it had. With a slight grunt and with exaggerated care, to remind the head of his loyal exertions the night before, he sat on the chair and looked up, his feet apart, his hands on his knees, the figure of an active, responsible, cautious, man.

'It's about those boys you chased, Mr Jarvis, the last two, the ones you nearly caught . . .'

'Yes?'

'You said you got close enough to them to see one of them, the boy in the black shirt, fairly clearly in a flash of lightning?'

'That's right, Mr Marshall.' The caution went. He was on solid ground here. 'I gave chase across the car-park as best as I could. The back one seemed nearly all in, and I reckon I'd have got him at the gate if his mate hadn't pulled him over.'

'But you got close enough to him to see him, and describe him?'

'Yes, I did. And that's the description I give the policeman. It all lit up perfect for a second, as bright as day. The only trouble was, he had his face turned away, else I'd have got a perfect look at him.'

'Yes, and I think you did very well to get that near.' The headmaster smiled, reassuringly. 'Now, you told the policeman that you were also near enough to hear them saying something, shouting at one another; you say that one of them said something about a television?'

The caretaker nodded enthusiastically, pleased to hold what sounded like important information which had nothing to do with the hall door. 'Yes, it was the big one who said it, I'm sure of that. The chap I was chasing couldn't have shouted "Help!" if he'd been drowning. He was real done in . . .'

'So what did the big one say? Can you remember the exact words?' Mr Marshall was leaning forward again, willing the slightly deaf caretaker to remember what he had heard.

Mr Jarvis closed his eyes and frowned, and turned his good ear towards the headmaster, as if he were trying to catch the words again, in the room. 'Well, it was something about grabbing hold of a television, as far as I can remember. But it was raining, and rumbling, and I couldn't be all that certain.'

'No, of course not.' It was sympathetic, but Mr Marshall pursued his point, like a lawyer leading a witness. 'But the television hadn't been touched, had it? The room hadn't even been entered?'

'No . . .'

'And the set is too heavy and bulky for someone without transport to steal, wouldn't you say?'

'Oh yes, definitely . . .'

'So what do you think they could mean? Why would they want to be discussing stealing a television set at such a crucial moment, when you were about to catch up with one of them?'

There was a short, doubt-filled, silence. 'I don't know, Mr Marshall. I really couldn't say.' The caretaker was slightly ruffled now, on the middle ground between defence and attack. He'd done his best, given chase, and reported what he'd heard. What was this all about? What else was he supposed to have done? Asked the boy to repeat what he'd said while he wrote it down?

'He used the word "grab", did he?'

'Sounded like that. Then something about a television ... an old television.' His voice suddenly rose half an octave as some subconscious mental activity brought another scrap of information to the surface. 'Yes, *old*, I'm sure of it, something about an *old* television.' He straightened his back, triumphant, as another of the seemingly crucial words echoed in the chambers of his memory. 'Yes, "old," he said. "Grab an old television," or something.'

'And what was the boy doing at the time? The one who was shouting?' Mr Marshall was smiling, a tight, satisfied smile.

'Why, he was holding out his hand for the small boy to catch hold of it. It was just before he pulled him over the gate ...'

'Yes!' Mr Marshall stood up, quickly, in a theatrical move, in the lawyer's triumph of skilled argument. 'He wanted him to *catch hold* of his hand; or to *grab hold* of it, didn't he? *Grab hold*? Eh? "Grab 'old!",' he concluded in a loud, accurate, cockney accent. He stood there, smiling, hands on hips, eyes blazing. In a play, Mr Jarvis would have leapt to his feet shouting, 'Yes! Yes! You've got it! Well done, sir!' But the caretaker had been cheerfully proven both deaf and wrong. So the best he could do was to grudgingly concede a quiet, 'Well, yes, it could have been, I suppose.'

With undaunted enthusiasm the headmaster went on: 'But he wouldn't call the boy a television, would he? "Grab 'old, Television." That doesn't make sense, does it?'

Mystified, Mr Jarvis shook his head.

'So could it have been something else you heard? Something meaning television, which your brain – quite naturally – interpreted as television? Something like . . . *telly*?'

The caretaker thought about it for a moment. Then he put on his bland not-prepared-to-be-impressed-any-more face, as he did when he gave up trying to understand his wife shouting at him in German. He'd lost him now. What was this all about, anyhow?

Mr Marshall paced up and down the small room, now beside him, now behind him, slapping his folded glasses into his palm.

'But wouldn't it make more sense if he'd shouted, "Grab 'old, *Tel*!"? Or some name like that? Eh? *Tel*? Something like *Tel*? The nickname for Terry?' He stopped pacing, round behind his desk again, and he looked earnestly at the caretaker for his reaction – but certain, as sure as Monday follows Sunday, that he was right. 'Eh? *Terry – Tel*!'

At last Mr Jarvis saw the point. Yes. Of course. That made sense. That did make sense. More than the television thing. He nodded, his mouth closed and twisted to one side in considered agreement. He was a clever old bird, old Marshall. No wonder he was headmaster, and Joe Sope was only the caretaker. 'Yes, it would, I dare say,' he said, careful thought still sounding in his voice. 'Yes, no doubt about that – so long as the boy's name *was* Terry . . .'

Mr Marshall was nodding, and grinning with a new seriousness. 'But if it was, Mr Jarvis; if it was, it would make a lot of sense then, wouldn't it? A lot more sense than shouting something about an old television?'

'Yes, I suppose it would. But . . .'

'Yes?'

'But only if they was good friends. Then it would, definitely.' He thought for a moment more. 'But of course, they would've been, wouldn't they? Doing all that together, and staying behind to help each other over the gate. They'd need to be buddies for that . . .'

'Yes, they would. I think you're right. They'd certainly need to be good friends for all those circumstances to fit.' He put on his glasses with a sigh, and looked down at Terry's record card, at 'Terence John Harmer', the full and uncommon way of referring to Terry that had first made him think about the name's abbreviations. 'Well, you see, that's what's been nagging at me for some little time.'

Jarvis didn't understand. But then he couldn't be expected to. Mr Marshall sat down again with an exhausted bump, dropping his body the last little bit as he'd dropped the telephone earlier. This was a difficult, responsible job to have: how much easier to deal with things, like Jarvis, than with people. 'Yes, I think that's more likely it, Mr Jarvis...' Still, when you had special gifts you had to expect to use them. And you needed to know quite a bit about the workings of the young mind, he thought with a responsible, experienced sigh, to really appreciate the likeliest truth in such a situation. 'You go and get some ointment on that bruise on your cheek. And tell Mrs Baker I'll see Terry Harmer as soon as he gets back . . .'

Chapter Twelve

A SURPRISE stream of warm spring sunshine seeped through the clouds and bathed Terry in a benign warmth as he walked back to school with the radio. The sudden heat on his head, the first of the year, momentarily took his mind off his situation and flashed trailers into his mind of the days ahead, of runs in the car with the windows open, of new swimming-trunks, of later bed-times, and of a thin denim jacket. It washed him with the same comforting warmth that his bath had, and he was filled with a fleeting feeling of rare contentment. For a few happy metres, as the sun washes out the car headlamp in day-time, so it seemed to reduce his remaining problem to insignificance. Like an ointment it soothed him and gave him relief from his hurts. Like a returning friend it put its arm around his shoulder.

It was Les who worried him; but as he walked along the dry pavements behind the sharpness of his shadow, he kept telling himself, over and over until he was convinced, that he'd seen the last of him; he existed no more than his own shadow could exist within the greater shadow of a house. It was Les who was really on his own now. Hadn't the others all run off, glad to get away, scot-free. Hadn't they gone empty-handed from the break-in? Could there possibly be anything in it for them any more? No, of course not. And they had no reason to come hunting for him on Les's behalf. That Mick had been riling him all the time, trying to score off him. And the black boy, and Plastic-head, and the little kid, they'd only really joined in for the kicks, for the aggro. O.K., they'd been a bit scared of Les when he had his knife, but it had all been acted up for his own benefit. No, Les, with his ugly, grimy face hadn't got so much going for him now, not as far as getting Terry was concerned. He'd got his radio and he'd have to be content with that. He was blooming lucky he hadn't been given away. He'd certainly have to whistle for this other one. It was going back where it belonged. Comforted with these thoughts Terry walked confidently along the street, almost whistling; and Les became less and less real, an evaporating nightmare in the sunlight. It was too warm to have worries. Not until he was turning into the school gate again did the sun disappear behind a thin cloud and a shiver sweep across the car-park, but Terry shrugged it off and broke into a run to the school entrance. It was almost over now, he thought.

But life, as he was about to discover, is unpredictable, full of surprises; and as soon as you get used to one idea you're being asked to change it. He fondly thought he would be returning the hero. But he was only a few seconds away from another new and unpleasant experience. It was when he got inside the door, and he was religiously wiping his feet on the flattened mat, that he suddenly found out what it was like to be notorious.

There was Mr Jarvis, standing with his back to the fish-tank, talking to Mrs Baker out of Mr Marshall's hearing, gesticulating with his hands and doing a mime of someone grabbing a pair of wrists; an agitated figure, the voice was tripping over itself in its eagerness to tell. But when the caretaker saw the radio in Terry's arms he froze in mid-sentence, and he stared with hostility at the surprised boy. Mrs Baker looked round sharply to follow his gaze, flicking her eyes like an ant-eater's tongue between the radio and the deepening red of the boy's face.

'Excuse me,' she said, and disappeared back into her room. The caretaker folded his arms and nodded his head disapprovingly at Terry, as much as to say 'I might have thought it'. Well, that was only to be expected, Terry thought, until it was all explained to everybody by Mr Marshall.

The secretary's sharp face reappeared round her door. 'Go straight in, please,' she said. 'Mr Marshall's waiting for you.'

Despite his innocence Terry felt very small and uncomfortable as he walked towards the office door. Suddenly, walking past the secretary was like walking past an open fridge. Mr Jarvis, still in a state of mild surprise, turned away to look at the fish-tank, while Mrs Baker stared him out as if he were a gipsy walking up her path with pegs. She stepped out of his way at the last moment. 'Go on through,' she said. She raised her eyebrows at Mr Jarvis, questioning what this world was coming to, but she followed Terry in, tut-tutting loudly as her door failed to shut properly.

Terry's second confrontation with Mr Marshall started like the first, in silence. Terry put the radio on the desk and stepped back modestly, with the air of one seeking no praise for what he had done, but nonetheless proud to have kept his word. Mr Marshall walked all round the radio. He stood on his toes to look at it from above, and he crouched down to view it from table level. Seeing no dents he peered at it

closely for scratches. Finally, satisfied with the look of it, he switched it on to see how it sounded. 'Amen,' intoned a fruity voice with perfect clarity.

The headmaster switched it off and grunted. 'So much for this one,' he said curtly. 'You can thank your lucky stars you won't have to pay for this to be repaired . . .'

Terry nodded, and swallowed. What was this all about? What if it had got damaged? It wasn't his fault, was it? If Marshall knew he'd been forced to take it, he must know he wouldn't be to blame for any harm that might have come to it.

'Now, what about the other one? The one your friend got away with? How do you intend to get that back?'

His tone had changed. This wasn't the sanctimonious voice of twenty minutes before which had given Terry the benefit of the doubt. This was more the throaty growl of someone wronged.

Terry shook his head in bewilderment. 'Please, sir, I don't know where it is. I don't know where he lives. And he's not my friend, I told you . . .' The moisture was pressing on his eyes again; his voice was in danger of being impeded by the choke of being misunderstood. What was this all about? What had happened in the past twenty minutes?

'You told me a lot of things, Harmer, and I made the mistake of . . . of believing you, boy!' Mr Marshall rose on his toes as his voice welled up on a wave of real anger. 'I took your word, Harmer, and I gave you the benefit of the doubt. And a perfect fool you must think I am, to have swallowed all that story about a knife, and threats, and being forced to take a radio home . . .'

Terry hardly heard the last words. His head went light and swimmy and he heard his voice shouting at the headmaster as if he were at home with Tracey. 'It's the truth! He did have a knife, and he made me do it! He did! On my mother's death-bed!' It was a sudden, explosive situation, and he couldn't help himself.

'Don't you shout at me, boy! And don't blaspheme! You won't bluff your way out of this the way you lied your way out before!' The head's face was suddenly all mouth and glasses on a column of blotchy red neck.

Terry opened his mouth to shout through his tears again. But he had no chance against the louder, faster, dominating voice of authority. 'I happen to know that this boy *is* a friend of yours. And you're only making things a hundred times worse for yourself by continuing to deny it. I wasn't born yesterday. I'm up to sorting the truth from a hundred little liars like you ...'

Terry's body shook with the sobs of frustration. The words he tried to use ran into a long, loud, unintelligible howl, as he rubbed his fingers in his eyes in a vain attempt to keep the humiliation in, tide-marking his face. But still the man kept shouting, giving him no chance, bullying, like a Les with a knife-edged voice.

'You thought you were so clever, didn't you? You and your friends? What a good idea! You could get together with a few ne'er-do-wells and help yourself to a few pounds' worth of school property. And if you were caught you could say they forced you into it! Well, let me tell you this. I don't believe a word of it. Not a word.' He glanced down at the record card again, with its 'Terence John Harmer'. 'Bully-boys don't go round calling their innocent victims by pet names, laddy! Only friends do that. Friends! Mates! So don't come the innocent with me, Sonny Jim!' He stood back, breathless, and adjusted his tie. He looked across at the miserable boy – the dirty face, the knuckled eyes, the heaving shoulders which seemed to be trying to throw off some burden.

'P ... P ... P ...' Each attempted consonant was caught on an impeding sob.

'I beg your pardon?'

'P . . . P . . . Pig-face!' Terry finally managed it before the next sob choked it off.

'What did you say?' The headmaster's ears flicked back visibly, like an aroused tiger.

'He called me "Pig-face" most of the time.'

But Mr Marshall's head was already shaking from side to side smugly, now more the toy dog in the rear window of a car. 'Well, that's not what I know, Harmer.' Suddenly his head stopped moving and he threw a fast, straight question across the desk. 'Are you denying that he called you by your nickname, then?'

'No, sir.' There was a world of miserable understanding in Terry's admission. He was beginning to see it now, the change of mood, the sudden animosity. Jarvis must have realized about that bloody 'Tel' business, and told him. Well, he didn't understand it himself, so how could he explain it to someone else?

'Please, sir, most of the time he just pushed me, or called me "Pig-face".' He'd got his second wind. The sobbing had stopped for a moment, and his voice sounded as calm and as reasonable as any liar's. 'But one or two times he called me "Terry"; and only one time, when I was getting over the gate, he called me "Tel". I don't know why. Most of the time it was "Pig-face". It's true!' The calm was suddenly over as he threw himself on the man's trust. Another sob shook him, and the tears welled up again in his eyes as he realized the hopelessness of trying to convince the headmaster of his innocence. Not to be trusted, not to be believed, this was a new pain. It made his misunderstandings at home seem puerile by comparison.

The effect was devastating. Suddenly he had that feeling that nothing mattered any more, that there were no more standards to live up to if he wasn't to be believed. Marshall couldn't know him at all, to think he'd have done all that on purpose. Terry didn't care about anything any more. He'd have thrown the rotten radio through the window, or at

Marshall's stupid head, if he'd been a metre nearer the door. Who cared? Stuff 'em all! His mum and dad knew he wasn't a bloody thief!

'Well, just listen to this, Harmer,' the headmaster said to the blazing eyes, 'and then you can return to your class. If you really want me to believe you're no friend of this boy, then you can tell me who he is!' Again he rose on his toes as if he were up to his chest in choppy water. 'I can't believe you don't know more about him than you've told me.' He dropped his voice to a low monotone. 'But if you're more scared of him than you are of me, if you're really in the predicament you say you're in – and I don't for a minute believe you are – then instead of giving him away, you can go and tell him, from me, that unless that radio is returned we will leave no stone unturned to find out who he is. And tell him this. I have a thing in my cupboard called an inventory. It's a list of the equipment in the school. And every item on that inventory has to be accounted for. *I* have to account for it. And I have one radio for which I cannot account! So tell your friend all that! It's a simple matter, Harmer; the good name of this school is at stake, and if you're not the liar I think you are, then I want the radio back, or I want the boy's name. It's up to you. Do you understand?' The headmaster stood there, chin up, and held the stern pose while he waited for the boy's answer.

'Yes.'

'Then get out. I've wasted enough time on this already...'

But Terry had already turned to go. He had to obey. But having to respect was something else.

Bunking-off from school, Terry found, is a tense and lonely pursuit. Like an escaped prisoner of war you walk through hostile territory on your own, in apprehension of every second glance. Everyone seems about to say, 'Hey, you, boy – why aren't you in school?' You wish you could maintain a convincing limp, or that you had the audacity to put a bandage round your head, issuing yourself with a sort of medical certificate, an explanation of your appearance out of school. But worse than running into a nosey stranger was the possibility of meeting someone you knew. Mrs Johnson from down the road with a, 'Hello, Terry, where you off to? Day off today is it?' Or Uncle Charlie, cruising silently up behind you in his big car. 'Gawd, it's all holidays for some people!' Worse, there was the chance old Marshall had phoned P.C. Peters when he'd found he'd bunked-off, putting a panda car on his trail. So he hugged the low copings, found the shadows when the sun shone, and tried to look as if a genuine mission was taking him down Fox Hill Road to the thinly populated common.

Once he had left the unpleasant atmosphere of the headmaster's office it hadn't taken Terry long to decide he was not going back to the classroom. There was no doubt what the knuckles had meant. If he couldn't produce the radio or the culprit he was in for a duffing in some shady corner of the playground at playtime. And anyway, who could concentrate on Red Indians when old Marshall was on the warpath? Who wanted to sit and be lacerated by all those sharp and hateful stares? There was only one thing to be done about trouble like this – you had to run away from it. He was getting used to doing that. When you're on your own against greater odds, he told himself, there's not much choice.

Getting away had been easy enough. The impulse to go had struck him as he had shuffled miserably out of the secretary's room into the entrance lobby, the instant he had seen the sun shining peacefully outside, glinting on the dusty polish of the bright cars. But he knew that to have made a break for it out across the car-park would have been a mistake. Marshall would have seen him for a start, and the last thing he wanted today was another chase: his body still ached from the night before. No, the best thing was to go back down the corridor to his own room, then carry on past it and go out of the pupils' entrance at the back. That way, Marshall would think he was in the classroom, and Mr Evans would think he was still in with Marshall.

A glance at the master clock had told him that there were two more electric jumps to playtime, and then a quarter of an hour's break when no one would have to account for him. There would just be time before the rest rushed out. So with a fast but legal walk round the school he had managed to get to the rear entrance just before the bells had rung, and from then on he had merely been the first boy out to play.

Once out, he hadn't known where to go. A first, natural thought, now he was in this much trouble, had been to run to the brush factory where his mother worked. She'd understand. She'd back him up and protect him. She'd put her arm round him and squeeze him and tell him it would all be all right. But as he had thought more about it he had realized how difficult it would be to get hold of her in the big factory – she was shifted from belt to belt according to the demands of production – and, in any case, she would never hear the last of the questions from the other women if he raked her out of there, in trouble. The same went for his dad in the office at the cableworks – although he hadn't given any serious consideration to that for one moment. He'd really rather his mum told his dad. Of course, there was always Gran Harmer – but she'd never cotton on to all the details he'd have to tell her. And that just left Uncle Charlie. Now, he'd probably understand, and he'd know what to do, and he'd support him by not driving him straight back to school or phoning his dad. But his dad was the fly in the ointment there. He'd be far from pleased if Terry got Uncle Charlie involved in any family trouble. His dad was bad enough when he came to tea and made his mum all silly with laughing. No, it was no good running to Uncle Charlie. Besides, Uncle Charlie was special, for good times, to be told about the goals he scored rather than the times he didn't get a game. So in the end he'd decided there was no one, not until his mum came home from work. And that left him with best part of the day to kill.

The house was empty, he'd realized. He could go home and sit out the hours there: he could watch the telly or lie on his bed. He had his key for emergencies, and if this wasn't an emergency, what was? It hadn't been until he'd got there, walked up to the front door and let himself in with the most casual, normal air in the world, that a very good reason for not being there had suddenly struck him. Standing there on the safe side of the stained-glass ship at sea, which was riding out its own storm on the front door, a vision of P.C. Peters had suddenly flashed into his mind. Once Terry was reported missing from school, he'd be round here soon enough, wouldn't he? Perhaps with Marshall, or Mr Evans, or even his dad. And that he didn't want. No, above everything else, first and foremost, he wanted a quiet and private quarter of an hour with his mum. That was essential. Then she could tell his dad. And after that the world could fight the whole blooming family. Meanwhile, he'd have to lie low, until his mum got back from work. The trouble was, where? He couldn't hide in the house. If one of the neighbours had seen him come in then they'd better see him go out – or else if someone official came and found out he was in there, they'd knock the door down to find him.

That left the common. The ravine. The Court flats site was all right after school, but it was no good when the workmen were there; besides, you had to pass the school to get there. And there was nowhere else. There were too many nosey parjees in the park, with their big brown hats and their habit of enforcing the park rules to the last full-stop. They pinned you down with their regulations as if you were litter under the spike: and there was probably some bye-law against going in the park in school hours. So, all ways up, the ravine it had to be, he'd decided. At least he could hang about down there, and time his arrival back home to coincide with his mother's return from work.

Then he could tell her everything, and at last, whatever anyone else said, it would all be all right.

He'd stood in the kitchen and heaved a long, heavy sigh. There was something rather sad about the kitchen, standing in there on your own. The empty room, silent but for the persistent drip of a hastily turned tap and the loyal hum of the fridge, was ticking over and waiting for real life to begin again when everyone came in. Suddenly, Terry had shivered as a strange feeling swept through him, one that had to be denied. Standing there, it had been as if the others were all dead, and he'd be left to cope alone: to put away the draining cups, washed and left there by his mum, to answer the official letter standing propped against the caddy, to brush the cornflakes off the floor and put out the note for milk. He'd shivered again; and as he'd shut out the sad, self-indulgent thought, he'd realized how lucky he was that it wasn't all true. He might fall out with them, they might all get on one another's nerves, and quarrel, and fight. But it was all within family boundaries, all fenced in with love. And he couldn't do without it, he'd been made to see; not yet; perhaps, like Uncle Charlie, some people could never do without it. This was another sort of fence he'd found himself climbing – by running off the way he had. He heaved a huge sigh. It'd take more than Tracey getting up his nose to start him climbing that again.

Terry spent the longest day of his life down in the ravine. Waiting for nothing to happen but for time to pass is a tedious business, he discovered. The first hour or so wasn't so bad: he had plenty to occupy him then, when every blue car appearing on the sky-line of road led to a scramble into the gorse, when every figure walking past the bandstand was a policeman to be eluded. But as the day wore on and the police cars reverted to being commercial travellers' and the imagined policemen shed their disguises and became old ladies again, Terry stopped bothering so much and just wandered in the sun and waited for the Co-op clock to chime the next hour.

He went over everything a score of times, in between bombing ants and tying trip-up loops in the longer grass, but one thought was recurrent, focused back into his mind by the dull reflection off the drain cover at the foot of the ravine. Les. He was supposed to meet him there at half-past four with the radio. There was no chance of that now, but as the single stroke of one o'clock became two, he found himself nursing another idea which grew overwhelmingly as he fed it with thought. Hadn't Marshall offered him one certain way out of this mess? Hadn't he said he wanted either the missing radio returned, or Les's name as a substitute? Like the cops on the telly, he was prepared to do a deal for that. The idea grew as he weaned it from fantasy into solid intention. Why not to go to Les and ask – no, demand – the return of the transistor? Even if Les refused, he could tell him how he was still protecting him. And he could keep him wondering whether or not he was some day suddenly going to be caught.

The more he thought about it the more convinced he was that that was what he had to do. Old Marshall had hinted that he hadn't been brave enough. He'd said that the first time, when he'd also said he believed him. Well, this would be brave, wouldn't it? If he somehow felt a bit ashamed about the way he'd given in last night – and he couldn't deny a sneaking doubt about himself – wouldn't this put him right? And even if it didn't work, he could truthfully tell his mum and dad what he'd done. At least he'd be left with something to be proud of out of the rotten business.

All at once Terry was impatient to be beginning. Just as he'd start off waiting for a cousin's visit at the front room window, then move to the end of the street and finally walk down to the bus stop, so he found himself inching his way down the ravine in the direction of the drain cover. And although his rendezvous with Les was half-past four he was sitting on the metal circle and listening to the deep gurgling of the previous night's storm water by the time the Co-op clock woke up to strike three.

Les wouldn't be there for an hour and a half, and there was a chance he wouldn't come at all; it was going to be a long and frustrating wait, Terry decided; and it occurred to him after ten long minutes that perhaps he'd be better off going home to his mum first, then doing this bit of business afterwards. The only snag with that was that once he got home, and his parents had been told about the trouble he was in, his future moves would be out of his hands. He certainly wouldn't be allowed to come out again to find Les. It was like driving along. He'd have to ride within the armoured vehicle his parents would be driving – while to redeem himself he needed to ride his own solo machine. He kicked at a smooth, round pebble. To do this, to do that, to do the other: he was fed up with thinking out what was going to be for the best. Well, perhaps when all was said and done he'd be best off letting his family steer him. But only after he'd made this one last attempt to make his own way back to grace.

Terry's impatience for his own course of action grew apace until by half-past three he was walking gingerly along the outer streets of the Queen's Dock Estate, spurred into the hostile territory by the impulsive thought that Les probably wasn't at school, but was wandering around near by. Hadn't he said something about bunking-off to find a buyer for the radios? Well, he'd still need to do that, even for two. Or he might be nervous about having nearly been caught, and the likelihood that someone would be going round the schools making inquiries. Napier mightn't bother, but Les already knew that Fox Hill was different. Looking around for Les certainly seemed to be a chance worth taking, Terry thought. And it wasn't as if he had something better to do. If he could find Les somehow before his mum came home from the brush-works wouldn't he have that much more weight to throw in on his side of the scales? If he'd managed to get the radio back before he told them everything at home, it'd be easier for everyone, wouldn't it?

In spite of the fright he'd had the night before, and the bruised and shaking state he'd been in, Terry could remember roughly which way the gang had taken him. He could more or less remember where the high dock fence began, and he had a very vague idea of where the old house had been. He could at least take a chance and stooge around in the general area down there for a while in the hope of seeing Les. Not that he wasn't still scared. Like an ill wind Les would always be a force to be reckoned with: but the bigger scare of the threat to his future at Fox Hill School which the break-in had raised, gave Terry enough of a feeling of resentment to spur him on to a confrontation with the bigger boy. Filled suddenly with the same feeling of determination which had sent him angrily down to the common the night before, he walked doggedly down the uneven pavements with his head down, but with his eyes everywhere on the look-out for landmarks.

Terry did not have to reach the docks to find what he was looking for. It suddenly loomed up before him like a signpost in the desert. 'Fags and Mags', the paper shop which Les had avoided, stood boarded and crumbling on the next corner. Les must live near here, he thought. Hadn't he said something about his dad coming up here for his paper? Perhaps he could hang around here for a bit. If Les was about, he wouldn't be far away. But to his own surprise, and before he could give himself time to worry about all the implications of his action, Terry suddenly found himself inside the shop. He'd pushed the rickety door open and he was in the gloomy electric glow of the dingy shop. A rack of glossy magazines smiled at him on one side, and a suspicious old woman rubbed her hands and eyed him from her seat behind the counter on the other.

'Yes, son?' she asked with a frown. She'd serve him with cigars if he had the money.

'I'm looking for someone,' Terry replied loudly, emboldened by the closed door behind him: had it been easy to get out he might have made an excuse and fled. 'Mate of mine. I think he comes in here . . .'

'Who's that then?' The kid certainly wasn't a copper: they hadn't got to that yet.

'A boy called Les. I think his dad gets his papers here. I want to find him . . .' Terry stood balanced between coming in and going out.

'Fourth 'ouse down on your right. Victoria Gardens.'

Terry's face opened, his eyebrows raised. It was as simple as that – if they were both talking about the same Les.

'He's got a . . .' Terry made a vague gesture across the front of his face.

''S'right. Fourth 'ouse down.'

'Oh. Thanks.'

There was no reply. The old lady watched him as he struggled with the door, then she kicked a saucer of crusted cat food into the flank of a fat tabby and turned her attention back to the painful cracks on the backs of her hands.

Out in the sun, over the road from the shop, the street sign told Terry that he was already in Victoria Gardens. It was a narrow, characterless, council road. It had none of the dingy flavour, none of the history, of the older disintegrating streets around it. It belonged anywhere, and nowhere. The small estate could have been where it was, by the side of the docks, or it could have been tacked on to some over-grown village in the country, were it not for the overall layer of London dust which took the colour from the privets and the tall front gardens. It was an untidy urban flower-bed, where babies were the annuals and the law did the weeding. But the pattern of the building was universal. The terraced houses were separated from each other by narrow alleys running through the centres of the buildings, the bricks were flat pink, the electricity cables were stapled to the walls and wire re-inforced hedges grew in the fronts to annoy the pedestrian and frustrate the nosey passer-by.

Very cautiously Terry approached the fourth house down. He didn't know what he was going to do. If he didn't see Les, would he knock? Or would he hang around looking casual till Les saw him? Who knew? He'd have to play it by ear. In any case the first thing was to get a look at the place.

Luckily, where the gate had once been, there was a gap wide enough to give Terry a reasonable view of the house as he walked past, eyes right. He stopped to inspect a fascinating privet leaf, then he turned and walked back.

At first Terry was puzzled by the apparent absence of a front door. But after the second, harder, look, he realized that it must be in the darkness of the central alley. These were gloomy, soulless buildings. Charity built and just as cold. The Victorian houses had at least had a sunny front step to sit on, a place to be social, out in the world. Here your front door was secret and hidden, off-putting, repelling, where the casual visitor would feel at a disadvantage, where he'd be at the mercy of the occupant's decision to switch on the hall light, or leave the doorway in darkness. One thing was certain now, Terry decided. He couldn't march up to the front door and demand to see Les. He needed to retain the safety factor of being in full view of the street. Once down in there you were lost to the world. Going visiting there would be more like pot-holing.

Attempting to look purposeful to the empty street, Terry walked back to the gap and took a longer look at the house. The dark curtains upstairs were drawn across the central window, and the two smaller upstairs windows were blanked across with plain net. The whole house presented a closed, repelling image. If there was anything on the doormat – if there was a doormat – it wasn't very likely to spell 'Welcome'.

Terry didn't know what to do. He bent down and untied and tied the laces on both his plimsolls while he thought. He shook an imaginary stone out of each. Then he decided. There were two alternatives, he told his left foot. He could hang around a bit longer for a glimpse of Les, walking up and down the street till he got bored, or too scared; or he could forget this business altogether and run off home and wait for his mother.

What was it to be? he asked a crack in the pavement. He was suddenly filled with an overwhelming urge to go home. Be blowed to this. He'd tried, hadn't he?

He stood up to go. But now again, like the night before, the situation was suddenly wrenched out of his hands. Again he had no choice. It was like the playground game of running up behind some unsuspecting girl and pushing her in the back. What brought the scream wasn't so much the hurt of it as the shock to the system.

'What the 'ell are you doin' 'ere!' The familiar breaking voice croaked unpleasantly in his ear. 'Old bag up the paper shop says my friend's come looking for me. I told you the stinkin' ravine!'

Terry's right arm was up his back in a painful lock before he could even turn his head.

'Get in the 'ouse! I ought to bloody kill yer!'

Chapter Thirteen

TERRY was right about the alley. After the brightness of the afternoon he suddenly needed to use his free hand to feel where he was going, and the pain of resisting Les burned into his arm as he instinctively slowed to a shuffle in the narrow darkness.

'Ouch! Let go! You're hurting!' he shouted loudly for someone, anyone, to hear. But it was cut off swiftly as Les clamped his free hand over Terry's mouth, and he pushed him roughly to the left, into the even darker area outside Les's front door.

'Shuddup or I'll really thump yer!' Les threatened. He removed the coarse, smelly hand from Terry's face and fumbled through the letter-box for the key on a string. 'What the 'ell you think you're playin' at, comin' down 'ere?'

Terry said nothing. He didn't want that hand back again. He was back where he'd started with this violent kid: he'd lost the initiative again.

Awkwardly, Les aimed at the key-hole and pushed the door open. It cracked with a shudder on the passage wall. 'Go on! Get in!' With a shove, the pain slightly less intense now with the release of the arm-lock, Terry stumbled into the darkened house.

Terry's first reaction, after the leading edge of fear had travelled across his chest, was one of surprise. He'd expected to be thrown on to a hard lino floor, in a passage of peeling wallpaper, his nose offended by a smell of mustiness and old greens. But it wasn't like that at all. His feet landed on a deep-pile violet carpet, and only at the last second did some instinct keep his hands off the sheen of the Vymura walls.

Whatever impression the house gave from the outside, it wasn't like that in the passage. There was no line of old coats, no awkward pram or tricycle blocking the way. The woodwork shone like painted glass, unchipped, dust-free, and the expected bare bulbs were, in reality, a series of modern, brass, wall-mounted shades.

'On yer left, in the lounge, and watch yer filthy paws!'

Terry managed to enter the sitting-room without another push. 'Stay there, and don't touch nothin'. I'm goin' upstairs to see she ain't comin'. We ain't got long.' The door shut, and there was silence for a moment. But it immediately re-opened, just a crack, for Les to say what he had to before they got down to business. 'You silly little berk!' The door shut again with a bang, and Terry was alone.

Standing motionless in the middle of the blue carpet, Terry looked around him, just his head moving. It wasn't the sort of room you felt free to move about in, to fling yourself down on the settee, or go bossing out of the window. It was well named 'the lounge'. It was no living-room. It was more an evening room, a room of promise. Everything in it seemed to be waiting for work to be finished and for pleasure to begin, rather like the foyer of a cinema. In one corner there stood a high, curved bar, with a quilted black front and with small bunches of plastic grapes suspended above. It stood ready, with Babycham glasses and plastic swizzle sticks on the top, for the first visitor who might fancy a drink. Not that Terry thought he'd stand much chance if he asked for a Coke. A poker-work motto stood among the various bottles on the mirrored shelf behind. 'Don't drink and drive. Just drink. You can always crawl home!' Under the window was a long, curved settee, too big for the room, like a grand piano in a bedroom, but in its lush orange velvet-look finish proudly proclaiming its comfort. As Terry's eyes moved round the room he noticed a large colour television, its sliding doors closed, and a low stereo unit under a transparent cover opposite the bar. It was all so different from what he'd imagined. The nearest Terry had got to imagining Les's home, and it was so far off target it wasn't true, was a vague picture of some sort of hovel, a dirty thieves' kitchen, with a Fagin of a father and a slut of a mother, the family all sitting round some newspaper-covered table planning their next shop-lifting expedition. Les, scarred and grimy, didn't fit in with this room at all. He was too grotty for this lush comfort. He was more like the crazy relation they kept in the dungeon in horror films.

Terry jumped as his mind was brought back to his predicament by the door slamming behind him. Les rushed round to face him.

'Well, where is it? Where've you 'idden it?' The older boy wasn't bothering to put on a swaggering front now. Someone else with more flair, Mick perhaps, would have leaned an elbow on the bar, or lounged cockily back in one of the orange armchairs. But Les wasn't like that, and he was in a hurry.

'They've got it,' Terry reported, simply. There was to be no beating about the bush now; there was no need. Although he was still apprehensive, this room, and Les's nervous behaviour, made him less fearful by the second. And there was no sign of the knife. That was probably hidden back down at the old house. Anyway, Terry thought sardonically, Les wouldn't risk blood on this carpet! 'Jarvis sort of recognized me last night. In my shirt. The caretaker. He heard you call me by my name . . . and they got me this morning.'

'God, no!' Les started to scratch his neck with his fast, nervous action.

'They made me get the radio. And . . .'

'Yes?' Les was anxious: hurrying him, and anxious.

'They wanted to know who you are. Where you lived.'

A pink reminder of the previous night's look of threatening violence flushed on to Les's face and his voice carried an echo of its old menace. But he didn't move any nearer.

There was no knife, or raised fist. It was all bluster now. 'You didn't say nothin', did yer? Did yer?'

'No. 'Course not. I said I didn't know who you were.'

Les's shoulders dropped a fraction with the small relief. 'That's right.'

'But they didn't believe me.' He might as well have it straight – and perhaps even a bit stronger than it had really been at the time. 'The police were there and all . . .'

Les just stared at him now, with eyes like darts.

'. . . They said that if you called me by a friendly name, sort of . . . we must've been friends . . .' A frown, worried and uncomprehending, replaced Les's piercing stare. 'At the gate. You called me "Tel", the nickname for Terry. They said that was, like, friendly . . .'

'Oh, did they?'

'They didn't think it sounded right . . . for an enemy . . .' This was all very difficult, this business of what was meant by a name. It was like scribbling a soppy message to a girl and having it intercepted by her friend. Some things were best not put into words.

Les's next move took Terry more by surprise than a lunge with his foot, or a bony punch, or a spit in the face would have done. It was totally unexpected. Les smiled. Not a cynical or sarcastic smile, another weapon in his armoury of threat and persuasion, but a genuine smile which lifted the heavy-hooded eyelids and curled back the lips.

'Well, we ain't no more, are we? Enemies? We done a good job together, di'n't we? 'Cept right at the end. Yer needed a bit o' persuadin', but once y'got used to the idea you mucked in all right, di'n't yer? You was more 'elp than the stinkin' rest of 'em . . .'

'Eh?'

'An' that is yer name, i'n it? What yer muckers call yer?'

'Yea, but . . .'

'An' anyway, what they beefin' about? They got one radio back. They only lost one. That ain't much, God knows . . .'

Terry took a deep breath. Why couldn't he see? Did it have to be spelt out for him? 'Yea, but they got me an' all. I'm right in it . . .'

But Les still couldn't see. 'They got your'n back. They can't blame you for mine.'

'But they do!' Terry's voice was raised now, half-way to a shout. It was like trying to make a foreigner understand. 'They reckon I'm right in on it, and they said – the headmaster – that I've either got to get the other radio back, or . . .' He breathed in noisily, signifying reluctance with his voice and his face. Les was looking at him, his head held back and to one side, ready to dismiss the ultimatum which was about to be delivered. But it had to be given. '. . . Or I've got to tell them who you are.'

Les said nothing. His brain fought with the message it had received, as if, like the stomach, it contained juices to help digest the hard gristle of what Terry had told him. His eyes narrowed again, then widened, his mouth chewed, before it settled into a glistening sneer. Then, for the first time, he chose to lean back confidently, cockily, on the bar. It could have been a pose, an act of unfriendliness to test the strength of what Terry would say in denial – or it could have been that what he had to say was passing through his mind for real.

'So you've come snoopin' down 'ere to find out just who I am – to tell your rotten 'eadmaster. That's it, i'n it?'

'Oh, God!' Terry sat down on the carpet and thumped it with a clenched fist. It seemed a stupid, babyish thing to do, but it was something, and there were just no words to convey the build-up of frustration he felt. He hadn't been believed about anything for two days. His mum hadn't believed what a smug bully Tracey was, the gang hadn't believed he wasn't hiding loot in the ravine, Marshall hadn't believed his story of the break-in, and now Les wouldn't believe his reason for finding him. He sat there, staring at the nylon tufts of the blue carpet, and cast frantically around in his mind for the right words to say. The irony was that Les's idea hadn't occurred to him, and there was no way he could ever prove it. Of course, it was true that he had him now – his address, everything but his last name. But Terry hadn't thought it out like that. That side of it hadn't crossed his mind. If it had he probably wouldn't have dared to come down here. But it was just like Les to think the worst. Just like all of them, it seemed.

'Well, now yer know, don't yer? Terry? My friend Tel? Eight Victoria Gardens, Queen's Dock Estate. An' the name's 'Icks. Leslie 'Icks. With a haitch.'

Terry banged the floor again, hard, with his fist. Les was rubbing his nose in it, making what he was doing sound so much worse than it was. Suddenly even the room smelt bad. He'd certainly come for a purpose, but not for the reason Les was dreaming up. 'NO!' When it finally came out it was louder than Terry intended, bringing Les leaping off the bar with a pained expression on his face and flat, quietening palms, like a football captain telling his team to calm down.

'Shuddup! They're a nosey lot next door. I don't want no one to know you're 'ere!'

Terry lowered his voice. Making a noise at least drew Les's serious attention. 'All I came for is the radio,' he explained. 'If I can get that back to school safely it's gonna be a lot easier for me, and you won't come into it at all.' Les's head went back on to one side, as if hearing better made thinking easier. 'But old Marshall wasn't mucking about. If I don't get that radio back they're really gonna have a go at me to get your name.'

'Huh!' Les smiled, but it was neither confident nor friendly. 'What can they do? They can't torture yer, can they? They can't get the rack out!'

'No.' Terry stared at Les. Now it had finally come to the crunch. Terry could spell it out, or he could shrug his shoulders. He wasn't blind, and he wasn't stupid. He knew that if ever he was going to risk real violence again it was now. It was a hard decision. And it was brave. He looked directly between Les's eyes and he gave it to him there. 'But I'll tell you this, Hicks – if it comes down to me going to juvenile court for this lot on my own, or you and the rest of 'em coming too, then you're all bloody coming. Knife or no bloody knife!' He reinforced the strong words by staring out the older boy, managing, by a huge effort of eye-prickling will, not to be the first to blink. That was it. He'd called Les's bluff. He'd also shot his bolt. There was no going back now. He was going to win, or he was going to be a very sorry loser. There wouldn't be any in-between, because Les was either going to have to give him back the radio or face up to being in it up to his scarred neck. And he wouldn't be very likely to stand for that.

Having lost the staring contest, Les blinked his eyes several times and started a furious rubbing of his neck. He might have paced up and down, but he didn't: all the movement was on his face.

'Yea,' he said after a while, 'great. But what you've forgot, sunshine, is the one little thing that matters. The radio. I ain't got it. I sold it. 'Smorning. That's why I ain't been to school. I got rid of it, quick, to this chap on two to ten, 'fore 'e went to work.'

Oh God! Terry felt sick, really sick; the bile rose in his mouth and had to be choked back down with an effort. It seemed that nothing was going to go his way. Nothing. It was like his dad sometimes said when he was in one of his down moods: 'Everything I touch seems to turn to stone.' The more he tried, the harder it was to get himself out, like a man struggling in quicksand. He was sinking deeper all the time, putting himself right under by giving Les an ultimatum that he hadn't a hope in hell of meeting.

'Can you get it back?'

'No, 'course not. 'E ain't there. 'E's at work, i'n' 'e? I told yer. 'E's on two to ten this week, down the . . . well, down some fact'ry. I can't get 'old of 'im.'

'I thought he had a shop . . .'

'Like a jeweller's?' Les laughed sardonically. 'Some fence with a direct tunnel to abroad? No, mate, 'e gets rid of 'is stuff round the fact'ry, on the nod. Ain't you ever 'ad a watch brought 'ome for yer birthday? No box, no guarantee? Well, that's where it comes from, a million to one. Yer don't 'ave to be bent to buy odds an' ends like that. They all come out the docks and into the fact'ry, an' it's blokes like this who takes the risks. Every fact'ry's got one or two. No one round 'ere gets nothin' big from a shop; only tellies, colour tellies; no one's worked out a fiddle over them yet. But everythin' else . . . You name it, they can get it . . .'

Terry stood up. However long Les went on it could only end up in a threat, or a duffing. There was no way out now. He'd run himself right into a dead-end. And Les had everything to gain by making sure of his silence.

'But there must be some way of getting hold of him before he sells it. If you could get it back for tomorrow . . . ?'

'No chance. 'E won't let me 'ave it back, anyway. 'E's got a customer by now, promised it to someone.' Les spoke in a dispirited voice. He wasn't just fobbing Terry off any more. These were real hard facts that affected them equally. 'All 'e 'as to do is file off the serial number tonight and stamp a new one on, and take it in tomorrer in the boot of 'is car. There's no chance we'll get it back now. 'E'll be choked enough I won't be gettin' the other one. 'E'll feel a right twit after promisin' that to someone an' all . . .'

Terry watched Les carefully; he put on a listening face, but he was watching, waiting. He was probably just half a step ahead in realizing that there wasn't much more to be said. There was no way out of it without the radio, and that meant, in his own words, that there was no way out of it for Les either. So Les's only possible hope now, either by threat or by action, was to shut Terry up. Terry wouldn't be safe until he was well away from this estate.

'So . . .' He took the first step of the million mile journey back across the common, one step towards the magenta door.

'Shuddup!' Les was standing stock still, frozen into an attitude of intense concentration. He was on the balls of his feet, his arms out from his sides, his head cocked again, his mouth open. Terry froze too. He hadn't prompted this nervous expectancy. It was something outside them both, outside the house. He stopped breathing to listen.

A pair of high heels clickety-clicked down the cement path from the gap in the hedge, towards the door, their hard flat tapping deepening to a dank echo as they entered the alley.

'It's me mum, back from bingo!' hissed Les. 'Quick! She'll suss us out if she sees you 'ere!'

There was a moment of confusion as they both tried to get through the door together, but Les made it first into the passage. They froze on their toes again as they heard the heels stop outside the door, and they saw the letter-box flap open to allow a thin hand to grope through the gap for the hanging key.

'Upstairs!' urged Les. 'She won't be long. She's down the "Denmark" by half-five Friday!'

Terry had no option. Les pushed him back and away from the front door to the rear of the narrow passage where a short corridor led off to the kitchen on the right. The stairs back-tracked at the side of the passage, and Les pushed Terry up them, hissing nervously and hurrying close behind.

'Sssssh!'

They tiptoed into a small bedroom somewhere above and behind the main door while down below Mrs Hicks let herself into the smart house in a rising cloud of perfume. With a click to coincide with the front door closing, Les shut them in. Terry breathed a faint sigh of temporary relief, and standing awkwardly with his weight unbalanced – but not daring to move for fear of hostile floorboards – he looked round the small room.

'Good God and little fish-hooks!' Terry couldn't help it.

It was pushed out of him as a punch in the stomach pushes out a gasp. One look at the room was enough. Les might be just a few metres away from Mrs Hicks at this moment, but a whole world of difference separated them otherwise.

Standing with his back to the door, motionless beside Les, Terry took it all in. It was a small room with very little furniture, and everything in it was piled on everything else. It was a real tip, with clothes all over the place, a scattering of odd boots and holed plimsolls on the floor, and a scruffy pile of old boxing magazines on the window ledge. It smelt a bit of dogs, too, Terry noticed. The room had been reasonably decorated; but the paper was just beginning to turn yellow, and the pattern had worn off by the door and above the bed. Compared to the rest of the house it looked as if it had been next in line for decoration a couple of times, but whoever did the decorating had decided to pass it over. The walls were covered with Les's dismal attempts to brighten up the room; not with girls, like his private den in the derelict house, but with crooked and crumpled paper sportsmen – boxing, men wrestling, and weird leather creatures leaning scowling over wide handle-bars. In their captured poses of dedicated pursuit, they looked a hundred per cent what they were, and a race apart from the unfortunate-looking creature that was Les. But the most dismal aspect of the whole room, the saddest item of all, and the focal point, was the bed. It wasn't a real bed at all. It was a wooden camp-bed, the sort you saw in tents in army films, this one with its grey bedclothes screwed back at its foot, its woodwork chipped and scratched, and in the middle of its canvas, where the weight of Les's body would lie, was a round hole which went right through to the clutter of junk beneath. Beds were things Terry rarely thought about: you had to be old to worry about posture-springing and the advantages of the duvet over the eiderdown: but this apology for a place to sleep struck Terry as the worst he had ever seen. How could anyone ever be expected to lie on that?

'It's comfy like that,' Les explained. 'I like my bed like that.' He said it in an enthusiastic-sounding voice, like a child in an infant school reading-book. But Terry didn't believe him; it sounded what it probably was, just a self-conscious apology for being caught with a secret shame exposed.

Terry nodded. 'Yea,' he whispered.

There was nowhere to sit. The bed couldn't be trusted, so they just stood there, unmoving and without speaking, listening to the sounds of Les's mother walking about downstairs. The lack of other noises, a radio, or the television, kept them as rigid as statues. She wasn't singing, and her tread, even on the fitted carpets, could be clearly heard in its heaviness. She obviously hadn't had a win at bingo.

'She'll put our tea out on the table, then she'll open the curtains in the lounge for my old man, then she'll clear off down the "Denmark". She won't be long. But we gotta plan what we're gonna do before 'e comes in . . .'

Terry looked round sharply at Les. So he was prepared to plan! That sounded better than a duffing.

Plates could be heard coming out of the drying rack and on to the kitchen table. The fridge door kept opening and closing. Cutlery clattered coldly onto the formica. It was a quick and clinical preparation of an instant meal. His own mum tried harder than that, Terry thought.

After a while the noises in the kitchen stopped and the door was clicked-to on its ball-catch. Les and Terry tensed, and cut their breathing back to shallow, surface movements. There was one door fewer between them and Les's mum now. And Terry, with two females in his own house, couldn't believe she wouldn't come up the stairs to her own bedroom before going out. The muscles in the backs of Terry's legs began to ache as he held himself rigid against the accidental creaking of a floorboard, and within seconds, already weakened by the activities of the night before, they began to shake.

'Tel!' croaked Les. 'Shift yer weight a bit or you'll bloody fall over!'

Terry made a slight balancing movement as the door of the lounge opened to cover any sound he might make. But his mind was buzzing now. She must almost hear the shouting going on in his head. '*Tel!*' He'd said it again: the friendly name that meant collaboration. A few minutes before he'd been frightened of what Les was about to do to him; now it seemed that Les, up against it with his mum, was trying to claim his friendship. No, Les had no right to that claim.

Terry suddenly saw that if he wanted out, now was his chance to get out. With his mum downstairs, Les couldn't stop him from just walking out of the room, down the stairs, and out of the house with a polite, 'Good afternoon, Mrs Hicks.' It could be as easy as that.

And as difficult. A word from Les and she might leap to gang up on this intruder with her son, to guard against any threat to Les's future. Their own family fence might be just as high as Terry's. He didn't move.

Quite distinctly, because the lounge door was open, they heard the curtains swish easily along their satinized runners. A ship hooted on the river, a forlorn sound like a night creature calling for its mate. Then there was a short silence while she fiddled with something, or looked out of the window, or straightened the mats on the bar.

'She might bring some friends back from the "Denmark",' Les explained. 'When my old man's on the petrol pumps tonight. You know, nothing in it,' he added quickly, 'just one of the other barmaids or a little gang. She likes it nice everywhere . . .' There was a sort of pride in his voice, and Terry got the feeling that she couldn't do much wrong in his eyes. He looked at the work-house bed again. He couldn't understand.

'LESLIE!' The name came hurtling up the stairs, riding on the back of a shriek. 'LESLIE!' It was totally unexpected, the name almost wounding in the viciousness of its harsh bite. 'Come down 'ere, you little swine! Come 'ere! If I 'ave to come up I'll ruddy murder you!'

Les's head had shot up from its bowed listening position, vulnerable-looking, and uncomprehending. How the hell . . . ? His eyes blinked, his mouth twitched, and his right hand clawed nervously at his neck where the rough skin joined the smooth. He didn't say a word; but on the first shrieked word of command, Terry noticed, his feet had started moving obediently to the door. There was clearly no second asking in this house.

Les opened the door. 'What?' he called down the stairs. 'What's up?'

'I'll give you "What's up"! Come down 'ere an' look at this carpet!'

The raised voice was harsh, cigarette-coarsened, and frightening. Terry could imagine the hard face and the blonde, nicotine-yellowed hair which went with it, and he could almost smell the stale smoky breath as it issued out of the wide-open mouth. Les went out of the room and shuffled slowly down the stairs.

'You little swine! You've got no business bein' in the 'ouse at all! Why ain't you at school? An' look at my carpet. Look! Look! Look at it!'

Terry heard the hard repeated thump of hand on head as Les reached the bottom of the stairs and he was forced to run the gauntlet between the banister post and his mother.

'Ow! Ow! Ow!' Les tried to cover his head, but she was skilled at this, her eye was good, and she landed a telling blow every time.

She dragged Les into the lounge by the wisp of hair on the top of his prematurely thinning head. He didn't resist, but he ran with her, keeping up her speed to avoid the extra pain. He was as big as she was, but he used no strength to resist. Like many a bigger man, he had to take it from her. The day he decided not to he'd be out on his own, for good.

'You rotten little swine! You know I like this room kept nice. I keep the sun off the carpet all day so it don't fade – and what do you do with it? You bring all . . . the mess . . . off the . . . street . . . on it!' There were pauses between her words as she saved her wind for hitting Les, punching him hard around the head and shoulders as he stood hunched and cowering like some bed-wetting creature in a nineteenth-century asylum. 'Look at it, on my carpet! I don't know whether it's dirt or dogs' mess till I sponge it. But I've got a bloody good idea!' She hit him again, and as she did, a fresh surge of anger over her violated carpet rose up within her, and as if a drill had reached oil it came gushing out in black temper. Climbing down off her shoes she threw one at his head and held the other up, on the verge of clubbing him with it. 'Pig! Horrible filthy pig! You're not fit to live with human beings! Never have been! Get out of my sight! Get out! Get out! Oh, for the chance to get shot of you!'

Les, bruised across the shoulders and head, and bleeding from a cut above his eye where the shoe had glanced off him, dived for the door – and like some mangy, beaten dog with its ears flat back and its tail between its legs, he scurried for the stairs and scuttled up them on all fours.

Terry heard the whimper as he reached the top. He put his plimsoll, the offending plimsoll, gingerly back on the floor, keeping the outside welt off Les's thin mat. God! He must have trodden in it on the common, or in the street. Strange he hadn't noticed it before. But then he had, hadn't he? And not recognized it. His stomach curdled with a churning mixture of fear and guilt. He'd heard most of what had gone on downstairs: all the words, and most of the actions, and he knew what he'd let Les in for.

The door opened slowly, ashamedly, and Les crept in. He was trying not to cry. But his eyes were red bubbles, his mouth was a distorted slit, like a weeping wound, and from the cut in his tight forehead skin, a thick dark slug of blood crawled down his face.

Visibly, Les gathered up the means to speak, a noisy, shuddering intake of breath. Terry waited apprehensively for the vitriolic attack – on Les's mother and on himself – which was bound to come.

Les shut the door. He cuffed his nose and wriggled his fingers in his eyes. He sniffed loudly, offensively, and he gained some control of himself.

'She don' really mean nothin',' he said. 'She says so 'erself. 'Er temper's 'er own worse enemy . . .'

Chapter Fourteen

Les made an effort to suffer his injuries quietly until his mother had gone, but it wasn't easy. The pain of the blows began to wear off, but the indignity of being the big tough guy hit in front of some kid went deeper and hurt more. Nothing cut as deep, however, as the shared knowledge of who had done the hitting. Terry hovered, not knowing what to do, feeling as helpless as the first man at a bad accident, and not daring to say anything to comfort Les in case he blew up in his face. Les dabbed at his cut forehead with a filthy handkerchief from his pocket, and that was the only movement in the untidy bedroom. They just stood there, and waited.

Neither of them realized just how early it was. Mrs Hicks banged about downstairs for what seemed like an eternity before she eventually slammed the front door with an angry finality and clicked her way up the path again. They both waited until she was well clear before they spoke.

'Sorry, Les . . .'

'I know what we'll do . . .'

They both spoke together, but Terry quickly submitted and shut up once he realized that Les wasn't going for him. Les wasn't seeking an apology, although the way Terry felt about what had just happened he felt both he, and Les's rotten mother, owed him one. But while the sobbing and the dabbing and the waiting had gone on, Les had obviously been thinking more of the future than of the past. That was good. The past was enough of a mess already.

'I know what we'll do,' Les repeated. 'We'll just 'ave to get that trannie back . . .'

Terry brightened. So it was possible? This was more like

it. Les had probably been bluffing about not being able to ask for it back. But if he could, it would solve a hell of a lot of problems. He'd be spared a lot of aggro at school, and he'd probably get away with just paying for a new lock, or something. He wouldn't be out of the wood, but he'd be able to see the daylight through the trees.

'We'll 'ave to go round 'is 'ouse when it's a bit darker . . .'

'Yea?'

'Before 'e gets in.'

'Yea?' Terry didn't understand; but he'd go along with Les if it meant getting the radio back.

'Then we'll get into 'is shelter an' nick it . . .'

'Eh?' Terry, who had been fiddling self-consciously with a boxing magazine, dropped it to the floor. 'What do you mean?' he asked, his voice high with disbelief.

''Is shelter. 'Is old air-raid shelter in the garden. 'E uses it like a shed, only it's more thicker. 'E keeps 'is stuff in there.'

'I didn't mean that,' Terry explained slowly, as if he were talking to a backward child. 'I know what a shelter is.' There were several of the hump-backed buildings squatting in back gardens down his own street, grown over with ivy or clambering with gnomes. 'I mean, what do you mean about nicking?'

'Well it's the only way, i'n it, Tel? Ask yourself.' Les finished dabbing at his forehead and sat balancing on the side of the camp bed, his face straight and earnest, the complete 'con' man. ''E won't give it back, God's truth. An' you reckon you've gotta 'ave it back. That only leaves one way – we gotta nick it!'

Terry looked down on to the top of Les's head, where the lifeless hair shared the thinning scalp with grime and a few bigger specks of grit. There was nothing he wanted in the world so much as to be able to tell Les that getting the radio back was his problem, that he'd have nothing to do with it. But it wasn't his alone, and they both knew that. Although the whole problem had been created by Les, things had happened quickly, circumstances had changed. Terry had acted in certain ways, and they were fast finding themselves dependent on one another. The fact that neither of them liked it was by the way. It was the same problem a million working partnerships shared.

'It won't matter much to you,' Les said slowly, staring down at the threads which were beginning to break up the pattern on the rug. 'But I've gotta stay out of this. You 'eard 'er. One more go up the juvenile an' they'll put me away somewhere . . .' He looked up at Terry to see what effect his words had had.

Terry was tempted to tell him that if he was that close to real trouble then he shouldn't have started on the raid in the first place. But he had no need to voice his thoughts. Les was quick enough to anticipate them.

'I just wanted a few things for me place,' he explained in a self-pitying whine. 'That's all I done it for. There ain't a lot to this 'ouse, not for me, an' I need a few bits for my place. It was the others done it for fun. I just done it for the money . . .'

Les was forgetting that Terry had been in on the raid from the start, from the first moment Les had dreamed it up: and that he had a few aches and pains and memories that said it was for the aggro and the cussedness of it, as much as for any other reason, that they'd busted into the school. And could he honestly say he hadn't taken pleasure in the violence? He looked at the ugly, bruised and battered head again. He wouldn't swap with him for a million pounds, with a mum like that. All shout and punch and kick him out of the way. He could see now how easily that permanent scar could have been scalded on to the young Les, when something he'd done had made her lose her temper. He could see her slinging a saucepan of water across the kitchen, or a hot cup, or something like that. You saw that sort of thing quite a lot on the telly. Terry looked at the silent boy with the running nose, still now, and different, like an actor off the screen, and he wondered, did Les turn the violence on to others, like himself, because of his mother? Or was it born in him as it was in her blood?

Les's brain was racing on, making plans. 'It won't be too 'ard,' he said, 'if you 'elp. All you 'ave to do is keep watch while I go over 'is garden and get in the shelter. I've got a stack of old keys down my place. One of 'em's bound to fit 'is padlock. You won't even be in it. They can't nick no one for just standin' on a pavement, can they?' Terry pulled an uncertain face. 'An' if it ends up with you an 'ero with the tranny, and me kept outta Borstal, it's worth a bit o' risk, i'n it? Eh, Tel?'

'Well . . .' There it was again. The oblique offer of friendship. Like Uncle Charlie said, learn your customers' names, then when they come in, use them and they'll come back; people like to be known, to be accepted. Perhaps Les was only doing the same thing. It wouldn't do to trust him . . .

'Go on. We'll 'ave it all over and settled by 'alf past six. An' if you go 'ome with the radio, no one won't mind if you've let yer tea get cold for once . . . Eh . . . ? 'Ow about it, son?' He leaned forward and smiled encouragement with his mouth, while his eyes assessed more coolly the younger boy's reaction.

'Well, I s'pose . . .' Terry could see the advantages. This did make some sense. From his own point of view he'd be better off. The fact that Les would be stealing himself another breathing space before the law finally caught up with him wasn't his concern. And if it really only meant standing on the pavement . . . Terry set his mouth in a determined line, and nodded. 'O.K.' He shut his eyes and squeezed a drone inside his ears to drown the sound of a voice which wanted to caution him against it. He was eager to get this business settled, wasn't he? Well, now was his chance. And wasn't he in trouble enough already? A bit more wouldn't hurt.

Les leaned back, and stopped smiling. 'Good ol' Tel. Right, so what we do is, we go down my place and wait till it gets a bit dark – outta the way of my ol' man, right?' Terry nodded. 'An' on the way we walk past the place we're gonna do to suss it out, an' I give yer the low-down on where to stand an' all that, right?'

Terry agreed again. It was ridiculous, he thought, but he agreed. If someone had told him two nights ago that he'd be willingly involved in planning a break-in to someone's shed – with a sick, doubtful character like this – he'd have told them to have their brains tested.

'Plus, Tel my ol' lad,' the croaky voice went on, 'you're gonna do me a favour an' make sure you wipe that stuff off yer boots, ain't yer?' Les looked at Terry with one of those looks which could be serious or could be teasing – the sort of look over which you made a mistake at your peril. Whichever it was, Terry thought, it took some guts to bring that business up again.

Slowly, Les's face wrinkled into a smile. 'I'm a bit partic'lar down my place,' he said. 'I get it from me mum.'

Mrs Harmer had never had a teacher in the house before, let alone a headmaster. When she had first answered the ring, it being a Friday, and seeing the crinkled outline of a man through the glass ship on the door, she had hurried back into the kitchen for her purse. You didn't keep the milkman waiting for his money on a Friday night. 'Just a sec!' she shouted. Then she had found her purse in the cutlery drawer and thrown the door open with a loud, 'How much, milkman?' Neither of them had known what to say after that.

Unlike some of the mothers who spent more time up at the school, Mrs Harmer wasn't too certain who this person was at first. He was familiar enough: but he could have been the annual insurance man, or perhaps a friend of Jack's, or even someone off the television. It was that sort of face. It wasn't until he said, 'Mrs Harmer?' in the slightly uncertain way he said it on Open Evening, that she suddenly realized who he was.

'It's Mr Marshall, isn't it? From the school?' She frowned, not in puzzlement, but in anxiety. Something had happened to Terry. Why else should he come? It was like the policeman calling after her father had died at work. You could hear your own voice saying things as if you were someone else. Your mind went in a hundred directions at once. But somehow you still went through the preliminary courtesies. 'Come in, please,' she said. It was lucky she'd Hoovered downstairs.

'Thank you, I won't stay long,' said the headmaster, with a restrained smile. He stepped inside. His expertise with parents of children who had been taken to hospital quickly revealed itself. 'Now please don't worry about his health,' he said. 'Put your mind at rest over that. He hasn't had an accident or anything . . .'

'Oh, thank God.' That was a relief. That was the main thing. He was all right. Perhaps the head had come about the Boulogne trip or something, she thought; he was going round giving the parents details.

'I'm afraid my husband isn't in yet. He'll be another hour or so.'

She ushered him into the sitting-room, pushing the door open and leaning round him awkwardly to hold it for him. She scurried ahead again and scooped Tracey's cookery apron off the settee. 'Please sit down.'

'No thank you, Mrs Harmer. I won't be long. Tell me, is Terry at home?' He looked round the room as if he half expected to see Terry crouching behind an armchair, or bulging, with just his shoes showing, behind a curtain.

'No. He usually is by now. But I expect he's in some boy's house or other . . .'

'Yes, he may well be . . .'

Mrs Harmer looked at him closely. There was something

a bit odd about the way he'd said that: he'd used the sort of double-meaning voice you're meant to query.

'Why, there's not something wrong, is there?'

'Well, yes, I'm afraid there is.' On an impulse Mr Marshall sat down on the settee, unbuttoned his tweed jacket, and crossed his legs. It wouldn't pay to be too formal over this. The woman was in for a shock, and he'd need to handle this very carefully. 'Did he tell you anything about last night, Mrs Harmer? Where he was, what he was doing?'

Mrs Harmer sat down too, next to him on the settee, but perched on the edge. If only Jack were here. It was so much more of an ordeal, dealing with trouble on your own. 'Well, he did come in late, soaked through he was. But he'd been

caught in the storm out to play, he said. Why? Was he doing something he shouldn't?' Her voice took on a slightly harder edge: just the faintest beginning of a defensive family wall. Attack one, it hinted, and you attack us all.

Mr Marshall was no fool. He rarely expected parents to believe what he told them about their children when it was unflattering. Not at Fox Hill. In years gone by, in a poorer district, his word had been law, but up here it was different. More often than not he ended up almost feeling he was the guilty party himself when he had some misdemeanour to report. He therefore began what he had to say to Mrs Harmer with a most diplomatic statement.

'Well, Mrs Harmer, it appears to be most out of character, something of a surprise to Mr Evans and to me, but I have a certain amount of strong evidence – a confession, in fact – to show that Terry was involved in a break-in at the school last night.' He wrinkled his glasses up his nose, while Mrs Harmer suddenly sat as still and as tense as a mourner in a crematorium. Only her hands, shaking slightly, but otherwise held forcibly in repose, provided any minor movement. 'The small gang of boys, of which Terry was a member, broke into my room and made off with two transistor radios. They were chased by Jarvis, the caretaker, but they got away. But one boy called out to your son, to Terry, and we were able this morning to confront him with the evidence of his name. Now, Mrs Harmer . . .' He leaned forward like a family doctor, and would have patted her hand had he been one, '. . . Terry admits all this, and he came home this morning to fetch one of the radios that had been taken. If you were at work, you wouldn't know.' Mrs Harmer shut her eyes and opened them slowly. 'Apparently he'd hidden it in the dustbin. But one other radio is missing. And the rest of the gang are unknown to us, and only Terry knows who they are. Unfortunately, he won't tell us.' He suddenly realized that he had finished for the moment; he had no more to report; no strong finish to his narration. Just for a few minutes he wanted to keep the news of Terry's running off to himself, until he'd got what further information he could about the night before. 'So, we have a problem, Mrs Harmer. And we'll need each other's help to solve it.'

Mrs Harmer couldn't take it in for a moment. 'I beg your pardon, Mr Marshall? Are you saying that my Terry's in a gang that broke into the school last night? Broke in? To the school? I'm sorry, but I can't believe it. I know Terry. He wouldn't do a thing like that!'

'I'm afraid it's true, Mrs Harmer. We couldn't believe it either. But your son admits it. Although . . .'

'Although what?' Her eyes were clearly, sharply, focused, searching his face indignantly for some sign of uncertainty in what he was saying. Her voice had risen a note nearer anger.

Mr Marshall continued as evenly as he could. Why couldn't parents accept that their children weren't always little angels? 'I was going to say, although he's got some story about being forced into it by a gang he met at the Court flats . . .'

Mrs Harmer's voice came down a peg. 'Well, that would seem to be a bit more like it – if it's true at all.' There was a moment's silence. She didn't quite know what to say, what it was diplomatic to tell him. Secretly, she and Jack had wondered and worried about Terry's activities the night before: and hadn't they scoured the streets and bothered the family over his whereabouts during the thunderstorm? 'He certainly didn't go out to play with his normal friends, whoever he sometimes meets up the flats. As a matter of fact, he fell out with his sister, and I had to be cross with him, and he slammed off in a huff. Then he came back later, soaked through.' Her voice took on its attacking note again. 'But I know Terry. And I know he wouldn't go breaking in and stealing in a million years.' She looked round about her, exasperated; boys from families like theirs just didn't do that sort of thing. 'He doesn't want for anything. We both go to work, and I keep the children nice.' Mr Marshall nodded:

he always did when they said that. 'Don't get me wrong, Mr Marshall. We're not rich. Not by a long chalk. But we're decent, and so's Terry. You must know that. You're his headmaster.'

Mr Marshall nodded. This threw a slightly different light on things because she was at least corroborating what the boy had said about going off after a quarrel, and that didn't sound much of a preparation for a planned raid on the school. But there was still this nagging doubt, the doubt he had nursed all along, and it had to be voiced.

'There's just one obstacle to me believing your son, Mrs Harmer,' he said, 'and I've told him so. I must be quite truthful. What made me crossest about the whole thing, even more than the loss of an expensive radio, was his insistence that these boys were complete strangers to him, when there is no doubt at all that one of the other boys, the leader it seems, knows Terry well. He helped him to escape, and he treated him as an old friend. And that I cannot tie up with what he told me. I'm sorry. Otherwise, there's nothing I'd like more than to believe him.'

'How?' Mrs Harmer's hackles were up. Family pride was at stake. 'How was he friendly? How do you know?'

'Simply by what he called him.' Mr Marshall knew this wasn't going to be easy: it was like the old days when he'd had to tell hopeful parents that their children had failed the eleven-plus. Everyone gets used to everything after a while – disappointments, failure – but this first telling is always the worst part to have to handle.

'The gang leader, the older boy, pulled Terry over the gate to safety. And as he did so he shouted instructions at him – and he used his nickname.' He paused to give it weight. 'He called him "Tel".'

'So?' Mrs Harmer wasn't having this: it was all cut and dried and Terry had been found guilty by this man before she and Jack had even been told about it. This wasn't justice.

'Well, it is a friendly way of referring to him, isn't it? It does indicate a certain degree of friendship . . .' It was obvious. Why couldn't the boy's mother be sensible and at least acknowledge a fact as a fact. They wouldn't get anywhere if she couldn't accept that.

The two adults stared at each other across the silence, each seeing the same reported event from a totally different point of view.

'I don't agree.'

Mrs Harmer spun round; so did the headmaster. It was Tracey, standing in the doorway. How long she had been there neither of them knew. She was still in her school uniform; but she looked suddenly older, with the pale adult strain of suppressed anger on her face.

'Tracey!'

'I don't agree,' she repeated, walking into the room staring so hard at the headmaster that her mother thought she'd bang into the settee. 'Hasn't anyone ever called you "mate"? Or "friend"?' Rank, profession, and difference in age counted for nothing. For Tracey, as well as for her mother, family pride was paramount. It blazed in her eyes, and it trembled out on her voice. 'Lots of people call me "Trace" who don't know me from the Queen. That doesn't mean I'm their friend. And it's the same with Terry. It's not his fault what someone calls him.'

'Tracey!'

'It's downright unfair to blame him for that!'

Both Mr Marshall and Mrs Harmer were standing up by now. The interruption had taken them both by surprise; but of the two, the headmaster was the more shaken. What the girl was saying gave him enough to think about – that particular interpretation hadn't crossed his mind – but more shocking was the angry, arrogant way he was being spoken to by this former pupil.

'You don't give anyone a chance!'

'Tracey, you've gone too far. That's enough now!'

Without a word, Mr Marshall walked towards the door. The women were always worse than the men; they were so much more emotional when it came to a show-down. He stopped a few steps short of Tracey. He didn't want to have to ask the child to stand aside.

'I think I'd better leave now,' he said, turning back to Mrs Harmer. 'I'd be grateful if you and your husband would come to school on Monday morning to discuss the matter with me.'

'Yes . . .'

'But what I must tell you, before I go, is that Terry ran off from school this morning. I kept hoping he'd turn up. But if he's not here at home then he's on the loose again . . .'

Tracey let out a snort. He made Terry sound like an escaped lunatic.

'Oh my God.' Gladys Harmer dropped her hands helplessly to her sides. She longed for her husband to come home. This was a terrible to-do, and she needed to share it with Jack, soon.

Near to tears, and trembling, Tracey stood aside with an exaggerated movement to allow the headmaster to pass, followed by her mother. 'If anything's happened to him,' she called after the retreating figure in the hall, 'it'll be your fault!' Mr Marshall ignored her. 'Mate!' she shouted, before she slammed the door.

Gladys Harmer ignored her too. Good for Tracey: she'd said something she daren't. Not to a teacher. Not in a million years.

For once in her life Gladys Harmer's heart dropped when she saw Uncle Charlie's Rover glide up to the house. Her first reaction was to search the interior of the car for some sign of Terry; but there was none. Her second was to hide. In her worried condition she just couldn't face the prospect of putting on a bright front for the astute old man. You could put on a false laugh and a pretend smile for one of his remarks, but he wasn't the thick-skinned rib-digger who would fail to miss your depressed mood for long. A lifetime behind a counter had taught him a lot about people.

Tracey, who had been rallying round by fetching her morning mug from the dressing-table, called down the stairs, 'Uncle Charlie's here!' It was a conspirator's shout, the look-out down to the safe blower. Tracey liked the old fellow, but she shared her mother's concern. They didn't want him here in the middle of all this. He had his place in the family, but it wasn't here, just now. Besides, as Gladys realized, Jack was coming in at any moment. There was much to be told – quietly and patiently – and much to do; and Uncle Charlie could only get in the way of all that.

Gladys thought seriously about not opening the door to him, pretending no one was in. But she had bad memories of using a similar trick one Saturday when she'd had a row with Jack. He'd gone off in a temper to meet his mother from the coach station after a holiday (rows, she'd thought, always happen when there's no time to resolve them), and she had been left in tears in the kitchen. Then Cousin Ellen from the other side of the water had called, out of the blue. It was a rare event for her to cross the ferry on an unheralded visit, but this had been on a sunny day, before telephones were so common. Gladys had frozen in the kitchen, refusing to answer the door, keeping as still as she could and peeping red-eyed through the door crack until the outline had moved away. Then she had only just relaxed enough to put on a kettle for a reviving cup of tea when Cousin Ellen had surprised her at the back door, looking through, waving, and smiling falsely under that ridiculous hat she used to wear. 'Cooee, Glad. Didn't you hear me, dear?' Gladys's answering smile must have been a sight for Ellen to remember. Gladys had certainly never forgotten. So today, after calling, 'Not a word!' up the stairs to Tracey and preparing her face with an acceptable smile, she opened the door to her uncle.

'Hello, Uncle Charlie. Come in.'

'Won't stay long, Glad, won't stay long. Just wanted to whisper a quiet word in your ear . . .'

'Come into the kitchen. I'm just making a cup of tea. Jack won't be long.'

The big man lumbered awkwardly through the doorway on his once dainty feet, grunting softly. 'Listen, Glad, it's none of my business, and you can tick me off for coming,' he began, as soon as the kitchen door was shut behind them, 'but I thought you'd best know as soon as you came in from work . . .'

If Gladys didn't know exactly what he was going to tell her, she had a shrewd idea who it was going to be about. 'Yes? What is it?'

'Well, it's about young Terry,' the big man said, easing his weight on to a kitchen stool, the highest seat he could see. He dropped his voice, remembering the diplomacy, and looked round at the door. 'Is he home yet?'

Gladys shook her head.

'No, I thought he might not be. You see, I saw him this morning, Glad, going down Fox Hill Road to the common. I was in my car, and I don't think he saw me. But it was him – in red?' Gladys nodded. 'And he had a look about him, Glad, that said he wasn't going on any message for the schoolmaster, or anything like that. I'm sorry, girl, but I've got a feeling he was playing hookey . . .'

Still Gladys said nothing; she just nodded very slightly.

'I know it's awkward; but I thought I'd best tell you. Especially knowing how worried you was last night . . .'

Gladys crossed to the sink and ran an already clean cup under the hot tap. 'Thank you, Uncle Charlie. There does seem to be a bit of something going on . . .' She drew a deep breath.

'Now, now, now,' the older man interrupted, launching himself off the stool with difficulty. 'I don't want to know. I'd no more interfere than fly in the air. You talk it over with Jack. A family problem's a family problem, and you'll want to sort it out yourselves your own way without the world knowing.' He hobbled to the kitchen door. 'But if you want any help later, you know where I am . . .'

'Thanks, Uncle Charlie. I think it's all a storm in a tea-cup; but thanks a lot . . .'

'That's all right, girl. And try not to worry. They wouldn't be kids if they didn't get in a scrape or two. Gawd, my bum used to be black and blue when I was at school!'

Gladys laughed nervously. She wouldn't willingly let that happen to Terry.

'Here, I nearly forgot.' Uncle Charlie let go of the door and, balancing himself, put his hand in his inside pocket to take out a slim white paper packet like a wallet. 'I brought a bit of ham for Jack's tea. It's a nice bit; thought he might fancy it . . .'

'Thanks, Uncle Charlie, thanks a lot . . . for everything.'

'That's all right, girl. You're welcome. That's what a family's for . . .'

Within half-an-hour Jack had heard the whole story. When he had first come in, Gladys hadn't known how to begin telling him, how to take the tuneless whistle off his lips; so before he had closed the back door, and before his mouth had opened to shout, 'Aye, aye!', she had started to unburden herself, talking she didn't know what rubbish at first, just to get started. Somehow she got it out. Telling him what she had been told by the headmaster was the hardest part, but he had stood still, brief-case in hand, and heard the whole story within a metre of the back door.

'I might have known,' he said when she had finished, surprising her with his lack of bluster. 'I damn well knew there was something up last night. I knew we had to find him. Something made me go out looking for him; and I know it wasn't just the thunderstorm. I didn't understand then, but I know it now . . .'

When Tracey came into the kitchen a few minutes later, fed up with discreetly staying out of the way in her bedroom, they were still standing there, her father still clutching his brief-case while he talked, like a door-to-door insurance man.

'I'll make a cup of tea,' she said.

'She knows then?' Jack asked Gladys.

'Oh yes,' Gladys was tempted to say more, but she kept the rest back. For the time being. You had to handle men with the skill of a snake-charmer, and the right time would come.

'Then for God's sake let's stop chewing the fat and get out and find Terry. Mind, I'm not worried like last night – that's over – but he must be feeling pretty rotten not to want to come home.' Suddenly, with an extraordinary action for him, he threw his brief-case down into a corner of the kitchen. 'Come on.' He strode back to the door, towards the garaged car. 'By the way,' he asked, 'does anyone else know about this?'

Gladys and Tracey looked at each other with eyes so filled with meaning that a bird could have perched on the line between them.

'No,' they chorused.

'Good.'

Through the strain, Gladys smiled at her daughter. Tracey was learning how to handle her father too.

Chapter Fifteen

LES was like a newly-wed showing off his new home. The walk from his mother's house to his own place had gone without incident, and he was just beginning to bubble with that nervous excitement that fore-runs a raid. He showed Terry all the rooms, the long knocked-through lounge running from front to back downstairs where he planned to have an air rifle shooting gallery, the old kitchen where, he proudly proved, he could still draw off a mug of clean water, and an old paraffin stove he was going to do up for next winter.

He led Terry all over the small house; just a house to Terry, with bare rooms of little interest; but Les could see them as they were going to be, and he took Terry's mild interest as an indication of the 'ooohs' and 'aaahs' of envy that were to come when kids like Mick and the rest of the gang saw it finished.

They were just killing time. They were right ready, impatient for the sun to dip across the other side of London and leave them to the shadows. It was annoying, Terry thought, how the sun did this. It got dark when you wanted light, and when you had a film show or something at school, and you were waiting for the black-out, it shone on for ages out of a cloudless sky.

Terry and Les had walked as normally as they could through the Queen's Dock Estate, for all the world like two Boy Scouts going to do some old lady a good turn. They had made a slight diversion so that Terry could see the house they were to raid, a corner house at the end of a quiet street, but little had been said, just 'Over there,' and 'Yea,' and then they had walked down through the deserted streets to the derelict house which Les had claimed as his own. They had walked along the cracked paving-stones neither seeking nor shunning attention, until, reaching the house itself, they had dived at the last moment into the corrugated doorway, with Les putting on a little act of swooping on a spider to stamp on it, just in case anyone was looking.

Once in the room upstairs they found a seat each – Les in his paper-bottomed chair and Terry on a thin cushion on a box – and they went over the plan for the second raid. It was simple and straightforward, and so far as both of them could see, it couldn't go wrong.

'We got this ball, see, Tel?' Les mimed its shape with his dirty fingers, his pale tissue-paper skin wrinkling over his face with enthusiasm. 'I got one 'ere, the rubber ball off the bog chain out the back. An' we're 'avin' this game in the street, right? Where I showed yer. We're goin' down the path throwin' the ball to one another, ain't we? Then, when we get outside Ron's 'ouse . . .' He suddenly stopped, and frowned. 'Oh cobblers, that's 'is name. I've told yer.' He laughed. 'Cut me tongue off! Anyway, when we get outside 'is 'ouse, by 'is side fence, I throw the ball to you, too 'igh, an' over it goes, right? So with 'im an' 'is ol' lady bein' out, I do no more'n bunk over the fence to get the ball back, don' I? Then you stand waitin' for me, all casual, till I bang the fence to say I'm ready, an' I 'and the radio over. It's as easy as that.'

Terry nodded. He couldn't fault that. It did seem to be a good plan – once given the situation where you're going breaking in to someone's place at all.

Les opened his palms to signify simplicity. 'If anyone comes, the fuzz, or some nosey parker, all yer do is bang the fence, pretend you're killin' a fly or somethin', an' I lie low till yer bang again. An' if it's Ron's ol' lady, comin' 'ome early, then yer bang bloody 'ard, an' run like the clappers. Don' worry! I won't be far be'ind! O.K.?' He sniffed. 'Can't go wrong, can it?'

'Yea, O.K.' Terry's stomach dive-bombed over again. The time was getting closer, and it took a lot of getting used to, this sort of thing. And it was the real thing this time. There were no excuses now. There was no knife in his back, no out-numbering gang scragging him along. He was well in it now. He was as far over that fence between right and wrong as Les would be over this Ron's. It was all or nothing. Double or quits.

Up the lot of them! He'd got to get that radio back and start square. And if he failed, well, he'd got nothing to lose, and he'd know he'd tried.

To dismiss these tedious questions of rightness and wrongness he asked Les about the house again. And as if he'd sprinkled sunshine and water Les opened like a flower, blossoming in the warmth of Terry's interest.

'Well, it ain't much, but it's me own,' he said; 'till they pull it down; but that won't be for years I don' reckon.'

'D'you get down here a lot?'

'Yea, much as I can, really.' He leaned back in his chair. 'See, I'm gettin' it the way I like it; I can relax in 'ere; I don' 'ave to watch where me feet go all the time; an' I can smoke, an' play darts, do anythin'. It's mine . . .'

Terry sat looking at the splintering floor, and for a brief moment, in the quietness of this room, he thought he could see what Les was all about. Last night he'd thought that prison would have been too good for him. Then, a while back, he'd thought that even Borstal would have been better for Les than life with that woman. But now he could see a way out for Les, the reason why Les needed this place, and some excuse for him wanting some money of his own. It was freedom: freedom to do what pleased him. And that, even in this small way, was a great thing. In that way Les could be luckier than most. Of all the people Terry knew, only Uncle Charlie had that sort of freedom, could just skip off and please himself when he liked, for an evening. Everyone else had duties and responsibilities that kept them bound to someone else. Like Marshall's radios, he thought suddenly. Almost everyone has to be checked, present and correct, every so often.

Les broke into his thoughts by creaking noisily out of his chair. 'I'm goin' out the back to get that ball,' he announced. 'Don' go away, will yer?'

Terry looked up. It was no threat this time; it was a request. He shook his head. No, he wouldn't go away. It was all very different tonight. They needed each other now.

For the second night running, Gladys and Jack Harmer set off in their car to look for Terry. But tonight there was more purpose, more shape, to their searching. Where the first hunt had been the result of Jack's intangible, brooding fears for Terry's safety, with the lightning as a substitute for some unnamed danger, this second hunt was as clear in purpose as the fine spring evening. Terry had got caught up in something, he'd been accused of being an accomplice, and he'd run away from trouble. Now he had to be found before he did something stupid. All the questions, all the debate, all the sorting of right from wrong and the laying of blame, could come later. Just now Terry had to be found.

If Jack was clearer in his mind tonight, and more composed in his attitude, Gladys was the reverse. She had only been involved at all last night because Jack was worried – and because her handling of the row with Tracey had first driven him off. But tonight it was more urgent. Poor little devil, he was wandering round somewhere, too frightened to come home, convinced that the world was against him. Tonight it was she who needed to wrap her arms around him most.

'Tracey, stay at home, and whatever you do, keep him here if he comes in. Tell him everything's all right. We believe him, tell him, and we're going to sort it out . . .' Her voice let her down as emotion took the strength from her words.

Tonight she was outside waiting when the car came round from the back. And inside, instead of looking from side to side as she was driven along, alert but relaxed, as she had the night before, she left off her seat belt and leaned forward, and gave the directions.

'Flats?' Jack said.

'No, common. And tonight can we drive down round the bottom of the ravine? We must check down there.'

Jack rattled the gear stick in neutral with the flat of his palm and engaged first gear. 'We'll find him, Glad. Don't worry. He can't have gone far . . .'

A ship's hooter sounded on the river; again, that plaintive call.

'I don't know. Kids get funny ideas in their heads. They do strange things.'

'Oh, come on, Gladys.' He tried to invest his voice with an unnatural lightness. 'Terry's got his head screwed on the right way. He'll be all right.'

Gladys turned her head away from her husband; tonight she wanted to keep her tears a private thing, even from him. 'That's what I kept saying last night, wasn't it?'

There was no answer to that, so Jack, wisely, didn't try to find one.

'That's a funny old ball.' Terry caught the lavatory chain handle and looked at it closely. It had a hole running through it where the screw had gone. Its hard mottled rubber surface was beginning to perish. It had the weight and the feel of a super-ball, but when Terry threw it on to the wooden floor it gave off more noise than bounce. 'Dead, isn't it?'

'It'll do. No one won't know. It's only for cover, anyway.'

Gran Harmer had had one like that for years, nibbling the plaster off the lavatory wall in a little arc at the circumference of the chain radius. More than once Terry had hurt himself by heading it. 'They're good, these,' he said, throwing it back to Les. 'They don't make 'em like that any more . . .'

It was a novelty, that was all, and only nervousness caused him to make the least significant object the centre of an exaggerated amount of interest – like kids and mothers did with the fat cat at the clinic.

'Not long now.' Les was looking out of the grimy window over the abandoned back-yards of the Queen's Dock Estate. 'Nearly time we got down there . . .'

They both stood still, waiting, while a persistent ray from the low sun penetrated the glass and picked out the falling dust particles in the air. Terry wanted to go to the lavatory; but he knew it was nerves: while Les scratched his neck through the front of his shirt. Waiting was always the worst part. Feeling tense already, Terry was perhaps less surprised than he would normally have been to hear his own voice suddenly asking the question that had teetered on the brink ever since they had left Les's house. It was frank and straightforward, unsugared with diplomacy.

'Your mum,' he said, 'has she always been like that? Hitting you, and that?'

Les didn't move. For a moment Terry thought he was standing still building up the energy to turn round from the window and hit him. But the right shoulder suddenly dropped, and Les relaxed, and he seemed to give in to the request to answer.

'It's just 'er way.' His voice was quiet, almost inaudible. 'With me. Me sister's different: she never 'it 'er, not so much. But . . . well, it's only nat'ral . . . me dad comin' along – this one, now – then me, all those years after finishin' wi' kids . . . keepin' 'er indoors, she reckoned . . .'

Terry hardly dared move. It had been a stupid question to ask. He felt like an intruder, like being in a room playing hide-and-seek, when people really don't know you're there.

Les ran his hand down his throat, over the ridge across his neck. 'But it's only 'er way. She gets ratty quick. Like most people's ol' ladies, don't yer reckon?' His voice had changed now, and he looked at Terry defiantly, daring him not to agree that his treatment at the hands of his mother was normal.

'Oh, yea,' said Terry. 'Show me the mother that don't get ratty . . .'

'Yea,' said Les. 'Too right!' The subject was closed. 'All right, then?' he asked. It was still much too early, but they'd waited long enough. And they needed a change of mood. 'We'll take it slow . . .'

'O.K.,' said Terry. 'Let's get it over with . . .'

'Yea,' said Les. 'Then we'll be all square, right?'

Terry looked into the hooded eyes. 'Yea,' he said. 'Yea, I suppose we will . . .'

By the time Uncle Charlie had finished filling the baby-food shelves with tins of mustard he realized that his mind had been a long way away.

'Dammit!'

He looked at ten minutes' wasted work. He could either leave the mustard where it was, and change the notice, putting the baby-food farther down the shop, or he could take the mustard out and start again. Changing the notice would be quicker – but the mothers knew where the baby-food was, and they went straight for it. Besides, someone might make a mistake and put a baby off eating for life.

He tottered over to his wooden chair and sat down, cursing. He wasn't usually so stupid. As if he were trying to recall a dream, he attempted to recapture the thoughts that had occupied his mind while he had stacked the jars in the wrong place. He turned and stared at the jars in a mock show of helping to jog his memory. But there was really no need. He knew. It was Terry.

A strange boy, Terry. Not a boy you'd take to straight away, if you didn't know him. He seemed to hold himself back, kept a bit of himself to himself. Not a boy to jump into your arms, or hold your hand. But then, he wasn't smarmy, either, like some he knew. He grew on you, over the years. You didn't know all he was thinking; you couldn't read him like a book, like some kids. He was his own man. Ploughed his own furrow. Quiet – but no man's fool.

And right now he was in trouble. It stuck out a mile. There was last night, for a kick-off. Old Jack wasn't the sort to panic: he might be a bit careful, a bit cautious; but he wasn't the sort to go to pieces. And he looked real worried last night. Something was going on, that had been clear. And there was the boy this morning. The way he was walking down Fox Hill Road, head down, keeping in the shade, daring anyone to speak to him; he was running away from something, sure as eggs was eggs.

'Poor old Glad,' he muttered to himself. One thing about never marrying, never having children was the worry you were spared. The times he'd been in someone's house, and the baby had cried, or messed, or fallen over – and the mother had been up off her chair with a tight, anxious face as if the end of the world had come. Or when they'd grown up, and they'd gone the wrong way, then it was all excuses – but underneath it there was always the responsibility. He saw it in the shop, when kids had been found lifting sweets. The apologies, the shame, and the strain; especially the shame: they rarely came in again. No, you were spared a lot of trouble, not having kids.

He looked round the shop at the darkening shelves. The sun was just going down, that period when it was light one minute and dark the next. He got up and moved awkwardly to the light switch. It was a bit like being a kid, he thought; light one minute, dark the next, then light again, all between tea and bed-time. He thought again of Terry, going through his bit of dark. Still, who was to know? Perhaps it was better than all this grey . . .

As he switched the lights on, slowly and carefully because he still had a strange idea that neon didn't like to be hurried, he took a last look out of the shop window, at his reflected face in the shadow of the street. It was that moment when the houses opposite stood on equal terms with his neon reflection, before they faded into the darkness, like one scene mixing into another in a film. A few more minutes and the street would have gone. And as luck would have it it was just that moment when Jack and Gladys drove through his reflected head, from ear to ear. Gladys looked towards him, at the white lights, waving with a quick and nervous gesture, almost as if she didn't want Jack to see. Uncle Charlie steadied himself to wave back. Gawd, she looked a sight. Out looking for the boy again, hundred to one on.

The old man stood looking at the window until the street had gone and he was surrounded by his shop. Then, cursing his awkwardness, he moved. Slowly, he drew the blinds, and leaving one striplight on for safety, he hobbled out of the shop and through to the room at the back. Blow the mustard. He was going to take the motor out.

It was chilly outside. The sun had carried a false promise of summer, for the days still concealed a sting in the tail. Terry shivered in his red nylon sweater, and Les rolled his shirt sleeves down to flap, buttonless, round his wrists. He looked a scruffy sight. His hair was wisped up by the merest whisper of a breeze, his face was blotchy with his mother's blows, and the cut on his forehead was turning black. Beneath the tide-mark on his scarred neck his shirt billowed out like a blouse, and his jeans pockets stood out sideways, clown-shaped, with the ball in one pocket and his stringed collection of keys in the other. By contrast, Terry, increasingly aware of his appearance these days, felt too smart for these streets. He rolled up one sleeve, and tried to walk with a bit of a slouch. He felt out of place enough as it was, down here, without drawing attention to himself.

Terry was glad they were on their way. He was beginning to get concerned over time. He hadn't got his watch on, but he guessed his mother would be home by now, and starting to wonder where he was. It was also quite possible, he knew, that someone had called from the school, or the police. There would be a big scene when he did get home, and the sooner he got back with the radio, and got it over with, the better. Not long now, thank God. How anyone could live through weeks of waiting to go to court he didn't know. Waiting overnight for trouble at school was bad enough. These thoughts helped his walk with Les, his impatience overcame some of his fear, and he was pleased not to have to talk any more; but when they turned the final corner into Ron's quiet road his heart began its fast nervous thud, his mouth dried out, and an annoying itch tingled at him, out of reach, in the small of his back.

''Ere, catch!'

The voice came from several metres behind him. He hadn't noticed, but Les had stopped a few steps back to put a throwing distance between them. Terry turned, just in time to get his hands up to the gently lobbed lavatory handle as it dropped heavily down the last few metres. It smacked, stinging, into his hand. It was hard, all right. He held on to it for half a second before it dropped with an unyielding thud on to the cracked paving slab.

'Bu'er-fingers!'

But it wasn't that. Terry wasn't at all a bad catcher. His eye had been distracted. He had seen a man cranking slowly round the corner from the front of Ron's house on a black, upright bicycle. He probably meant no harm, he didn't even look at them a second time, but it was the first stranger he'd seen for quite a while – and he was suddenly reminded of the existence of the rest of the world. Plans were all very well in abstract, but they had to be operated amongst people like this. The man was getting on in years, with a flat cap and a grey face, and he pedalled slowly and methodically past, each push of his leading foot a slight effort. His eyes stared vacantly ahead as he pedalled, apparently without seeing anything of the street on either side, neither the ball in the gutter nor the boarded-up houses.

Terry took a pace towards the man. It was no good getting jumpy now. He picked up the ball from the gutter and put extra show into the return throw.

'Coming over, L . . .' He just stopped himself in time from using the boy's name.

Les's quick frown cleared. The kid was learning . . .

Jack and Gladys drove along slowly, worried and irritated, in the stream of home-bound traffic which was skirting the common. Jack groaned. It was all flashing red stop-lights and clutch, clutch, clutch. His left sole ached with pushing it out for so long; yet if he changed into neutral to give his foot a rest, everything started moving again, and he was left to scramble into gear.

Gladys, beside him, was displaying her anxiety in physical movement. She wriggled in her seat, leaning forwards, backwards, and sideways, she craned her head round and over Jack, she wound the window down and up, and she leaned out, she sat back, and she irritably condemned the whole line of drivers for using the road at the same time as she was.

'Oh, come on, come on, come on!' she muttered through clenched teeth as they stopped again. She found she was even becoming irritated with the shape and the smug angle of the back of the man's head in the car in front: an irrational, but real, irritation – the sort sometimes revealed in times of stress. 'Oh, go on, you stupid idiot!' she called out, when he stalled his car and the rest of the line in front went forward. 'Every minute counts for us!'

'All right, all right,' Jack tried to calm her. 'You just have to be patient in traffic. It seems to take longer than it really does . . .'

Gladys clenched her fists in her lap. He could be so annoyingly reasonable at times, when it suited his mood;

when at others, like last night, he'd be leading off like a lunatic.

'Pity you can't drive it straight across the common! The circus people are allowed to. We'd be across the other side in half a minute.'

Jack tucked his chin on his chest, held his steering-wheel straight and steady, and while Gladys looked out to the left across the common, he resisted the half-serious temptation to take an illegal short-cut, and slowly followed the car in front.

Uncle Charlie double-locked the shop door and teetered across the pavement towards his car. It wouldn't do any harm, he thought, to cruise around for half an hour, and keep his eyes open for the lad. No need to make a big thing about it. No need to interfere. If he saw him he could just give him the gipsy's warning, tell him to get back home before his mum and dad got too worried. They were bound to keep checking back at home.

Nearly forgot! He turned round to push the shop door, to try it for safety. It was habit, years of habit, and tonight he'd nearly forgotten. He must be getting old. He rattled the door, and satisfied, he turned back to face the car. But his legs were old, and arthritic, and nowhere near as nimble as his brain. He had mentally turned and begun to walk before his stiff joints could obey his brain's command, and like a man with his bootlaces tied, Uncle Charlie, knotted from the waist down, lost his balance and fell in a shocked silence to the pavement. Only the years of physical activity – dancing, boxing, tennis and humping cartons of canned foods – together with a certain amount of luck in the way he fell – allowed him to take the fall on his hands and his elbows instead of his head.

'Gawd!' His hands hurt, and his left elbow seemed to be well-grazed if the warm feel of blood in his sleeve was anything to go by. But miraculously, he was otherwise unhurt.

His head was untouched, and he could still think clearly. He knew who he was, and what he was doing, and he knew what people would think. He also had the presence of mind to know, without taxing his heart in trying, that he couldn't stand up unaided. He kept his head; he didn't panic; he lay there looking like a beached seal, waiting for the rescuing wave that was bound to come. His mind was alert, and when the first car turned the corner, a light-blue and white

police panda, he was ready with a handkerchief to wave and an arresting message to shout.

'Timber! Over here!'

The panda drew up alongside him. 'Hello, what've you been up to, Charlie?' The middle-aged policeman knew the shopkeeper well. Who didn't, around here? But his knowledge didn't prevent him from getting close enough to sniff the old boy's breath as he helped him up to lean against the wall. 'A bit early for you to be out for the night's jollifications?' He was all right. The old boy was as clean as a whistle. 'Come on, it's inside with you; or up to the Casualty . . .'

'No, I'm all right, thanks mate. I'll be all right in the motor . . .' The old man lunged forward off the wall to demonstrate his determination, and his ability, to do what the policeman wanted. But his legs were weaker than he thought, shaking with the shock of the fall, and his insistent commands were disobeyed.

'Oh no you don't. My job wouldn't be worth a light if I got you into that car. They'd throw the book at me for being a real fool . . .'

Uncle Charlie said nothing – the first sign of that defiant streak the family possessed. He'd get indoors and have another try later.

'Is there anything I can do for you, Charlie? I'm just cruising round for a spell till refreshments. If it's something worrying you I could leave a message, or pick something up. Providing it's legal!' He laughed; but he knew Charlie; there was nothing bent about this old boy.

Uncle Charlie leaned against the wall and thought for a moment; and something – a combination of age and shock, perhaps – led him in his weakened condition to break his word to Gladys, to make the mistake of putting his self-imposed duty before what cold sense would tell him was best.

'Well, I suppose if you're just cruising around, it wouldn't hurt to cruise round the common, down that way. You could keep your eyes open for my nephew, young Terry. In a red roll-neck sweater.' His voice rose in a warning. 'He's done nothing,' he said. 'But he's gone missing. Just send him home, that's all.'

'Will do, Charlie.' The policeman winked sympathetically at the old boy. He'd got a son of his own. He knew all about these family worries. 'We'll get you indoors first, then I'll have a little poodle around the common. Show the flag down Queen's Dock. That never does any harm . . .'

'Thanks,' said Uncle Charlie. But he said no more. He was just beginning to feel the slightest bit faint.

Chapter Sixteen

LES looked across the steeply cambered road at number thirty-one. At one time, when the docks were flourishing and people really lived in the area, Ron's end-of-terrace house was considered to be superior to all the others. With a long side fence carrying cinema posters (and complimentary tickets) and a side gate to the bigger corner garden, the local children always expected better carol-singing and Guy Fawkes takings here than at the run-of-the-mill terraced houses farther along. And when it came to elections, in the old days when there were enough people living there, this house was always the Labour Party Committee Rooms. It was that sort of house: a part of the terrace, but that fraction more important than all the others.

A difference still remained between this house and most of the others: this house was occupied, while the majority of the rest had been closed and boarded-up, and their tenants had been removed to higher things. And Ron lived here, too – canny, fingers-in-the-pie Ron, with his shelter full of stolen goods – the sort of man who would live in apparent poverty all his life, and then retire to Bermuda. Les knew all about Ron. He'd taken note. Ron was the sort of person he had ambitions to be.

Terry looked across at the fence. It was about two metres high, with long straight over-lapping boards, nothing much to get a grip on. But Les should be able to manage it, he thought, if he took a run from well over on this side of the road. As for getting back, there was bound to be something in the garden he could stand on. He switched his attention back to the ball which they continued throwing at one another, with easy well-judged lobs instead of the hard or high testing throws that would normally have developed by now. They said nothing. The only sound was a steady smack, smack, as the improvised ball stung into careful pairs of hands.

Les looked up at the sky. It really wasn't dark enough yet; but they'd been stooging around there for quite a while already. To hang about much longer would look unnatural. And you could never tell. Someone, in one of the few occupied houses, could easily be spending half an hour at the front-room window.

''Ere, mate!' he called in a falsely normal voice, avoiding Terry's name. 'Get over on the other side. See if yer can catch one from over 'ere.'

So this was it, at last. Terry took a deep, noisy breath through his nostrils, extra oxygen to help cope with the mild attack of nerves. The words were like a secret code to a spy. Here we go! He ran over the road on uncertain legs and positioned himself in front of the long side fence, at a point where the top looked smoothest for Les to jump at. He threw the ball back across at Les, and he looked round. The road seemed clear; there was no one about, and no movement of net curtains so far as he could see.

'All right?' he called.

Les eyed the whole length of fence and he noted Terry's position against it. It looked all right. He was not too far from where he knew the shelter door to be, yet far enough down the garden to avoid Ron's skeleton of a greenhouse.

'Yea,' Les shouted. ''Ere, catch this.'

He threw the ball at Terry. Terry, who felt sure it was meant to go over his head, put his hands up mechanically, just a gesture towards catching it, and he was surprised when he ended up having to make a real last-minute catch.

''Old it then!' shouted Les. ''Ere, back to me!'

Terry's whole arm shook with nervous anticipation as he returned the ball to Les. It must be this next time, then. The first was just for show. He watched Les catch the ball. With

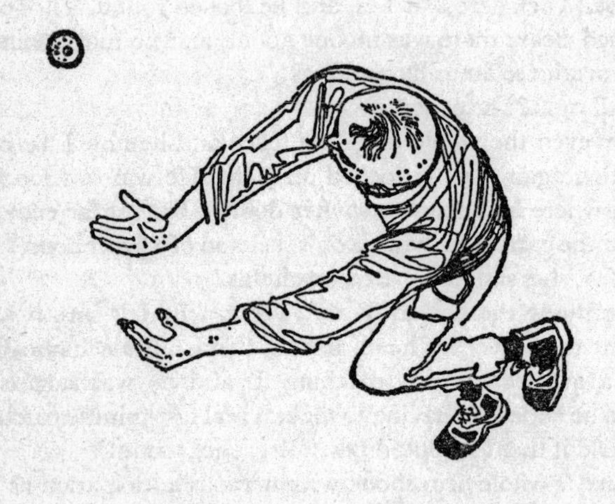

a quick glance in each direction Les pretended to drop it, rolling it forward in front of him like a goalkeeper getting round the four-step rule. When he was on the crown of the road he put his foot on it and picked it up.

'See if yer can catch this 'igh one,' he shouted in a moderate voice, loud enough to satisfy anyone who might be watching, but soft enough not to draw unwanted attention. Under-arm this time for accuracy, he threw the lavatory handle carefully in Terry's direction, this time in a high lobbing arc which carried it neatly over the fence to land without a sound in the long grass of Ron's back garden.

'Oh dear!' called Les, in the least sincere voice Terry had ever heard. 'Ain't I a silly?'

'Yes,' said Terry, in the same talking-to-baby tone. 'You'd better go and get it.' In spite of the tension, he wanted to laugh. And in spite of wanting to laugh he felt a sudden and strange glow in the warmth of doing this together; it was the feeling he'd envied Mick and Dennis and Plastic-head and Blondie the night before. It made him shiver. It was some sort of friendship, he supposed.

Les, with a strained effort-ridden face, was running at him. He lacked the technique and the training of someone about to do a Fosbury Flop, but he skilfully collected his energy into the movement he wanted, and with a well-timed leap his hands reached up and gripped the top of the fence while his toes crashed into it beneath. A wriggle, a heave up with one leg, and he was straddling it, smiling down at Terry; then another grunting push and he was gone.

There was silence for a moment, then Terry heard the swathing sound of feet walking through long grass.

Not knowing what to do with himself, Terry walked over to the fence and made himself small by crouching at its foot. He looked up and down the street. It was still empty. He watched an ant, struggling to pull the body of something larger back to the nest. It seemed strange, he thought, that wherever you landed – like that ball thrown over the garden – you found yourself surrounded by some pattern of organized life. Ants, wasps, bees, termites, all going about their business like this one: all conforming to the laws of their colony. There was nowhere in the world where you wouldn't find this. Even down here in the Queen's Dock Estate there were law-abiding ants!

He heard the muffled jingle of keys. Les was at work already. Not long now and he'd have the radio back in his own hands, be back on the road to being normal again. Meanwhile, feeling awkward and vulnerable, he wished he had a small placard to hold up. 'This boy is waiting for his friend to get his ball back from someone's back garden.' Everything was easier when everyone knew exactly what was supposed to be going on.

The Harmers' car crawled along the edge of the common, still in the restriction of the queue. This must be worse than usual, Jack thought. A hold-up of some sort. There could have been an accident farther up. A boy run over, perhaps? He was cross with himself for thinking such a mawkish thought. Come on! People from the bus, which was two vehicles in front, were getting off and walking: it was quicker.

Gladys suddenly pulled at her door handle. 'I'm sorry. I've had enough of this. I can't stand it any longer, Jack. I'm going to walk down over the common, see if I can't see him. All the time we're sitting here he's walking about somewhere, miserable, thinking all sort of things, planning silly plans . . .'

'Oh come on, Glad, don't be silly yourself. We won't be long now.' He twisted his head out of his window and looked up the outside of the line of vehicles. A newsboy was approaching, walking down the crown of the road, selling *Standards* to the drivers. Jack relaxed a bit. This must be a normal hold-up or he wouldn't be here. He suddenly brightened. 'I'll tell you what. We'll get out of this lot and take the next on the right and have a look up by the Court flats. That's where Marshall said he was last night, wasn't it? It's much more likely he's up there than down on the common. We can check indoors on our way, and come back this way later, if necessary . . .'

'No.' Gladys was firm. Uncle Charlie had told her different. 'I've just got a feeling about it, Jack. I think he's down this way.' She buttoned her coat. 'I'm going to walk across the common and down the ravine; you can meet me in that road at the bottom with the car.' Jack stared ahead at the stupid neck of the man in front. It wasn't a time to argue. 'At least I'll feel I'm doing something!'

'All right, all right, you go. I'll meet you round the other side, where the gully used to be.'

'All right.'

Jack exasperated the driver behind him as he allowed a gap in front to develop while Gladys got out. But it was all stop, go: and before Gladys had half-run twenty metres across the grass, the cars had caught up, then stopped again, as someone way up front kept in with the law by letting a panda car enter the queue from a side road on the right.

It seemed like an age to Terry, crouching there. Every time he heard footsteps he froze, his nose on his knees, smelling the wool in his trousers, while his eyes hurt with the strain of staring sideways without moving his head. There were more and more footsteps as people started coming home from work, cutting through Ron's road to the occupied areas of the Queen's Dock. A woman walked right past him, hurrying, with the look of someone who has a cat waiting for the fish in her thin shopping bag. She hardly seemed to notice Terry. She probably thought she was lucky not to be sworn at or spat upon. A couple of motor-bikes roared, unsilenced, past the turning; then a short line of cars followed the popping of a cripple carriage. Terry sat still.

There was no sense acting a part. The charade with the ball seemed pointless now.

Come on, Les.

A man with heavy footsteps turned the corner and walked along towards Terry. From his crouching position Terry first noticed the old-fashioned black polished shoes, squeaking their way home; he looked up to see who it was, to check it didn't look like anyone who might be Ron. The man wore a tightly fastened suit jacket, with grey trousers which didn't match; his top pocket was clipped to death with pens, and in his hand he carried a thin plastic attaché-case, its stomach flattened like a snake's now that his mid-day meal had been digested. No, Terry decided, it wasn't Ron. Anyway, he thought Ron had a car. But it was some sort of busybody for sure. For God's sake don't thump now, Les! The man stopped by Terry. He stood and stared for a few seconds, as if Terry had to account to him for being there.

'Hello,' he said. 'I don't know you, do I?'

'Hello,' said Terry, looking up at him and staring him out, disregarding his question.

'What're you up to down here, then?'

The words sounded like a policeman's introduction, polite but nosey, and the man was obviously trying to give himself some air of authority by the way he was standing, with his case clasped in his hands behind his back.

But he got nowhere with Terry, not on the outside. 'I'm not up to nothing,' he said. He stuck at that. Why mention Les and the lost ball? Les was well over the fence by now, should be on his way back any time. This bloke needn't know anything about Les unless he knocked.

'Oh,' said the man. There was a long silence, which Terry refused to fill. He crouched there with a cocky look; although more than anything else he wanted to get up and run. But that, he decided, was just the sign this berk was looking for. The man took two steps along the pavement, then he stopped again and turned back. He clearly wasn't

happy with Terry's uninformative answer, but he didn't know what to do about it. 'Well, so long as you're not,' he said firmly. 'Because some of these houses are empty, it don't mean they all are.' He walked on again, even more slowly, stopping and looking back every few paces as if to give Terry some sort of warning signal. Bluff. It was all bluff. Terry, more cockily still, put his head on one side and stared back. He wanted to sneer. It was only because he was on his own. If the rest of the gang had been there this bloke would've run a mile. Terry spat across the pavement.

Come on Les, for God's sake. The next bloke might be more persistent. He sighed and looked back at the ants again. They never stopped, never gave up. They were in some sort of a trail, carrying sugar granules one way, and going back down the empty line for more. When Terry trod on one the others just skirted round it and went about their business. He became absorbed, and tried to flick one or two in a trailing line off their course; the line soon repaired itself, he discovered. But passing the time like that, to ease an anxious wait, he kept his eyes on the pavement for a crucial thirty seconds; and what he failed to notice in his temporary absorption was the blue and white of a panda car passing across the end of the street on his right.

Gladys Harmer almost tripped over something, up by the bandstand. She hadn't seen it from a distance. There were more people about tonight. It had turned into a fine spring evening, with the sun dipping behind Highgate Hill, all London before it, the Post Office Tower silhouetted like a modern sculpture, black on gold. On the common dogs were being walked, small loud groups of children played, and a Darby and Joan couple walked contentedly back home. Gladys hurried on. A young woman with two daughters who ran round and round her was sitting on a park seat, watching them, responding to their every remark, tiring them out before going back to her room in someone else's house. Gladys was by no means alone in having a problem to face.

She kept her eyes about her, inspecting every group of children for a boy in a red nylon sweater. But he wasn't there. She thought her looking was in a disorganized fashion for a while, but wherever her searching took her, she found herself somehow being drawn to the common's central structure, the bandstand, and like the moon round the earth her searchings turned out to be in orbit about it, and she was gradually pulled in to the centre. It was when she finally got there, and she decided to search on the bandstand itself among a giggling group of boys, that she almost tripped over this something on the grass before her. Her first impulse was to step over it, or kick it aside. But the pattern on it said something to her. It said, 'Terry.'

'Good God, Terry's duffel bag!'

It lay there, sodden, like some decomposing animal in the grass. She stooped to pick it up, and with a quiet sucking noise it came, sending a shiver the length of her spine as she discovered that a slug had already fastened itself to the dark damp underside. Uggh! That hadn't taken long!

Gladys flicked the slug away, and trailing the bag by her side she began to run across the last few metres of flat common towards the ravine, down towards the drain cover. He wouldn't have left this behind to rot, not unless something was up; yet she knew he hadn't been lying to Marshall. She was more certain than ever that he was in some real trouble, some bother that he couldn't see his way out of. She hurried as fast as the slope would permit her down the steep-sided ravine. There was never any time to lose. The effort of running sounded loud in her head, the jarring footsteps, the panting lungs; but in any case, she was too far away to hear the boys in the bandstand.

'Pig-face!' they shouted.

By the time the knock came Terry was patrolling up and down the length of the fence like a goalkeeper across the penalty area: nervously alert, ready to move when the signal came. When it did, the knock was loud and urgent, and Terry ran to the centre of the sound, all sense of precaution gone: there was no more play-acting.

'Tel?'

'Yea?'

'You there?'

'Yea.'

'It's too 'igh! I ain't got a foot'old this side.'

'You got it?'

There was a slight pause, an exasperated sigh. 'Yea.'

Terry's shoulders moved in a huge sigh of relief. Thank the Lord for that! They were almost home and dry now.

'You'll 'ave to get up on the fence.'

'What?'

'I can't give it to yer if y'don't get up on the fence! I told yer, I ain't got a foot'old this side!' The desperation in being stuck in that garden like an animal in a pit evened Les's voice to an unpleasant monotone, sending faint echoes of last night's fears sounding in Terry's mind. Les could soon turn very nasty if he wanted to.

'All right. Hold on. I'll get up.'

''Urry up then!'

Terry did what Les had done before and began his run from somewhere in the middle of the road. He remembered to check that the coast was clear, looking in both directions before beginning his run. He waited for a moment while an old car filled with cigarette smoke and four men passed across the turning. Then, when it was all clear, Terry broke into a run. He ran for the kerb, across the pavement, and with a leap he stretched for the top of the fence, scrambling desperately with his toes until he'd got his weight pushing down on his straight arms, and cocked one leg over to sit uncomfortably on the thin plank end. He looked down. Les was there beneath him – farther down than he'd thought because the level of the garden was lower than the pavement – standing flat against the fence and holding up the radio at the end of one long arm. Terry glanced quickly along the backs of the houses: he was well visible from any of the back bedrooms, if anyone cared to look out – if anyone lived in any of them.

'Quick! 'Ere y'are! Put it on the pavement for a minute an' come back for me! I wanna 'and up!' There was a sudden concern in the caked slits of eyes as Les handed the radio to Terry, the thought transmitted with the look. Terry had got the radio now. Why bother helping Les? Why not just run off while he could? 'It's too low over 'ere, an' there ain't no foot'olds. I'll make the 'ell of a row shiftin' the dustbin!'

'All right. Hold on.'

Terry balanced himself carefully while he used both hands to shift his grip on the radio. He'd drop it before he got down, the way he was holding it now. He manoeuvred the carrying handle into his left hand, then he clutched the fence with both hands and lifted his foot back over. A simple drop, with a controlled landing, would be sure to keep the radio safe.

'Shan't be a minute.'

He looked down at the pavement to judge the distance. But his eyes only flicked there for a second before they were drawn away by a large blue and white shape in the road, and his ears heard the quiet crunch of the panda car's tyres as they eased into the kerb not ten metres away.

Terry froze. He was paralysed. His waist was gripped with the cold hands of fear and his limbs went numb as he sat there, legs dangling like Humpty Dumpty, incapable of moving.

The policeman was out of his car and standing beneath him within seconds. Terry could see the professional eyes registering the radio, his clothes, the guilty expression on his face.

'Terry, is it?'

'Yes.' So Marshall had told the police. They were out looking for him.

'Live here, do you?'

'No . . .' It was all perishing cat-and-mouse with the law.

'But you have got the owner's permission to climb over his fence?'

Terry's voice dropped. You couldn't win. 'No.'

'And that radio. Yours, is it?'

What was the answer to that? Strictly speaking it was 'no' – but it belonged more with him than where it had just come from. The fuzz should know that. 'It's our school one. I'm just getting it back. From who had it.'

If the policeman felt this was getting a bit beyond him, he didn't let on. Jigsaw pieces: this was what police work was. On their own the pieces made no sense, but they always pieced together in the end. More or less.

'Well, you'd better give it to me, before you drop it.' He held his hand up for it, and Terry lowered it carefully. He began to feel a bit calmer. This wasn't how he'd thought it would be: he'd wanted to see his mother first: but it could all be explained in the police car, he supposed; how he'd bravely got the radio back to redeem himself.

It was the next question, just as he was shifting his weight to get down, that almost made him lose his footing.

'Anyone else with you, over there?'

Terry stopped, then he pretended to shift his weight to make his descent easier. He was playing for time, his mind racing. If he gave Les away they'd be linked together in this break-in, and he could see that that could go either way with Marshall. And he'd wanted the return of the radio to be his own work, without involving the other boy. Now, would Marshall believe his motive in doing this? Or would he think he and Les really were mates, who were trying to dig themselves out of this together? And who knew what Les would say? How would his mind be working right now?

'I asked you a question, son. Are you by yourself, or aren't you?'

The quick, and the easy, and the truthful answer was 'no'. This kid who'd started it all was over here. Last night he'd have shopped him like a flash. But it was a bit different today, somehow. For a start Terry could put himself in the clear without Les, now he'd got the radio: and he was in no mind to trust what Les would say in his own defence. So there was nothing practical in it. It just came down to how he felt. Nothing was simple. No decision was easy. You couldn't just make up your mind for yourself, it seemed. There was always someone else to think about, someone else who'd be affected by your decision, whether you wanted it or not.

In spite of himself, two pictures of Les flashed into Terry's mind. For a second it was Les, with his cut forehead in his apology for a bedroom, wanting to be friendly, responding to Terry's grudging moments of being helpful by calling him a familiar name. And then it was Les with a flick-knife at Terry's throat, mouthing obscenities, bullying his way into the school, spitting at him and shouting 'Pig-face.' Neither was a comfortable sight. Neither of these two Les's made for an easy decision.

Terry looked down from the fence at the older boy; a special view, seeing both sides, the policeman, and Les. And the Les he saw staring back at him, alive and real and not just in his mind, was demanding by his actions that Terry should leave him free. Terry's mind was made up by what he saw. It took just that one look to decide him. There was no room to manoeuvre, no time to compromise. He gave his answer in a clear, honest-sounding voice.

'I'm on my own,' he said.

'I see,' said the policeman, without moving a limb. 'On your own? So you're just looking down at the plants, are you? Come on, tell him to come out. The game's up.'

Chapter Seventeen

THE drizzle forced undignified entrances on everyone: the magistrates, the policemen, the social workers, and the accused and their families, they all scurried from their transport into the court building with their heads down and their coats flapping. But once inside, the elements were forgotten, and in the court-room itself the huge sky-light coloured everyone with a peaceful green tint which hardly varied come sunshine or storm. The court officials sat calmly beneath it in their uniforms, their suits and their dresses, unaware of the outside environment except when it was thought to have affected the behaviour of the accused. And only these, and their families, were expected to appear as they had arrived, in their wet, outdoor clothes.

In the corridor outside the magistrates' court it was all confusion. Policemen without helmets stood in blue-black groups and laughed like schoolboys, with occasional glances over their shoulders. A sergeant with long hair and a very indoor look about him stood by a wide green door in the tiled corridor, carrying a clip-board and a worried frown; and all the others stood about – wet and dry men and women, children of all ages, wide-eyed or tightly-scowling, edging away from their worried parents; and, standing out as a defiant gesture of defence, two members of counsel with shining faces and black morning suits, carrying long folded papers in their hands and loops of pink string dangling from their little fingers. There were nowhere near enough chairs, just two or three, and there was a continual squeeze and shuffle in the narrow corridor. It was an organized confusion of those who knew the ropes and those who didn't – and this Wednesday morning it was little different from any other lawful gathering of those concerned with justice in the borough.

Gladys and Jack Harmer stood in a corner with Terry, as far out of the way as they could. Terry, his eyes all around him, had already seen the policeman who had found him on the fence with the radio; he had his back half-turned and he was smoking a cigarette. And Jack had seen, and nodded to, the plain-clothes policeman from the Juvenile Bureau who had called at the house.

Gladys had seen them both, each for the first time since their enforced interventions in the affairs of the Harmer family. Standing isolated by her thoughts in the clamour of the corridor she recalled the meeting of the two cars that evening down in the Queen's Dock Estate. When they had seen Terry in the panda, and waved it down, the policeman had been polite enough, but very, very straight; and when he had asked them to follow his car to the police-station, keeping Terry in the panda with the other boy, she had thought Jack would cry with the frustration of the policeman's denying him a parent's right to talk to his child, having to content himself instead with following the back of Terry's head through the streets. Sadly, she recalled the policeman telling them how Uncle Charlie had put him up to looking round for Terry, and Jack's stiff reaction, and the new coldness between the two men which had kept the old boy away from the house for the past three weeks. It was ironic, she thought, how Uncle Charlie's attempts at helping them had left him more cut off than before.

The officer from the Juvenile Bureau had been straight, too, but erring more to friendly than polite. In his fur-lined driving-coat, sitting where Mr Marshall had sat, with the air of a man who wasn't being bought by the cup of tea he was drinking, he'd seemed honestly concerned as he had explained the situation.

'The first thing to understand,' he had explained, 'is that you're not to think of Terry as a criminal – even if he took part willingly.' At least two pairs of eyebrows had risen at that. 'No child under fourteen can be treated as a criminal: in the law they're children, and people think today that they need treatment rather than punishment. However,' he had included Terry in his no-nonsense look before continuing his set speech, 'that doesn't mean that in extreme cases we mightn't ask for a child to be put on probation, or even ask for him to be removed from his home in order to help him . . .'

Jack had coughed into his cold tea at that, and Terry had taken a bewildered and helpless look round the familiar family room.

'Not that anyone would want that for Terry.' The policeman had put his cup and saucer down and begun to hand roll a cigarette, while Jack had scooped an ash-tray off the television. 'Normally, this would rest with me, unless the school insisted on a prosecution. If Terry admitted his part in it, I'd get a report from his school, I'd talk to all of you, and I'd make damn sure Terry never did anything so stupid again.' His blue eyes stared the message at Terry. 'And that'd be that. No fine, no court, no stigma.'

The room had filled with the fragrant smell of the tobacco Gladys's father had always smoked. She hadn't smelt it for years, and in the living-room at that moment of domestic crisis it had brought a strange, unreal feeling of security. The man's tobacco comforted her even more than his words.

'However, in this case, Terry has denied complicity.' He had rested his arms on his knees and looked earnestly at Terry again, this time to explain the difficult words. 'You say you were forced into it – the first break-in, at least . . .' Terry had nodded. 'Then that means Juvenile Court. That, and the fact that the other boy's being jointly charged.' He had smiled. 'But I shouldn't worry, Terry. A lot of boys get involved in something they can't handle. That's what the Bureau and the court are for – to help them out of it in time.'

That had been three weeks ago. For Terry, standing at last in the building he'd imagined so often in the past three weeks – a mixture of all the television court-rooms he'd ever seen, and so far nothing like any of them – it had meant two weeks of school and a week of Easter holiday. And, despite the policeman's reassuring words, it had been twenty-odd nights of tossing and turning, and twenty-odd uncertain, bad-tempered days.

Marshall hadn't been too bad. Once the other radio had been returned, intact, and Terry's father had stuck up for him, he'd been more or less all right – as far as he was ever anything. He'd spoken to Terry once since, in the corridor, when he'd said something about growing as tall as 'your sister' (instead of 'Tracey', so he knew what she had said had got up his nose); but otherwise he'd been all right. Mr Evans had been O.K., he'd given Terry a couple of first-team games, and it hadn't been his fault that Terry hadn't played too well. And the other kids, once they'd heard he was going to Juvenile Court, had treated him as someone who had earned a bit of respect. No, the only trouble with school, as far as he could see, was that whenever Mr Evans couldn't tune-in 'Singing Together' properly on the radio, everyone turned and looked at him.

Worse than anything, playing on his mind something rotten, was what was about to happen any minute: Les's arrival at the court. It didn't seem right, somehow, that they should be dealt with together, especially when Terry was officially against Les. He would much rather have had his own bit in court on his own. He oughtn't to have to meet him again. As it was, Les would come with his mother any time now, and he might speak or he might not, and Terry had to be ready with what he was going to do – either speak back to him, or ignore him. What did you do under the circumstances? Introduce him to your mother? And what would their mothers want to do? Talk politely, or scratch each other's eyes out?

Terry stood and watched the top of the stairs. People seemed to be arriving all the time. His heart thumped and his throat pulsed drily as he waited for the moment. And as he waited it suddenly struck him afresh what all this ritual meant, both for him and for the boy he was waiting for. This court business wasn't going to be pleasant for Terry Harmer, but it was going to be a lot worse for Les. Terry had no doubt that he'd be going back home with his parents, where they'd lick their family wounds and try to forget; but Les, he'd be coming here with his mum, and if what was said was true, he'd be going off without her – to Borstal or somewhere. Terry closed his eyes and pushed a droning sound into his ears. Well, he thought, didn't it serve him right? And anyway, wasn't it for the best? He'd be away from his rotten mother – even if it did mean losing his private place in the old house. So, thinking his thoughts, he stood next to his parents and waited apprehensively for the boy's arrival at court.

When Les did come it was hard to think how anyone could ever have been frightened of him at all, he looked so scared himself. And by nearly being late he was in the wrong before he even got into the court. Terry's full name had been called and marked off on the clip-board list the sergeant carried; and 'Leslie John Hicks' had been paged impatiently up and down the corridor several times while the sergeant kept a custodial eye on the time.

'I hope the blighter comes,' Jack Harmer had said. 'We don't want the case put back after all this . . .'

'Can they do that?' Gladys had asked. 'Won't they get on and deal with Terry? He's been through such a lot already . . .'

'They won't do one without the other. They're jointly charged; so they must be heard together.'

As soon as Terry saw the frightened eyes he realized that he need not have worried about the reunion with the other boy. By almost being late he was a welcome sight at the top

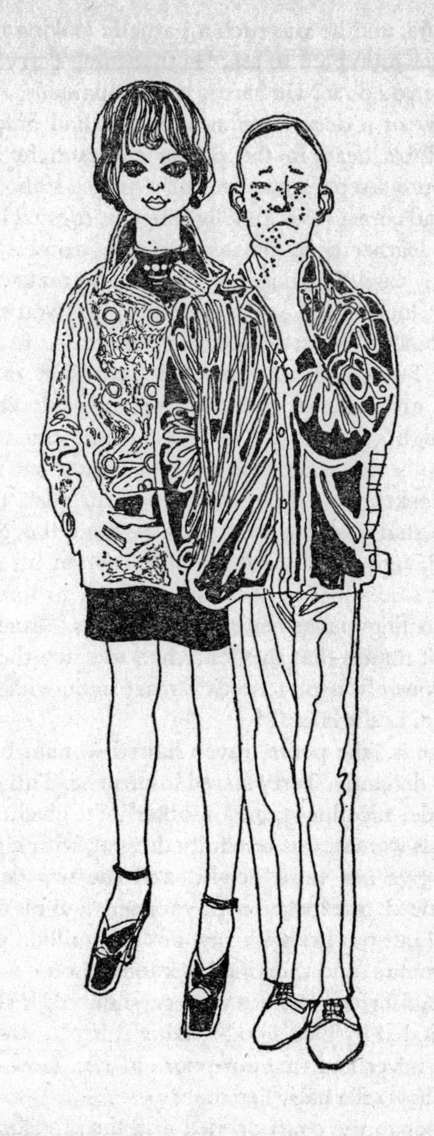

of the stairs, and he was such a pathetic looking figure that Gladys was prompted to ask, 'Is that him, Terry? The one who made you do it? He hardly looks capable.'

Terry went a deep burning red. She had only seen the back of Les's head in the panda car, and he had been whisked into a separate room at the police-station until his mother had come. Now, the slight figure, dressed in a brown imitation leather wind-cheater and grey trousers instead of turned-up jeans, looking shorter than normal without his big boots, looked like any law-abiding boy you might find around somewhere on a Wednesday morning in the school holidays. But closer up, the thin taut skin of his face, wrinkled around the eyes and showing blotchy in the drizzled light, the wispy hair laid flat and thinning on his wet head, the downcast look, and the hands, one in a wind-cheater pocket, the other nervously at his neck, these were the signs that drew second glances from the policemen. Awkward, ugly little devil, trouble written all over him, their eyes said – before they turned back to their nervous change-rattling policemen's conversations, dismissing Les with silent thanks that they only had to catch them; and it was someone else's job to decide what to do with them . . .'

'Are you Leslie Hicks?'

'Yes, he is,' the petite, raven-haired woman behind Les answered defiantly. Terry stared in surprise. This wasn't the big, blonde, nicotine-stained mother he'd given Les in his mind. This woman was tastefully dressed, with high wedge-shoes to give her extra height, and she was very pretty, Terry noticed. She looked a lot younger than his own mum. You wouldn't put her with Les, not in a million years. Seeing the woman, and thinking back to the house she lived in, Terry's half-formed feelings were crystallized. If she liked to be surrounded by nice, good-looking things, it was no wonder she'd never had time for poor old Les. How could you proudly show off a baby like that?

The door to the court opened and the sergeant called to

quieten the corridor noise: everyone obeyed instantly but the policemen.

'Terence Harmer and Leslie Hicks.' He looked about him until he saw someone moving towards him. 'This way. Yes, and parents, please. Come along.' His voice dropped to a confidential aside as the boys and the parents passed him in the doorway, as if they were all in it together against the magistrate. 'You lads to the front, in front of the big desk. Parents sit behind. We don't use the dock for juveniles.'

The five of them filed into the green light, the parents exchanging tight nods of acknowledgement, the boys avoiding each other's gaze like soldiers on parade. Gladys clutched Jack's arm tighter as she looked up and saw the big panelled box in front of them, the solemn faces around them, and the huge coat-of-arms on the wall. It was the atmosphere that got you. Like going into a hospital, the very feel of the place made you accept the doubt you felt about ever coming out.

The sergeant who had called their names stood by the boys and waited patiently while the grey-haired man behind the desk finished his whispered conversation with the two magistrates who sat above him. The man's back was turned to the court, revealing the elegantly tailored line of his suit, like an actor's, too good for real life. By contrast, the magistrates looked down-to-earth enough. There was a man and a woman, the man occupying the larger, central, chair. He was owlish-looking with a full face, horn-rimmed spectacles and a dandruff-sprinkled blazer; while the woman, who was slim and rather pale, looked even more decidedly scruffy, with untidy hair and the look of someone who has left a cigarette burning away in an ash-tray somewhere. She kept looking up, and round the court, and turning her head away to cough. After a few moments the Clerk of the Court ended his conversation with them and turned back to sit down on his plumped-up padded armchair, looking down his long nose at the papers before him. There was a long silence. No one ventured to do anything until the Clerk of the Court was ready. The male magistrate looked round the court, smiling widely at someone sitting with the people from the Juvenile Bureau; and his colleague coughed at the social workers.

Respectfully, the ushering sergeant held his silence until the Clerk of the Court looked up at him through his gold spectacles. He nodded for the proceedings to begin. Mr Powell ran a well-disciplined court. The social workers always had their reports, or some very good excuses, ready, and the magistrates made sure they were never held up in traffic.

'Case number one on your sheet, sir. Leslie Hicks and Terence Harmer.'

With a Stationery Office pencil the policeman indicated which boy was which before respectfully retiring to the back of the court.

'Leslie Hicks?' Mr Powell smiled, chin up, at Les.

'Yea.' Les's voice was quiet, and sullen.

'And you're fifteen, is that right?'

'Yea.'

The smile, which had faded a fraction, was renewed for Terry. 'Terence Harmer?'

'Yes, sir.'

'And you're eleven?'

'Yes, sir.'

Mr Powell looked down at his papers for a moment. He turned back a page to clarify something, then he addressed the boys together.

'Now, the charge being brought against you,' he explained in the sort of patient voice he reserved for explaining something just once, 'is that you broke into Fox Hill School in order to steal transistor radios, that you did a certain amount of damage, valued at eight pounds, and that you then made off with two radios, which were subsequently returned. Now, first of all, do you understand the charge?'

Both boys nodded, Terry a little more vigorously than Les.

Mr Powell turned to Les alone, like a vicar at a wedding ceremony. 'Now, Leslie, do you want to say to the court that you did do all this, or that you didn't do it?'

There was no pause: like the eager bridegroom Les answered before the question had been fully put, nodding his head jerkily once. 'Yea, I did it.' His voice was quiet, but throaty.

'Thank you,' said Mr Powell. He turned his attention to Terry. 'Now, Terence, do you want to tell the court that you did it, or that you didn't?'

Terry could almost feel his mother sitting up behind him with the straightest of straight backs, ready to shout his innocence. But it was a difficult question, the way they put it. It called for a straight yes or no answer – yet 'no' was a lie, and 'yes' only made him sound the same as Les.

'Well?'

'Yes, sir,' said Terry, 'but . . .'

'Now just a minute. You say, "Yes"?'

Terry nodded, and Mr Powell wrote something on the sheet in front of him.

'We can go into the reasons in a moment.' He smiled.

Abruptly, Mr Powell turned his back on the attentive court and stood up to the magistrates. 'You have the reports, sir . . .' Then slowly, with a faintly bored look around the room, just nodding to a policeman to switch the lights on, he turned back and sat down – while everyone in the court, it seemed to Terry, read through a wad of pages at their leisure. There was not a sound to be heard but the rhythmic rustle and turn of pages, almost all together like children in an examination, until, one by one as they finished everyone folded their arms and looked up. Mr Powell, meanwhile, had sucked and chewed a pastille for his mouth ulcer, while Terry and Les had stared ahead at the bench, the one in a conformist stand-at-ease position, the other, already knowing the outcome, leaning over off-handedly with his weight on one side.

Although the eyes of the court returned to him, Mr Powell said nothing. He remained staring straight ahead, indicating clearly by the angle of his head that he was not expecting to be the next to speak. The magistrates took his cue and whispered together, managing to avoid the eyes of either boy. Just once they turned back to refer to something in the reports. Then the woman coughed and the man spoke.

'Well, we've read your reports,' he said, in a well-modulated and cultured voice, trying to give an eye to each boy, 'your own versions of what happened, the reports from your schools, and the reports on your home backgrounds prepared by the social workers.' Terry remembered the call; it had been brief, and, clearly, the young woman (who had looked younger than Tracey) had been quite satisfied with what she had seen.

'Now, Leslie.'

Les looked up at him from beneath his hooded eyes, more like an eskimo in the green light than a London dock boy.

'You have admitted the charge, so there is no need to call any evidence. You have been before this court before, haven't you? More than once. Well, you know, people get very cross when boys like you refuse to help themselves. It can be perfectly fairly said that you've been given every chance you can expect to have. You haven't been going to school, have you?' There was a slight pause, but the magistrate didn't really expect to be answered. 'Well, we still want to help you, Leslie, if you'll let us, and there are various ways, which we needn't go into, in which we could attempt to do it. But the reports lead us to suppose that a period in a community home would be the best thing for you.' He paused again. He wanted to say more, it was clear; to give the boy some advice, or to explain his action more fully; but he seemed unable to find the words. Instead, he looked farther back and addressed Mrs Hicks, who had been prompted to stand. 'We're not satisfied that home is the best place for him at present. Do you understand?'

Mrs Hicks nodded, but she didn't.

'Committed to the care of the local authority at Cambridge Lodge, for two months.' He didn't bang a gavel, but it seemed very much like it to Terry.

Les didn't budge. It could have been someone else the magistrate was talking about. Mrs Hicks was motioned to sit down again.

Terry's heart threatened to thump up into his throat and choke him as the magistrate turned over a page and looked up at him. 'Now, Terence – or Terry, is it?'

'Yes, sir.'

Jack and Gladys Harmer stood up.

'Well now, Terry. The report tells us that you have a good and loving home background, for which I hope you are duly grateful . . .' he looked down at Terry as if he had given that gift himself '. . . that you attend school regularly, that you're doing well there, and that your headmaster thinks highly of you.' His voice had risen to a congratulatory peak. But Terry took the words in without moving a muscle, like winning a prize and not showing pleasure. Somehow, in a court, you learned to take a surprise, and perhaps even a complete change in your life, without showing any emotion. But one thought went through his head like a flash of lightning. Good old Tracey. She'd opened Marshall's eyes.

'And you say, don't you, that you were an unwilling party to all this? That you were forced into it by this other boy and four others?'

Terry kept his head dead ahead, not daring to look aside at Les as he nodded.

'I beg your pardon?'

'Yes, sir.'

'Yes. And incidentally, don't think that all the others –

or the man who received the stolen radio – will be getting away scot-free.' The magistrate smiled, like the cook at school dinners when you've complained about the custard to a teacher. 'But that is not our concern today. My colleague and I . . .' he indicated the lady magistrate with a sideways dip of his large head '. . . are inclined to accept your story.'

Terry's spirits rose in a sudden flight of relief, up towards the green sky, like flying; it was almost physical, the sudden feeling of floating on air. And he could feel, behind him, two other soaring spirits.

'However, there is one aspect of the matter we'd like you to clear up for us, if you would . . .'

Bump. He came down to earth again. Now for the catch. It had all gone too well so far.

'. . . We can understand why you felt impelled to retrieve the stolen radio from the house in Queen's Dock, but can you tell us why, when you were caught on the fence, you lied to the policeman about the other boy's presence? We cannot understand why you should try to conceal him at that stage, if he had been such an enemy to you. It's the one point on which your story breaks down: the one thing which prevents us from wholeheartedly' (and he emphasized and expanded the word with affection) 'from wholeheartedly exonerating you . . .'

Terry stood there, silent. How the hell did he answer that? They'd read the reports. Couldn't they see already why he hadn't given Les away?

He looked at the floor. There was a growing embarrassment when it became clear that Terry was going to say nothing. The silence hung in the court like a wet sheet on a windless day. A group of policemen laughed outside the door.

Mr Powell spoke with his mouth full of pastille in an attempt to end the impasse. 'Please answer the question, Terence.' To make it easier he re-phrased it for him. 'The court wants to know why you didn't tell the policeman Leslie Hicks was there in the garden, if you were an unwilling part of his plans. The radio was back in your possession by then, so what had you to lose by turning Hicks over to the police?'

Terry looked at his feet. He saw the shine on his shoes, the pattern on the wood-blocks, a minute red spider skating across the surface of the polish.

The magistrate supplemented his own question. 'Was it because you were still afraid of him? Frightened of something he'd said he might do to you? If so, we ought to know.'

Terry still said nothing, still his eyes searched the floor. Yes, that was part of it, he supposed; but it wasn't the whole truth, not by a long chalk. That answer didn't sum up the situation. He couldn't honestly say that. He became aware of a general movement of impatience as the whole court sought to advise him, by coughing or by rustling paper, that he ought to answer the magistrate's question.

'That was it, wasn't it? You were scared.'

Slowly, hardly moving, hoping that the one other boy in the room mightn't see, Terry shook his head.

'Oh, come now, Terry.' There was more than a hint of exasperation in the magistrate's voice. 'You say you weren't in on it, yet you refused to give him away when you had the chance. I say that could only be because you were afraid of him. I say you were afraid of what he'd do to you. That's the only acceptable explanation, isn't it?'

Terry swallowed. He could see the man was trying to make it easy for him, but he wasn't. He wasn't seeing. Why couldn't he see, with Les standing there listening to it all, that this one last bit of the story was best left untold; best for everyone? He couldn't say anything more, why couldn't he see that?

It was that terrible frustrated feeling again; that feeling when he was being chased by the man in the nightmare, when he couldn't speak, couldn't shout, when his mum and other people were near and he couldn't make them hear. This was the same, only he wasn't running, he was being chased by questions. His mum was there, his dad was there, but he was on his own against the man, and he couldn't speak. Why couldn't someone get him out of this?

'You were sorry for him, weren't you?'

It was the lady magistrate. She was stifling a cough, but the cough didn't matter, her eyes were fixed on Terry. Terry tried to shrug his shoulders, but it was a half-hearted attempt. 'In the report it says you were on the fence, looking down into the garden, when the policeman asked you if you were alone. You looked down again, and something the other boy was doing made you decide not to give him away. Now, you've shaken your head to say you weren't afraid of him any more, so he wasn't pointing a gun at you, or a knife, was he?'

She left her voice in the air, expecting a reply, and getting it.

'No.'

'And he wasn't shaking his fist?'

Silently, slowly, and with the minutest movement, Terry shook his head. So nothing was to be left secret out of all this. It all had to be paraded before these people, every last private action, someone's life being put on like a show.

'Then what was he doing, Terry?' Her voice was soft, and persuasive, and there was no not answering her. She knew anyway, more or less.

Terry looked at his feet again. He couldn't look up and say this.

'He was . . . he was . . . standing up against the fence, and . . . he was scratching his bad neck, until . . . till he made it bleed.' His voice faltered, dropped to a whisper. 'Please, miss, he was just looking at me, asking me not to tell, and trying to smile . . .'

There was a long silence in the peaceful green room. Les

shifted his weight to the other foot. Terry continued to stare at the floorboards which were misting up in front of his eyes. A social worker dropped her ball-point and spent a long time retrieving it.

In the silence the magistrates put their heads together. All the eyes, though, were on Les – the centre of attention, the silent object of everyone's pity, like some lunatic who could be discussed in his own hearing. At length the man looked up, while the lady magistrate parted her hair with her fingers.

'Thank you, Terry. The court is grateful to you. Unconditionally discharged.'

And that was that. Everyone turned over a new page on the pile of papers before them, and the policeman ushered the boys and their parents out.

As they re-entered the noisy muddle of the corridor, Les and his mother were discreetly filtered off into a side room with a heavy, scarred door. But just as Terry passed, both eyes riveted on the back of Les's neck, the older boy turned, and saw him. His eyes were dry slits, and his hair, where it had dried out in court, was wisping up again. Terry looked at his own parents quickly, then back at the boy.

'Cheerio, Les,' he said.

Les pursed his lips, then rolled his cheeks as if he were drawing up a gob for Terry's face. But then he swallowed, and he sneered. Or it might have been a twisted smile.

'See you, Pig-face!' he said.

And the heavy door was closed between them.

OTHER PUFFINS BY BERNARD ASHLEY

All My Men

A lonely boy in a new school learns that life can be richer outside the bully's gang. Careful and realistic.

Break in the Sun

Patsy hates the new London flat and her cruel, lazy stepfather. She'd much prefer to be back with just her Mum in that little house at Margate. But just when things seem desperate, a quite unexpected chance of escape presents itself.

A Kind of Wild Justice

Ronnie finds himself caught up in a confusion of events which finally leads him to a choice of beating the Bradshaw brothers at their own game or delivering them up to the law.

The Trouble with Donovan Croft

A fostered West Indian boy steadfastly refuses to speak to anybody in this powerful and realistic story.

Dodgem

An absorbing novel about the relationship between a resourceful boy and his troubled father – played out against the background of city streets, a 'care' institution and a travelling fair.

Dinner Ladies Don't Count

Two children, two problems and trouble at school. Jason storms around the school in a temper, and then gets the blame for something he didn't do. Also, Linda tells a lie, just a little one – and is horrified to see how big it grows. Just as it seems that things can't get worse, help comes for each of them in surprising ways.

Plus – for older readers

Running Scared

When a sinister woman corners Paula and gives her a warning to pass on to her grandad, she's pretty shaken up. What Grandad reveals to Paula alone is that he has been an unwilling witness to an armed robbery by a ruthless local gang, and has a vital piece of evidence that both they and the police are desperate for. The crooks will go to any lengths to get what they want, and Paula finds herself in a very dangerous position.

High Pavement Blues

Misery for fifteen-year-old Kevin meant setting up his mother's market stall on a bleak Saturday morning to the taunts of Alfie Cox and his dad on the next pitch. Kevin has to do something about it – but what?

Janey

Dominated by her bullying, violent stepfather, Janey breaks into a house she thought empty and discovers what appears to be a dead body. But the old lady's cries for help soon convince Janey of her mistake and the resultant friendship helps her in her struggle to free herself from the domination of her stepfather.

Other Puffin Books

The Finding
Nina Bawden

Alex doesn't know his birthday because he was found abandoned next to Cleopatra's Needle, so instead of a birthday he celebrates his Finding. After inheriting an unexpected fortune, Alex's life suddenly becomes very exciting indeed.

Racso and the Rats of NIMH
Jane Lesley Conly

When fieldmouse Timothy Frisby rescues young Racso, the city rat, from drowning it's the beginning of a friendship and an adventure. The two are caught up in the struggle of the Rats of NIMH to save their home from destruction. A powerful sequel to *Mrs Frisby and the Rats of NIMH.*

Nicobobinus
Terry Jones

Nicobobinus and his friend, Rosie, find themselves in all sorts of intriguing adventures when they set out to find the Land of the Dragons long ago. Stunningly illustrated by Michael Foreman.

Frying as Usual
Joan Lingard

When Mr Francetti breaks his leg it looks as if his fish restaurant will have to close so Toni, Rosita and Paula decide to keep things going.

Drift
William Mayne

A thrilling adventure of a young boy and an Indian girl, stranded on a frozen floating island in the North American wilderness.

Come Sing, Jimmy Jo
Katherine Paterson

An absorbing story about eleven-year-old Jimmy Jo's rise to stardom, and the problem of coping with fame.